Advance Praise for *Face of the Enemy*

"With consummate skill, Sandra Barret weaves together a lesbian love story and a full-throttle interstellar science fiction adventure. For fans of either romance or sci-fi, Barret never disappoints!"

~Rick R. Reed, author of *IM* and *In the Blood*

"Sandra Barret's *Face of the Enemy* pits the seduction of the warrior spirit against the surrender of a young woman's turbulent heart in this exciting space fiction drama. A sweet read."

~ F.R.R. Mallory, author of the lesbian erotica titles, *Not Quite Forbidden* and *Rhapsody*.

Face of the Enemy

Sandra Barret

Quest Books

Nederland, Texas

Copyright © 2007 by Sandra Barret

All rights reserved. No part of this publication may be reproduced, transmitted in any form or by any means, electronic or mechanical, including photocopy, recording, or any information storage and retrieval system, without permission in writing from the publisher. The characters, incidents and dialogue herein are fictional and any resemblance to actual events or persons, living or dead, is purely coincidental.

ISBN 978-1-932300-91-8
1-932300-91-0

First Printing 2007

9 8 7 6 5 4 3 2 1

Cover design by Donna Pawlowski

Published by:

Regal Crest Enterprises, LLC
4700 Hwy 365, Ste A
PMB 210
Port Arthur, Texas 77642

Find us on the World Wide Web at
http://www.regalcrest.biz

Printed in the United States of America

Acknowledgments

This story could not have been told without the help of Miriam English, Mathew T. Hagan, Kimiko Koopman, F. R. R. Mallory, Donna Pawlowski, Rick Reed, Kerry Smith, Lisa Smith-Nell, Sylverre, the psychocommagirls who provided so much great feedback, and all the folks who listened, advised, and encouraged me along the way.

For my kids, who put up with a writer-mom.

"Beware, all too often we say what we hear others say.
We think what we are told that we think.
We see what we are permitted to see.
Worse, we see what we are told that we see..."
~Octavia Butler

Chapter One

"PULL UP, DRAY! This ship'll burn on reentry."

A determined grin spread across Helena 'Dray' Draybeck's face as she angled their FX-27 star fighter into the upper atmosphere of the Novan planet. Her copilot shouted obscenities through her headset, but she ignored him. Ford was an unimaginative putz. She drummed her fingers on the flight console, beating out a mindless tune while she waited. The holographic readouts flashed warnings across her field of vision.

Ford was frantic as he screamed through the headset. "Pull up, or I'll take control of this ship!"

Dray's fingers stopped. "Touch my flight pattern, and I'll stuff you down the waste recycler." *Putz.*

Ford slid down in his seat harness. "Damn it, Dray. Why does every test flight have to be a freaking death match between you and Jordan?"

Dray's grin widened. "Because she's the only competition I have around here. Now prep booster three."

Dray watched her readouts, calculating the precise trajectory she needed to pull off her stunt. Jordan Bowers hit them from behind with small weapons fire. The ship's hull rattled around Dray. Three seconds, two seconds. One.

"Fire booster three!" she shouted.

Ford fired the booster, while Dray redirected the FX-27, timing a perfect atmospheric bounce that threw them up and over Jordan's star fighter in a dizzying roll that turned Ford an interesting shade of green. Dray switched to the rear viewers and watched Jordan's fighter turn into a yellow ball of fire as it burned through the Novan atmosphere.

"Yes," she whispered. Dray let Ford handle their return flight and landing on Buenos Aires Base Station, while she basked in her triumph. Six months after joining the Terran Military's officer training program, she was at the top of her class. Beating Jordan proved that. Dray waved goodbye to the pinpoint lights of the titanium mining colony on Achilles-5's moon as Ford coasted into the landing dock on Buenos Aries. A minute later, the lights in their cockpit changed from amber to green. Ford pushed open the hatch and rushed out.

Dray stepped out of the flight simulator and was accosted by the cheers and congratulations of her fellow cadets. She pulled off her helmet and ran her fingers through her short hair.

Jordan and her copilot emerged from the adjacent flight simulator. Jordan pulled off her helmet and let loose her shoulder-length black hair. She saluted Dray as her own well-wishers came over to console her. Dray's gaze lingered on Jordan, mesmerized by her light brown skin and deep-set brown eyes. Jordan was gorgeous.

They'd both enrolled in the officer training program at the same time, both going for their pilot and officer credentials. Their first meeting remained one of Dray's most revisited memories. Sitting in the same battle strategy class, Jordan's tall figure and perfect Terran Standard accent had captured Dray's attention. Then Jordan trounced her in their first head-to-head simulated battle. Brains, beauty, and an itchy trigger finger. What more could a girl ask for?

The shouts of congratulations brought Dray's attention back to her own cluster of friends. She didn't beat Jordan every day, and Dray was determined to make the most of it. Maybe she'd finally have the guts to talk to Jordan about something other than their classes. She knew almost nothing about her main competition. But she didn't have a chance before Major Fenton, their chief instructor, slammed open her office door.

"Cadet Privates Draybeck and Bowers, in here now!" Fenton barely showed her gray-haired head before retreating inside her office.

Jordan gave Dray a wry smile as the two entered Fenton's dungeon. The white composite interior of the major's office carried no warmth, much like its primary occupant. Fenton sat in her black-mesh chair, thick arms folded over an ample chest. Dray's breathing was steady; she was called to task in this particular office every other day.

"What is the purpose of this program, Cadet Draybeck?" Fenton asked in her usual raspy voice.

"The program trains officers to serve in the ADF, Ma'am." Draybeck knew the drill, but refused to make the lesson any easier. She hadn't done anything wrong this time, strictly speaking.

"That's it?" Fenton asked. "What about you, Cadet Bowers? Are you here to become another weapon of destruction for the Allied Defense Force?"

Jordan stared at the wall above Fenton's head. "We're here to learn how to lead the ADF, Ma'am."

Dray suppressed a sigh. Jordan played by the rules as usual.

"Precisely, Cadet. You train to be leaders. Terran Military personnel form the backbone of the inter-species ADF officer corp. And what kind of leadership mentality did you both show in that last simulation? Either of you?"

Dray sensed Jordan's discomfort under Fenton's glare. Fenton was a thick-necked, administrative pain in the butt.

"Cadet Draybeck, you have something you want to say?" Fenton's cloudy gray eyes turned to her.

"Ma'am, the simulation was over. We crushed the Novan outer defenses." Dray stared back at Fenton.

"And you thought you'd have a bit of fun trying to kill each other, eh?" Fenton's voice oozed disapproval.

"With respect, Ma'am. The simulations can't match the challenge of one fighter against another," Dray said.

"With respect, Draybeck? Spare me. The only person here who garners any of your respect is Cadet Bowers."

A blush crept up Dray's cheeks. She forced herself not to look at her fellow cadet. "She's a top pilot, Ma'am."

"Hmph. What about you, Cadet Bowers? Do you also think you're too good for the simulators?" Dray held her breath, waiting for Jordan to toe the line and cave under Fenton's icy glare.

"Yes, Ma'am." Jordan's quiet answer shocked Dray. She was agreeing with Dray against Fenton? Dray turned to her co-conspirator in time to catch Jordan's wink. A warmth flooded Dray that had nothing to do with Fenton's critical attention. Fenton glared at each of them in turn. Dray kept her expression neutral, but inside, she was celebrating. *She's on my side.*

"Don't pat yourselves on the back too hard. All you beat was the second-level flight aptitude simulation." Fenton's fingers tapped on the thickest part of her upper arm. "The two of you have no idea what it's like out there on the battle lines. No, don't interrupt, Draybeck. I know your family history, but you personally, neither of you, have seen what one Novan Legion-class can do to a squad of FX-27s. They're death traps. No simulator can mimic what they are capable of."

Dray hated Novans. Not because they were a mongrel offshoot of humanity, but because her mother had died fifteen years ago in the last Novan war, fighting against Legion ships. Dray didn't need Fenton, locked inside academia, to tell her the realities of what faced them if war broke out again. Besides, Dray didn't think they were clueless. They'd studied all Novan military tactics. The key to defeating the Legion ships was to cripple the master ship at a distance before it was close enough to launch its collection of fighter drones.

Fenton stared at Dray. "Your mother came through this same program, Draybeck. I stood beside her, where the two of you are right now, when she chose fighter-pilot training."

Dray clenched her jaw, fighting back her roiling emotions. She knew her mother had graduated from Buenos Aires. That's why she'd requested admittance here. And that's why she wanted to be a fighter pilot.

"You've got her skills in the cockpit, I'll give you that. And her pain in the ass attitude," Fenton said. "We spent two years together in a Novan prison camp before she got us and four others out. They don't mention that about her anymore, do they? Not after Turin." Fenton leaned forward. "She died too young." Fenton's eyes held Dray's for a moment. In their gray depths, Dray thought she saw a trace of sympathy. Or maybe it was pity.

Dray didn't want either. "I'm here to be a fighter pilot, Ma'am." She could see Jordan's questioning expression beside her.

"I see." Fenton unfolded her arms and stood. At two and a half meters tall, the older woman towered over the two cadets. "Follow me." Fenton led the way out of her office and through the hushed gaggle of cadets waiting in the simulator classroom. Even without a glance from Fenton, the cadets knew enough to disperse. Dray followed Fenton and Jordan, regaining her self-assurance. She would be a pilot, a damned good pilot. Just like her mother.

They marched through a connecting tunnel to the adjacent circular corridor, one of the seven concentric rings that formed each of the forty-three levels on Buenos Aires. Fenton bypassed the elevators and marched them down three flights. She pressed her palm to the chip-ID reader and the access door, marked 2-11D, slid open. Fenton walked a short distance down the corridor and entered the program administrator's office. She ignored the front desk clerk and marched into the inner office. Dray followed, pushing back thoughts of her mother as she faced the man seated behind a broad, cluttered desk. He was older than Fenton, with a flabby face and belly, suggesting he'd been at his desk job for too long. Someone who'd probably never seen real battle.

"Jim," Fenton said to the commander. "You wanted two more for the 28th squadron, right? Well, here's your two."

Fenton gave them a smirk and walked out. Dray and Jordan stood in stunned silence as the commander eyed them over his silver reading glasses. Dray kept her eyes locked on the vid-screen behind him, watching the small gray specks that were real fighter ships streaking across the blackness of space beyond their base station. She wanted to be out there, in a real ship.

"So, you passed your first pilot training proficiency test, eh?" He pointed to the screen behind him. "That's the 28th squadron you see. The real 28th. They're part of an inter-species ADF flight wing composed of five squadrons."

That last simulation was a test? Dray knew the instructors could choose any training exercise to rate pilot potential, but she hadn't expected it so soon. She looked at the ships again and couldn't help grinning. She was one step closer to her goal.

"You'll train on a variety of ships next, some attack, some tactical, and your flight tests will get a lot harder. Most of your training group will never make pilot grade or see active duty." His voice held a sarcastic edge. "Most of you will graduate and retire your military career within a year to return to your home worlds in a pampered government job."

Dray understood his meaning. The program had been the best during the Novan war. It was still the most sought-after school, but now it catered to the politically well-connected families in the ADF.

The commander stood up and stretched out his hand. "Welcome to the 28th trainer squad and congratulations on your promotion to cadet private first class. You'll train on a real ship starting tomorrow."

Jordan reacted faster than Dray, shaking his hand. "Thank you, Sir."

Dray shook his hand next, unable to voice her gratitude. Her grin was matched by Jordan's. They were being promoted. Dray wanted to run through the halls, shouting her new status, but had to wait for the commander to dismiss them.

"You'll move quarters tonight to the pilot training wing. Since you came in together, you can bunk together. See the chief petty officer to reprogram your chip-IDs for the appropriate base access and get your new uniforms."

The commander returned to his chair and his work, dismissing them without another word. Dray led the way out, and Jordan followed. They walked past the front desk and back into the hallway.

"It's ridiculous, you know," Jordan said, riding the elevator up to their level. "Assuming we're all here just to get military credits on our resume. It lowers the school's standards."

"It's still the best pilot training school." Dray absently eyed her right palm, wondering how far the reprogrammed chip-ID would get her when she wandered the station on her breaks. "And I'm not here for my resume. I was born military, and I'll die military."

Jordan glanced at her. "Why did Fenton bring up your mother?"

Dray tripped as they walked down the hall and had to use the wall to regain her balance. "No reason. She fought. She died. End of story."

Jordan must have sensed her discomfort because she changed the subject. "And now we're promoted. I thought we'd get detention for sure."

"Not for us," Dray said, pushing back thoughts of her mother. "We're the best."

Jordan laughed. "Modest, aren't you?" she teased. "Come on, let's find our new quarters." She turned back when Dray didn't move. "You don't mind bunking with me, do you?"

Deep brown eyes studied Dray, and a flush crawled up Dray's cheeks. *Get a grip*, she thought. "No, don't mind at all."

Jordan started back up the hallway. "You're cute when you blush," she said, grinning.

Dray knew her face was red, but no amount of self-control would keep the heat rising in her cheeks from Jordan's attention. She wanted the chance to get to know Jordan better, but bunkmates? Jordan would see her with bed hair and death breath in the morning. Dray faced her future like she was facing a squad of Novan Black March troops.

JORDAN RUSHED INTO the room she shared with three other cadets, relieved to find it empty. She turned on her vid-link and keyed in the one connection she had pre-programmed. She established a secure link with cipher codes even the ADF couldn't crack. They assumed she needed the secure link because of her mother's status, and the excuse worked in Jordan's favor. Paranoia was second nature for her, and her mother was the only person she could be truly open with. After a short interval, the video displayed an older woman with dark skin and deep-set eyes that matched Jordan's. The display flashed a name at the bottom, Chandrika Bowers, Ambassador to Gilgar.

"I've been promoted, Mother," Jordan said. "I'm cadet private first class now."

Her mother smiled. "Well done. Your father would be proud."

Jordan didn't believe her, but she smiled. Her father had been a philosopher and pacifist, before he died. Somehow, she didn't think he'd want her in Terran military training.

"I have my first real flight soon," Jordan said.

Her mother toyed with her Catholic Universalist medallion, the duplicate to the one Jordan wore around her neck. "Be careful. Don't give them any excuse to doubt who you are."

Jordan suppressed a sigh. She knew how to pass. She'd been doing it for years now. "No one thinks my reflexes are better than any other cadet's." She didn't go on to say that the only cadet she ever let win against her was far better than all the rest in the program.

"Don't take anything for granted, Jordan."

"Yes, Mother." A simple genetic test would expose her, but she wasn't worried. Terran law considered DNA testing an invasion of privacy. They couldn't test her without a court order. And she'd never give them an excuse to get that. "I'll call you after my first flight."

DRAY COULD NOT suppress her surprise over the number of cleaned and pressed uniforms Jordan hung in the closet in their new quarters in the pilot training wing. Dray had picked up the standard two gray-blue uniforms, two flight suits, and a spare pair of boots. Jordan must have paid extra to purchase three spare uniforms. And, Dray noticed, two extra flight suits.

Their new dual room was half the size of the quad room Dray had just vacated. The two bunks were attached to opposite walls, with a pair of study desks and two computer consoles separating the beds. A shared closet and bathroom facility made up the rest of the small room. Dray managed to tuck her one crate of personal belongings under her drab gray bed frame opposite Jordan's before a heavy thud on the door announced a visitor. Jordan gave Dray a puzzled look and opened the door to reveal another training pilot. His brilliant red hair and burnt orange skin contrasted with his gray-blue uniform. A Tarquin male, Dray thought. His uniform was adorned with one yellow bar, signifying he was a cadet corporal, one step away from graduating.

"Good evening, ladies." His deep green eyes took in Jordan's lithe figure. A hint of deeper orange rippled across his exposed skin.

Jordan invited him inside. "Hello, I'm Jordan Bowers."

"And I'm Dray." She shook the hand the Tarquin extended. Dray sized up her competition, knowing he had more training than she had. He turned his large green eyes on Dray and smiled, revealing white teeth and a pronounced set of canines.

"A pleasure." He placed his lips to the palm of Dray's hand before she could jerk it away from his smooth grip. He ignored her discomfort and pressed an orange hand on his chest. "I am Red Baron."

Dray couldn't stop the laughter that spilled out. Even the ever-polite Jordan couldn't contain her grin.

"Red Baron? You've got to be kidding," Dray said.

"Alas, no. My proper name is not pronounceable to the human

tongue. Your Terran enrollment officers seemed to enjoy their pun on my natural skin color." He grinned, diffusing any notion he was offended by his name.

"Are you in the 28th squadron?" Jordan asked.

"Yes. We will train together. Have you downloaded your new schedules?"

Jordan nodded. "How long have you been in the program?"

Red stood a polite distance away from Jordan, but his skin continued to ripple his attraction to her, much to Dray's dismay. She'd be competing with him for more than top cadet status.

"Just under one year," he said. "I am glad you are both here to join us. I look forward to many lessons, taught and learned between us." His eyes lingered over Jordan once more, causing her to blush, before he let himself out of their room.

Dray sat on her bed, fidgeting now that she and Jordan were alone. She wanted to say or do something, but how could she compete with a Tarquin male more advanced in training than she was?

"We're small fish in a bigger sea now," Jordan said, echoing Dray's thoughts.

"Are you nervous?" Dray asked.

Jordan's hands fidgeted in her lap. "Maybe a little." She looked up at Dray. "How about you?"

Dray smiled. "No. We'll hold our own."

"Always the voice of confidence," Jordan said, grinning.

"Yep. Stick with me, and we'll blow this place apart." Dray didn't feel as confident as she pretended, but she wouldn't let Jordan or anyone else see that side of her.

Jordan flung her pillow at Dray. Not the response Dray had hoped for, but at least the ghost of Red Baron no longer stood between them, for now.

"How many different species do you think we'll train with?" Dray asked.

"The majority will be Terran, but I'd expect Aquarans, definitely, and Chameleon. Tarquins are rare since they have top training facilities of their own. I'm surprised Red's here at all."

Dray considered her competition. She didn't know much about Chameleons or Tarquins, but her father's military staff included two Aquarans. "Do the Aquarans have cyber enhancements?"

Jordan crossed her arms. "I don't know anything about the enhancement rules."

Dray leaned back on her bed. "I know Aquarans need implants to live on Terran facilities. Moisture regulators at least, and vision enhancers. I hope the program regulates any other implants, the same as they do for Terran cadets." She propped herself up on one elbow to look at Jordan. "What's the first enhancement you're going to get?"

Jordan blanched. "What?"

"I know we're not allowed any until we're officers. Haven't you thought about what cyber enhancements you're going to sign up for?"

"No."

"Really? I've got my first three planned out. Reflex enhancers come first. They're a must for pilots."

Jordan walked to the bathroom door. "I'd like to go to sleep now."

"Oh, sorry." Dray said, embarrassed she'd been carrying on about a subject Jordan had no interest in. Jordan was a damned good pilot, but if she wanted to be the best, she'd have to think about her tech options. Dray rummaged in her new closet and pulled out sleep clothes. She'd have to work on Jordan, get her up to speed on the best enhancements available to recent grads.

JORDAN LAY AWAKE in their dark room, Dray's talk of implants still rolling through her mind. Terrans used implants to compete against the other half of humanity, the Novans, who specialized in genetic manipulation to overcome natural human limitations. *Two human subspecies torn apart by cultural taboos on what is or isn't an acceptable way to twist the human body,* Jordan thought. Sometimes she just wanted to scream in frustration.

Against her mother's wishes, Jordan had met some Novans on Gilgar. The Novans recognized each other by a unique biochemical scent that the Terrans could not detect at a conscious level. There were even small communities where Terrans and Novans lived side by side, something they never achieved on Earth, where both subspecies orignated. If they could manage peaceful interaction on a larger scale, there would be far less need for the vast Terran military. Instead, it was a race between the two, Novan genetic experiments and Terran cybernetic enhancements, to see which human subspecies could dominate.

Jordan couldn't sign up for enhancements. Her father would have forbidden it if he were still alive. And it would reveal she was not the full-blooded Terran that she pretended to be. It would end her career and strip her and her mother of their Terran citizenship.

She rolled over to face Dray's bunk. She could just make out Dray's profile in the dark. Her short blond hair framed a narrow face and small nose covered in freckles that Jordan couldn't see. She remembered watching a flush of color highlight those freckles earlier when she'd made Dray blush. Jordan closed her eyes, keeping Dray's image in mind as she drifted off to sleep.

DRAY ARRIVED AT their training launch bay early because she wanted the freedom to examine the ships before the rest of her squad showed up. The bay's ceiling formed an enormous arch above her. It was large enough to hold three Tamil-class destroyers in dry dock. Five Cygna frigates and a row of attack ships took up the rest of the launch bay.

The 28th training squad arrived at the launch bay in small groups. Chief instructor N'Gollo, a tall, dark-skinned woman, stood on a platform in front of the squad, tapping instructions into her com-board. "Listen up," she said. "We'll be training on the Cygna-class frigate today."

A disgruntled sigh arose from the group surrounding the instructor.

"A Cygna?" someone groaned. "It's a moving crate."

N'Gollo silenced the cadets of the 28th with a wave of her hand. "Yeah, it's no star fighter. Neither is most of the fleet. And the majority of you won't qualify for fighter pilot so you'll be piloting one of these larger ships."

Jordan slipped through the group and stood next to Dray. Her fingers worked the edges of her crisp, uncreased uniform as her eyes studied the Cygna frigate behind the instructor. Dray straightened her stance and ignored the wrinkles in her own uniform. She'd tossed it at the base of her bed before falling asleep the previous night.

N'Gollo scanned her com-board. "We'll go out in five groups, six cadets to a frigate. We'll rotate two copilots at a time once we're clear of the station. We will not be using the jump engines on this mission. It's local flying only today." She looked up from her com-board. "Where's Draybeck and Bowers?"

Dray and Jordan raised their hands. Excitement coursed through Dray. So what if the other cadets thought it was a crate? She'd still be piloting a real ship.

"As the newbies, you'll each be assigned to a more experienced cadet who'll act as your mentor and be responsible for anything you do for the first twenty days, got it?"

"Yes, Ma'am," they said in unison.

N'Gollo nodded and looked back down on her com-board. "Okay. Draybeck, you'll be with Tomiko on Cygna 324, and Bowers, you're with Baron on Cygna 187. The rest of you know your groups. Get on your ships and prepare to launch in five."

Jordan waved at Dray and trotted toward her ship. Dray's heart sank as she watched Red's tall orange figure gathering his group and Jordan onto his ship. Just what she needed, to have the Tarquin dominating Jordan's first days of real pilot training. She watched in frustration as Jordan ascended the ramp into her ship with Red chatting at her side.

"Draybeck? Helena Draybeck?"

Dray winced and turned. A small Asian woman with long black hair pulled into a tight bun stood beside her.

"I'm Jenny Tomiko. I'll be mentoring you." Jenny offered her hand, and Dray grasped the small hand in her own.

"Call me Dray," she said, letting go. She pushed back her frustrations over Red and focused on her first assignment.

"Great. Our ship is the first in line over here."

Jenny led the way past the other frigates to Cygna 324. Dray ran a hand along the ship's cool hull. It was a wide, gray ship, seventy-five meters long and less than half as wide. A real ship. No more simulations. So who cared if it was a twenty-year-old model used for tactical command and control? It was real and she'd be flying it in space today.

They entered mid-ship, and Jenny led Dray down a long, narrow corridor to the command center. Dray strapped into one of the crew seats lining the interior of the command center. Two other cadets sat to her left. The taller of the two, an Aquaran, bore the distinctive blue-green skin and wide flat nose of his species. His hair, or what Dray assumed would be called hair, resembled pictures she'd seen of deep red sea kelp. It dangled just past the collar of his uniform. Jenny sat on the opposite side of Dray, and the other two cadets sat in the copilot seats at the front. The main pilot seat remained empty. Dray nudged the Aquaran next to her. "Who takes over as commander on these runs?"

The cadet jutted his chin toward the door. "She does."

A tall, blond woman marched into the command center wearing the solid blue uniform of a junior pilot. She ignored the cadets and slid into the pilot's seat. Strapping on her com-link, she began to speak rapid-fire commands to the two copilots.

"Lieutenant Malory Grace," the Aquaran continued.

"Junior pilot. Friendly?" Dray asked.

He huffed. "What do you think?"

Dray watched the cool, distant lieutenant as she supervised the launch of their ship. The woman kept her gaze fixed on her holograph control panel, ignoring the visual experience of watching the ship pull clear of Buenos Aires. Dray didn't ignore her first real launch. The outer hull of the base station drifted by her view port, reflecting the light from Achilles, their star. She grinned, feeling the engines beneath her shift from dock speed to ion thrust. Simulators couldn't match that.

They flew past the proximity markers, a mesh of beacons surrounding the station. Dray saw a wing of fighters appear from the station's dark side and fly off in formation toward the asteroid belt. Some day, she'd be flying one of those.

A hand came into her view. "I'm Bello," said the Aquaran beside her.

Dray shook the offered hand and felt the webbing between his fingers. "Dray," she said.

His pupils narrowed to horizontal slits as his gaze bore down on Dray, reading her name tag. "Draybeck," he repeated. Then, as if in afterthought, he said, "Welcome to the 28th squad."

"Thanks." Dray recognized the anger in Bello's eyes and assumed he didn't like newbies. She returned her attention to the front of the ship as the pilots maneuvered away from the other ships, heading starboard.

"How far out do they take us?" she asked.

"Just shy of the asteroid belt around Achilles-7," said Jenny. "We each have a go at responding to Lieutenant Grace's flight patterns."

"Cool."

Bello grimaced. "You won't think it's cool once you're strapped in up there. Lieutenant Grace likes to test-drive her new pilot implants on these training missions. Nobody can keep up with her orders."

The first two copilots flew past the base station's proximity beacons and through the navigational test routines set by Lieutenant Grace. As the newest cadet, Dray had to wait until the final maneuvers before her turn came up. Lieutenant Grace's smooth voice filled her com-link. "Draybeck and Tomiko, strap in."

Dray nodded to Jenny and took her seat in the left copilot seat. She'd barely buckled in and attached her com-link when her heads-up display flashed to life and a stream of commands from Grace filled her ears. Her hands flew over the controls, matching Grace's navigation decisions. A grin spread across her face as her eyes flicked between her display and the front view port. She was piloting a real ship. She could see the distinct trails of three other ships within her view, each maneuvering closer to the base station as the lessons progressed.

"Tomiko, you're bleeding rear engines two and four. Check your throttle."

Grace's voice locked Dray's focus back on her own readouts. She noted the minor decreased efficiency on Jenny's maneuvers, but the results were within the accepted limits. Jenny pulled back on controls, and the readouts responded.

"Watch your port side, Tomiko."

Dray's stomach clenched. Was Jenny compensating for mistakes Dray was making? Dray saw nothing on the readouts to match Lieutenant Grace's warning. She looked through the view port. They weren't within fifty clicks of another ship. At their current speed, it would take twenty minutes to be within collision distance. She saw the tension in her copilot's expression as Jenny responded to Grace's critical commands.

By the time they docked back on Buenos Aires, Dray had listened to Grace level a barrage of criticisms at her new mentor. Dray made a few mistakes, but she was convinced her flying hadn't been that bad. When they were docked, Lieutenant Grace marched out of the command center without another word. Dray looked to her mentor, but Jenny avoided eye contact. Dray turned instead to Bello and grabbed him by the elbow as they made their way down the corridor.

"What gives? Is Grace harsh on everyone?" Dray asked.

Bello yanked his elbow back and waited until the rest of their group drifted away before answering. "She's got it in for Tomiko. They were lovers until Grace made lieutenant. " His eyes narrowed again. "Do me a favor and bug someone else with your questions."

Great, Dray thought. Her mentor and training pilot hated each other, and she'd already pissed off one of her teammates. That had to be a record.

Chapter Two

JORDAN CHANGED FROM her flight suit to a clean uniform. She walked into the packed mess hall. Ten different training squads used the common mess hall and the cacophony of conversation and cutlery was overbearing. By the time she made it through the dinner line, Red and Dray were seated at a table near the back of the mess hall. A small Asian woman sat next to Dray, holding an animated discussion. She introduced herself as Jenny, Dray's mentor.

Red stood up as Jordan sat and gave her a slight bow. "Good evening."

"Are you always this polite?" Jordan asked. Dray gave a slight huff to her left.

"Red couldn't be disrespectful to save his soul," Jenny said. "Could you, Big Red?"

"You know me too well, my friend." He sat back down.

"How was your first flight?" Dray asked.

"It was okay," Jordan replied.

"It takes time to adapt to real flight after six months on the simulators," Red said. Jordan gave a noncommittal nod. She'd made two deliberate mistakes during the flight, just to be on the safe side. She knew she could have controlled three Cygnas simultaneously, but the ADF didn't work that way, not after Turin.

Red changed the subject. "Jenny was just describing your Terran home world to us."

Jordan swallowed a mouthful of her stew. "You're from Earth?"

"Born and raised. I grew up in the Alberta farm state."

"Fascinating," Jordan said. "I think you're the first native Terran I've met."

Jenny laughed. "Yeah, we don't get off-world much. I think it's genetic. Those folks who stayed on Earth when colonization started centuries ago passed down a strong distaste for long-distance space travel. I know space jumps make me ill."

Jenny was joking, but Jordan wondered if the hypothesis wasn't at least partially true. There were entire cultures on Gilgar who refused to acknowledge space travel existed. Their government sheltered them from all external contact.

"Have you ever met a Novan?" Dray asked.

Jenny laughed. "Yes, I've met a few Novans. Earth is their home world, too."

"What are they like? Do they smell funny?" Dray asked.

Jordan stared at her plate, clenching her jaw. She recognized Dray's prejudice. She'd seen it before from other Terrans. They were the most xenophobic culture in some ways.

"Actually, they're human, just like us. We're attracted to their scent, but I think the biggest difference between Terran and Novan is political," Jenny said.

"Politics? " Dray said. "What about generations of screwing with human DNA until they're hardly human anymore?"

Jordan had all she could stand and slammed down her spoon. "They're just as human as you are. Same species, different sub-species. Terrans gave them that designation—*Homo sapiens novus*, remember? Novans."

Dray's eyes widened. "Okay, maybe I was being harsh. But you have to admit, they've done some crazy things with their genetics programs. I hear they're incorporating DNA from other species now."

Red spoke up. "If I may, I have met both Terran and Novan. And I find both equally attractive." His skin color rippled as he smiled at Jordan.

Jordan's eyes widened. Was he inferring something about her not being a full-blooded Terran? Her mother had thoroughly investigated all species in the ADF and assessed the risk of exposure Jordan would face in the military. Had her mother been wrong? Jordan focused on finishing her stew so she could return to her quarters and find out.

"What are you eating?" Dray asked, staring down at Jordan's stew.

Jordan looked down as something slithered through her viscous broth. "Silekian stew. It's delicious. Do you want to try some?"

"No way," Dray said. "It's still moving."

"That's just eel-plant. It reacts to heat by bending and twisting." Dray's look of disbelief didn't change. Jordan scooped up some of the broth in her spoon and held it out for Dray. "Trust me. It's delicious." Dray still hesitated.

"It is very good," Red said. "The chefs make excellent vegetarian meals."

Dray narrowed her eyes at Red and leaned forward, cupping Jordan's hand in hers to bring the broth to her lips. She gulped the spoonful and swallowed it like it was medicine. Jordan suppressed a nervous laugh. The touch of Dray's fingers wrapped around hers held her attention. Jordan's gaze locked with Dray's for a heartbeat. *Such intense blue eyes*, Jordan thought. Why did Dray have to be so close-minded about other cultures and species?

"Did you like it?" Jenny asked.

Dray let go of Jordan's hand. "It's kind of spicy, but good."

Red slapped a wide, orange hand on Dray's back. "You see? There are many food options with no animal carcasses."

Dray looked up at him. "Nothing personal, but you're that big and you eat no meat?"

He patted his chest. "I will not sacrifice a living creature to satiate my hunger."

"Right. But you'll join the military and blow up how many people?"

"An interesting dilemma, I assure you." Red's broad smile convinced Dray he hadn't been insulted by her question. "I see my career focusing on strategic defense. It is one of the reasons I joined an ADF program and not Tarquin military. My own people have a history of conquest and aggression. I chose a path that reflects our warrior nature, but embraces a more moderate approach."

Dray didn't know much about Tarquins, but given Red's tendency to be the peacemaker, she could see why he'd want to distance himself from them. Dray turned back to Jordan. "So, where did you get such exotic tastes in food?"

"My mother and I travel a lot." Jordan did not want to elaborate. She enjoyed not living under the shadow of her gregarious mother. She blushed as Red explained for her anyway.

"She is the daughter of the Terran Ambassador to Gilgar," he said.

Dray stared at him. "How do you know that?"

"We were given an introductory file on each of you when we became your mentors." He placed his hand on Jordan's shoulder. "I read about your father and looked up some of his writings. He had some profound ideas. I am sorry he died."

Jordan looked up to see Dray's gaze locked on her, waiting for an explanation. Jordan steeled herself and told the story as briefly as she could. "My father was kidnapped by terrorists. They tried to force my mother to break Gilgaran neutrality with the Novans. She refused. His body was never recovered." Part of Jordan's reason for joining the military was to escape the legacy of both her parents. "Gilgar remains neutral in all Terra/Nova disputes."

"Tarquins could learn much from Gilgar," Red said. "We were

neutral for decades until the Novan genetic program incorporated Tarquin DNA for its rapid healing abilities. Still, I am not sure the unauthorized use of genetic material warranted military intervention." Red shrugged his broad shoulders and shifted the conversation away from himself. "Jenny likely knows more about Dray than the rest of us," he said with a grin.

His words were not unkind, but Jordan didn't like the idea of Jenny dredging up painful elements of Dray's personal history as Red had inadvertently done to her. "She's the daughter of General Draybeck," Jordan said, hoping to prevent any further discussion delving into either of their families.

Dray looked at her in amazement. "You know my dad?"

A blush of embarrassment crept up Jordan's cheeks. "I saw a picture of him. You have his eyes."

The smile on Dray's face lightened Jordan's embarrassment, but her cheeks felt even warmer. She lowered her eyes to her stew and scooped up a spoonful to distract from her sudden shyness. She avoided direct eye contact with Dray for the remainder of the meal. Something about those blue eyes made her feel like jelly inside, but Dray made it obvious she would never be attracted to Jordan if she knew Jordan was anything other than a full-blooded Terran. That was the reason Jordan isolated herself from any romantic involvements.

DRAY TOOK A long trek through the base station. She had two free hours before her next test flight and didn't want to spend it moping over how she'd failed to qualify as pilot on their upcoming test battle. Besides, the rumor was spreading that someone had returned to the base station with an intact Novan Legion-class fighter. If it was true, Dray wanted a look at it. She'd tucked a pair of binoculars into her pocket, just in case. Her chip-ID blocked her from accessing any classified sections of the base station, but if the rumors were true, the Novan ship would still be in the landing dock and, as a pilot in training, she had open access. As she drew closer to the landing docks on Level 3U, she tried to stay out of sight of the officers. Nothing was supposed to be classified at this level, but she was sure anyone who outranked her would make her turn around.

She took the steps leading up to a series of catwalks hovering over the landing dock and peered over the railing at the top to scan the ships below. She saw a couple of short-range vessels and a Tamil-class transport that had recently landed on the near side of the dock. There was no sign of a Novan ship. She hopped onto the middle catwalk and walked the length of it. She caught sight of a mid-sized, black-hulled vessel on the far side of the landing dock. She studied it through her binoculars. It bore the elaborate markings of a Novan ship. Dray trotted off the catwalk and down the length of the upper corridor to get a closer look.

A hive of activity buzzed around the ship. Dray didn't dare get too close, but pulled out the binoculars for a better look at her first enemy ship. This was the fighter ship they targeted in simulations, a Novan Legion-class fighter controlling a wing of drone fighters.

Muffled voices from behind her prompted Dray to give up her vantage point. She stuffed her binoculars back into her jacket pocket and turned to escape up to the catwalk before anyone found her. Two men deep into an argument blocked her way. Dray glanced around but saw no other way for her to go but past them. She stuffed her hands in her pockets and walked with a quick, nonchalant stride. As she got closer to the two men, she overheard part of their conversation.

"That's not good enough," said the taller of the two. "I need solid leads or a lot of people are going to die. I'll be back here in three days."

Dray recognized the voice, but couldn't believe it until she saw the taller man's red head come into view. "Kelvin?" What was her brother doing on Buenos Aires?

Kelvin flinched and turned to her. His eyes narrowed, and he walked toward her. Whomever he was talking to didn't follow. "What are you doing here?"

"I live here, remember?" Dray crossed her arms. "What are *you* doing here?"

He brushed a hand through his hair, letting out a slow breath. "Sorry, it's classified. You shouldn't be up here, you know."

Dray shrugged. "It's not a restricted section." She looked over her shoulder. "And I got to see my first enemy ship. Worth the trip, I think."

He looked back at the ship. "Legion-class. If we can reverse-engineer the control system, we can put up a fleet of Terran Legion fighters ourselves."

Dray studied her brother. "This is your program, isn't it?"

"One of them, yes."

"You'd put a Terran pilot in control of an entire wing again? After what happened to Mom?"

Kelvin glared at her. "Turin was different. Mom controlled a wing of manned fighters. This would be drone-class fighters only. There's no reason a Terran with the right implants couldn't control more than one ship."

"And if the pilot fails?"

He shrugged. "Then only one person dies. Not like Turin."

Dray turned away from him, unsure how to react. On one level, he was right. The Battle of Turin had hung over the ADF for too long, but at the same time, should someone bearing the name Draybeck be associated with this program?

He put a hand on her shoulder. "How's the training going?"

"Well enough. I was just moved up a rank." She showed off her new uniform and he gave her a half-hearted pat on the shoulder. "Faster than you made it through the program," she said.

Kelvin stepped back. "I didn't have your single-minded focus on being a pilot."

Dray looked at his black uniform and triple bars marking him as a Colonel in the Terran Military Intelligence Division. It was a branch of the military that kept him as far away from their father as possible, and that was Kelvin's single-minded focus, Dray thought. Most everything he did was classified, so she'd get no more interesting information out of him. "How long are you on the station?" she asked.

"I ship out in an hour. Sorry. If I'd had more time, I'd have looked you up. I've only been here three hours, and I'm on a tight schedule."

Dray tried not to take offense. Her brother was as deep into his career as their father. "Well, good thing I'm nosy, or I wouldn't have seen you at all."

He glanced over his shoulder and then back at her, grabbing her shoulders. "Keep safe, and...just keep safe." His anxious expression faded. "I need to go. Say hi to Cara for me."

She didn't know how to react to his sudden protectiveness. "Sure." Dray planned to talk to their little sister in a day or so. Kelvin didn't mention their father, and Dray didn't expect him to. She wasn't sure what stood between the two male Draybecks, but it was a long-standing feud she and Cara kept out of.

Dray's watch beeped, reminding her if she didn't hurry, she'd miss her next class. That motivated her to say goodbye and rush back to her own section. She glanced down the connecting corridor, but whomever Kelvin had been talking to had disappeared.

DRAY SAT IN the back of the lecture hall with the combined 28th and 14th squadron, listening to the instructor review the battle capability of the FX-27. The instructor was a young man fresh from military college. His excitement over his lesson material did not filter to the rest of the cadets, who only wanted him to finish so they could get on with the mock battle. She'd be flying gunner instead of pilot in this battle, but she was determined to make the most of what she considered a secondary position.

Dray refocused on the discussion when the instructor shifted to battle tactics and started a history lesson on close-range fighting. Her fists clenched the edge of her desk, dreading what she knew he was about to discuss.

"The F-128, the predecessor to the FX-27, had been the mainstay of the Terran attack force during the last Novan war. The F-128 operated in a mesh network with all other fighters in a wing. A glitch in the system allowed a master-slave override where the chief pilot could lock all fighters in a wing into a preprogrammed battle maneuver. It was decommissioned after the battle of Turin when the chief pilot led three squadrons to their deaths." His eyes flicked to Dray and back to the rest of the class.

Dray bit her lip, trying not to react. Her ears burned, and she heard none of the rest of the lecture. Jordan must have noticed her turmoil because as soon as the lecture ended, she cornered Dray.

"What's wrong?" Jordan asked.

"Nothing." Dray tried to push past her, but Jordan held her arm.

"Please, don't block me out. Something upset you in there."

Jordan studied her, and Dray let out a long breath. "He was talking about my mother."

Jordan frowned. "I don't understand."

"That chief pilot on the F-128. Lieutenant Commander Katherine Draybeck. My mother died at Turin."

Jordan's face paled. "I'm so sorry. I didn't know."

Dray shrugged. Maybe she'd imagined the instructor singling her out during his lecture. "Most people don't remember the name of the pilot they blame Turin on. And they don't remember how many Novan Legion-class ships she was up against, either." *Or how many she destroyed before she died.* Dray walked past Jordan and marched to the launch bay. She needed to focus on the training exercise ahead.

THE 28th SQUADRON stood on one side of the fighter launch bay and the 14th squadron was lined up next to them. N'Gollo stood on a crate in the middle, addressing both teams. Jordan and Dray were in the back row since they were arranged by rank and seniority. Jordan wanted to talk to Dray about Turin and her mother, but Dray had made it clear the subject was off limits for now. N'Gollo's instructions brought Jordan's focus back to the training mission and the thrill of her first mock battle in a real fighter.

"A little background for the newbies. Each training FX-27 is equipped with electronic detectors that will register a hit on your ship and rate the damage based on simulated small weapons fire or missile attack. Your fighters likewise have been altered to carry four simulator class-two Singer missiles and two quad-packs of simulated ammo. If your fighter registers as destroyed, you'll slink back to base with your tail between your legs and hope the rest of your team does better."

A ripple of laughter spread across both teams. The 14th squadron had no new recruits on their team, and they would use that to their advantage. Jordan's excitement wasn't dampened by the notion that she and Dray would be the first targets out there, assumed to be the weakest links. She knew what they were capable of, and their mentors agreed. Red and Jenny would be flying with them. And they'd practiced all the 28th's strategic flight patterns. They were ready.

"The last team to have surviving fighters wins. The 28th are coded blue on your electronic readouts and the 14th are red. Oh, and for the newbies: the losing team gets to refuel both sets of FX-27s after the battle."

A few heads turned back to Dray and Jordan, but Jordan ignored them. She wouldn't be the weak link on their squad, and neither would Dray.

"Pilots to your ships and good luck."

N'Gollo hopped off her crate and trotted off the launch area as the two squadrons scrambled to their ships in an effort to be the first team launched. Jordan and Dray were in the sixth launch team. They split off from their red adversaries as soon as they cleared the base station, flew out past the station's control zone, and sped up to their rendezvous point.

The fighter felt just like the simulations, Jordan thought, easing into position with her squad. Red, as lead for the 28th, set their initial attack pattern, putting Dray and Jordan side by side as an opening taunt to the 14th. Bello guarded their back, while two of the 28th's top pilot and gunner pairs waited on the opposite side of the formation to strafe the 14th's exposed flank.

A beep on the remote com-link signaled the start of battle. Jordan felt a rush of adrenaline as the star fighters streaked across the empty gap between the two teams. She flew in formation with Dray, heading for the nearest pack of red fighters. As expected, a cluster of fighters came after them, anticipating two easy kills. What they got was a flood of well-aimed small weapons fire. As the red fighters scrambled to evade the attack, Bello fired off one of his Singer missiles, taking out two fighters and all but crippling a third.

"Excellent!" Red shouted over the team's private com-link.

As the pilot for the 28th's lead cadet, Jordan had to follow

Red's navigation guidance so he could control the attack. Dray, as gunner in her fighter, had more freedom to strike at their opponents and took full use of it. In the first ten minutes of battle, Jordan watched her strafe three fighters and send another sulking back to base.

"You've got two on your tail, Jordan," Bello warned.

"I see them. If you take the second fighter, I'll do a reverse pattern and take out the first." Jordan banked to her left as a diversion and flipped her fighter. She was facing the 14th's fighter now, and Red fired off a round that eliminated it.

Bello missed his mark, and the second fighter still shadowed Jordan. "180 and swap with me," Jenny said, appearing as a blue dot on Jordan's proximity detector.

"You got it." Jordan followed Jenny and Dray's flight pattern and then pulled out, making her attacker follow her and ignore Dray, who came in firing on his flank. The mistake cost him his fighter.

"I owe you one." Jordan sent her fighter back into the fray.

"WE'VE BARELY GOT the lead." Jenny read out the numbers of remaining ships on either team.

Dray saw one of the 28th's fighters illuminated under a direct hit. "Not any more. Only four fighters left for each of us." Dray's eyes switched between her tactical display and the view port, watching for the red dots of a fighter from the 14th. Her perimeter warning clanged to life. Where was Bello? He was supposed to be guarding her flank.

"Move out, Dray! She's got two above you!" Jordan's warning came too late as the other fighter set off a simulated Singer missile. Dray fired off her last shots, including her Singer, before the enemy missile struck. The simulation impact crippled her fighter. Jenny dropped them out of the battle zone, defeated.

"Not too shabby," Jenny said over the com-link. "You scored a total of three hits."

As Jenny spoke, Dray watched the other three red fighters streaming after Jordan and Red. She clenched her fighter's controls, wanting to fly to Jordan's defense, but she could only watch and listen as the mock battle continued without her.

"This is Bello. We're coming at them from within your shadow. They'll never see us coming."

He'd deserted Dray when she needed his protection, but he was there now for Jordan. Obviously, he didn't hate all newbies. Dray watched as Bello pushed it to top speed and came up behind Jordan's fighter.

"Shadow to Leader. We've got two Singers and are ready to play," Bello said.

"You got it, Shadow. On my mark." Jordan's voice echoed in Dray's ears as Bello matched Jordan's maneuvers. The 14th squad hadn't detected him yet.

"Now, Bello!" Jordan dropped speed and position, bringing one enemy fighter with her.

Bello's fighter came within view of the other two enemy fighters. "Smile, boys and girls, I've got candy enough for everyone. Fire missiles, gunner!" Lights illuminated both fighters in wide patches, and the defeated ships dropped out of the attack zone.

Jenny landed their ship, and Dray missed the rest of the battle, but the 28th had won. She checked the battle results and was surprised to see that she'd taken third place as gunner.

Jenny saw her score as well. "You'd make a great weapons officer, you know."

"It was fun, but I'd rather be a fighter pilot."

Jordan and Bello took one triumphant lap of the now empty zone before returning in formation to Buenos Aires. Jordan and Bello emerged from their fighters to the hearty cheers of the rest of the 28th. Cadets swarmed around them, but Dray pushed her way through. She congratulated Bello, but he ignored her.

"You did it," she said, grabbing Jordan's arm. Jordan threw her arms around Dray, picked her up, and swung her in a wide arc. When Dray's feet again touched the ground, Jordan's soft lips caressed her cheek, leaving Dray speechless.

"Of course we did, we're the best," Jordan whispered in Dray's ear.

The grin on Dray's face had nothing to do with the mock battle they'd just finished. She barely acknowledged when Jenny hugged her and left with Red.

She turned to Jordan, who was frowning as she watched Jenny leave. "What's up?" Dray asked.

"Hmm?" Jordan glanced at her and back to Jenny. "Nothing."

"Should we follow our mentors?"

Jordan stuffed her hands in her flight suit pocket. "I think I'll just go back to the dorm."

Dray's grin disappeared. Was Jordan upset because Red left with Jenny? She looked like she needed someone to talk to, but when Dray touched her arm, Jordan pulled away.

"Okay, I guess I'll see you later." Dray hesitated, but Jordan turned away and walked out of the launch area without another word.

JORDAN'S LONG STRIDES took her out of the docking bay and down a side corridor. When she was out of Dray's line of sight, her shoulders slumped and her pace slowed. She was not in any rush to get back to her quarters, but she had to get away from Dray's critical stare. Her cheeks burned with embarrassment at her petty, jealous reaction when Jenny hugged Dray. What right did she have to get upset if someone else showed an interest in Dray? It was not like she was giving Dray any clear indication of her feelings. She knew Dray was attracted to her; she recognized the signs as she had from numerous other cadets, male and female. Jordan couldn't trust their attraction. And Dray had made her prejudice against non-Terrans obvious. Dray would never accept Jordan as mixed-breed Terran.

By the time Dray arrived, Jordan had gotten over her jealousy. She sat on her bed, trying to ease herself into a relaxed state so she could practice her meditation.

"Are you sure you don't want me to leave?" Dray asked.

Jordan opened one eye. Dray leaned against the small table holding their shared vid-link. "I'll be fine. I've practiced this since I was three years old. A little background noise is fine."

"Even if I call my sister?"

Jordan smiled. "Even if you call your sister." She shut her eyes again and rolled her shoulders. Renewing her meditation on a regular basis was both welcome and necessary. She had never practiced in front of Dray, but she'd meditated in crowded public squares before. One person should not upset her equilibrium. She focused on her breathing, slowing and deepening it. The sounds of Dray settling into a chair and speaking softly into the vid-link drifted around Jordan. She used those sounds to block out any other stray thoughts, centering herself on Dray's deep voice.

She heard another voice filter through, an excited, higher-pitched voice. Curiosity overruled Jordan's self-control and she peeked one eye open. On the vid-screen, she saw a younger version of Dray, with reddish-blond hair: Dray's younger sister, Cara. Jordan's one-eyed gaze drifted to Dray's profile. Dray's hands moved as she talked. Her whole body posture was relaxed, a glimpse of Dray that Jordan seldom saw. Thoughts of meditation disappeared as she watched. Why couldn't Dray be this at ease when they were together, instead of the tough posturing she presented to Jordan?

Dray turned to Jordan and caught her staring. "This is Catholic Universalist meditation?" she asked with a grin. "Looks more like snooping to me."

A flush of embarrassment flooded Jordan's cheeks, and she looked away. "Sorry, I didn't mean to intrude."

"Come on over," Dray said, smiling. "I want you to meet my sister." Jordan unfolded herself from the bed and walked over to stand beside Dray. "Cara, this is my bunkmate, Jordan."

"Hey," Cara said. "Dray's always talking about you."

Jordan looked at Dray. She saw the relaxed expression turn to embarrassment in an instant. She winked at Dray and saw her blush deepen. "Well, don't believe everything she says."

"Trust me, I don't," Cara said.

"Are the two of you finished talking as if I'm not here?" Dray asked.

Jordan laughed and walked back to her bed. She stretched out on her side on the bunk, no longer pretending to do anything but watch Dray. She knew her attentions were being noticed, but she didn't care. Seeing Dray interact with her sister was better than meditation any day.

DRAY MUNCHED ON the remnants of her dinner while the news-vid droned on multiple screens around the mess hall. She ached in every muscle she possessed. After months as a cadet on Buenos Aires at 95 percent standard gravity, she hadn't been prepared for their most recent exercise. She went with the rest of the 28th to spend a day on the surface of Achilles-7, which had one and a half times standard gravity. 'Multi-atmosphere training,' they called it. *More like torture*, she thought as she tried to shift her aching thigh muscles.

She lost count of the number of times she'd tripped over minor obstacles on the planetary surface. Granted, she was in a full atmosphere suit which made her movements bulky and awkward, but the increased gravity meant her coordination and timing were sluggish. That led to half her bruises, even through the suit.

"What's on the vid tonight?" Red asked as he and Jenny joined her at the table. Dray was glad to see Jenny ease uncomfortably into a chair. At least she wasn't the only one aching from alternate gravity training.

"Another terrorist attack on a Terran transport factory," Dray said.

Jordan pulled up a spare seat and joined them. "Was it Novan?"

"Probably. They've hit three other sites in the past month." Dray noticed Jordan looked a lot less stiff than the rest of them. "Does anyone else feel like they've just been pushed through the trash compactor?"

"Most definitely," Red said. "We are going to the hot tubs. You are welcome to join us."

Dray turned to Jordan, who nodded her agreement. "Sure thing. We'll meet you there in about ten minutes."

They all eased out of their chairs, including Jordan. So she was just as sore as the rest of them, despite her fluid movements, Dray thought.

"Make that twenty," Jordan said with a weak laugh.

Two rows of steaming communal hot tubs lined the rehab room on 2-14D. Other members of the 28th were already soaking in the first tub. Red and Jenny were waiting for Dray and Jordan in the last hot tub in the room. They passed a mixed collection of cadets, enlisted personnel, and officers. The tubs were one of the few places on Buenos Aires where rank and formality disappeared in favor of swim suits and relaxation. Dray wore pylex shorts and a tank top, preferring the fast-drying material to a simple nylon suit. She didn't know what Jordan wore, since her roommate had wrapped a terrycloth robe around herself.

"Come on in," Jenny said. "The jets are doing wonders for my aching back."

Dray dropped her towel on the floor beside the sunken tub and lowered herself into the steaming water. She turned as Jordan took off her robe. A sleeveless nylon body suit clung to her from mid-thigh to neck. On someone else, the suit would have been modest to an extreme. On Jordan, it was a sensual vision. The suit covered her, yet revealed every detail of Jordan's fit body. Dray was glad the hot water gave her an excuse for the flush rising to her cheeks.

"So, you two are on your own tomorrow." Jenny said, breaking the silence. Jordan lowered herself into the water with a sigh. Swirling, bubbling water covered her to the neck, giving Dray the ability to pull her eyes away from Jordan's body for a time. She turned to the other two and saw an appreciative look from Jenny, and Red struggling to hide most of his tell-tale rippling skin under the water. Dray almost felt sorry for him, but she remembered, as of tomorrow, they would no longer be mentor and cadet. With the mentoring period over, she dreaded the freedom Red would have to fully express his feelings for Jordan.

Red sat up in the water, having regained control of his skin tone. "Yes. There are four new recruits in the 14th squadron starting soon. You will have someone to pick on."

Dray laughed. "We learned a lot from you guys, but I'll be glad to have someone else bear the brunt of the newbie jokes."

A young man asked to join them. He was thin in an androgynous way, with kinky black hair and skin so brown it bordered on black. Old-Earth African came to mind, but Dray knew no Terran carried such pure features anymore. The Pan-Africans were the first culture to experiment with genetic manipulation to fight off an ancient epidemic that had ravaged the continent. All their descendants were Novan.

Jordan introduced him to Dray. "This is Sahar Ubae. He's from the 14th squad."

Dray shook Sahar's hand, wondering just how many men were showing an interest in Jordan. She was surprised to see that Sahar's main focus was on Red.

"I would have made lieutenant by now, but I had to take time off to return to Tarquin," Red said, answering one of Sahar's questions.

Dray's eyes widened. "I thought if you left the program, that was it. Your spot was given to someone else."

"Tarquins are given special dispensation for our Min'Tak ceremony."

"What's that?" Dray asked, wondering why Jordan was blushing.

"It is our ritual for sexual maturity." He clasped his hands behind his neck, warming up to the conversation. "It is a hard concept for Terrans to understand, since most of you are born to your permanent gender. Even though all Tarquin are born as what you would consider immature females, we learn our real gender long before sexual maturity."

"So, when did you know you'd be male?" Sahar asked.

"I knew before my fourth birthday."

"Is the ceremony painful?" he asked.

"It is a natural process for us. Our bodies mature much the same as yours, only we do it in a matter of weeks instead of years. Human maturity takes such a long time. Very inefficient," he said with a wide grin.

Dray laughed. "And not very enjoyable, believe me." She remembered her own awkward puberty and shuddered. It also brought back memories of her first and only girlfriend. She winced at the memory of how that particular shrew-in-the-making had mocked Dray's clumsy advances. Dray didn't like failure, and even she had to admit she was a failure when it came to romance. She watched Jordan's reaction to Red and felt a familiar frustration inside.

"So you just became a full-grown male this year?" Sahar asked.

Dray found it hard to believe Red had been a Tarquin female less than a year ago. His muscle definition was a stark contrast to Sahar's more androgynous frame.

Red gave them a flamboyant bow. "Full male for three months now."

Sahar got out of the water and wrapped himself in a towel. "Sorry, the water's too hot for me. Is that mark on your chest part of the transformation?"

Dray noticed the blue tattoo in the shape of a small flame that was centered on Red's hairless orange chest.

"It is the mark of the Flame. It symbolizes the fire within, connecting all to the Eternal," Red said.

"Tarquin religion?" Jordan asked.

Red puzzled over her question for a moment. "You mean like your Terran religions? I suppose there is a similarity, though I like to think the Flame burns in all true religions."

"What sort of rituals go along with belief in the Flame?" Jordan asked as she lowered herself further into the steaming water.

Red smiled. "Many, but few are required. You accept the Flame or not. If you accept it, the Fire within guides you. There are many Terrans who accepted the Flame, but they must renounce all technological enhancements. Mind and body must remain pure."

Jordan nodded. "Catholic Universalists don't forbid all implants, but we're discouraged from anything not medically necessary."

"Count me out," Dray said.

"Most Terran implants won't work for me anyway. I'm only part Terran," Sahar said. "My primary parent was Terran and my secondary parent is Chameleon."

"Primary and secondary?" Jenny asked. "You're an F-K baby?"

"Yes, but not for the reasons you think," Sahar said. "Chameleons are the only species that don't require the Fletcher-Koopman procedure to mix their DNA with Terran DNA to produce offspring. We can reproduce naturally with most species, but both my parents were male and my Terran parent refused to copulate when my Chameleon parent became female for the sake of reproduction."

Now his old-world African features made sense to Dray. Chameleons could change their physical features on a whim. "So why do you look like one of the Novan races?" she asked.

"My Terran ancestors were African, before the Terra/Nova split."

"Couldn't you just shift your appearance to look more Terran?"

"It is my way of respecting both my parents. Besides, I can't morph as easily as a full Chameleon. And looking Terran wouldn't get me full Terran citizenship anyway. This makes sure of it," he said, waving his palm.

His chip-ID would mark him as part Terran. The Terran Purity standards applied second-class status to all Terran mixed-species offspring to protect the stability of the Terran genome. She watched Sahar leave, wondering if he'd end up in one of the covert ops departments. With his looks, he'd make an excellent Novan spy.

A loud, annoying voice interrupted her thoughts. One look at Jenny confirmed Dray's suspicions. She turned to the source and saw Malory Grace hanging on the arm of an unimpressive-looking woman. The two of them cavorted in the next hot tub in a manner unbecoming for a public place. All color drained from Jenny's face. Dray couldn't tell if she was offended by her ex-lover's public behavior or hurt by the obvious lack of tact Malory showed in an awkward situation. Dray's initial dislike of Malory turned more serious. A plan formed in her mind which would give a certain obnoxious junior pilot something to think about.

Dray looked at Jenny in the hot tub. "How are the aches?"

Jenny stretched and rolled her head. "I have a nice knot between my shoulder blades. The jets don't really help."

Dray stood up and walked around the tub. She repositioned herself behind Jenny with one leg dangling in the water to either side of her. Dray and Malory were eye to eye across the span of two hot tubs, and her movement had garnered Malory's attention.

"Lean back and let me see what I can do about that shoulder knot," Dray said.

Jenny leaned back, sliding between Dray's legs. To Dray's amusement, Malory sat up on the edge of her own hot tub to get a better look at what Dray was up to, all but ignoring her own companion. Dray massaged Jenny's shoulders, easing the sore muscles. Jenny's head lowered, relaxing into the massage. When Dray pushed through the knot between her shoulders, Jenny let out a low moan.

"That's better than sex." Jenny rolled her shoulders with ease.

To Dray's amusement, Lieutenant Malory Grace hopped out of the hot tub and marched out of the steaming room, leaving her confused companion behind. Dray withheld a long laugh until after the door closed shut behind Malory. "So much for that distraction," Dray said.

Dray's amusement ended when she made brief eye contact with Jordan. Her roommate's brown eyes bore into her for a heartbeat, then turned away. Jordan stepped out of the water and grabbed her terrycloth robe. Water dripped off the ends of her long black hair.

"I'm heading back," she announced.

"I'll join you," Dray offered.

Jordan grazed her with an icy glare. "Don't bother. Red's walking back with me."

Red glanced from Dray to Jordan. "Yes, of course," he said, his voice subdued.

Dray sat by the edge of the hot tub in stunned silence,

watching Jordan leave with Red at her side. Had Red made his move for Jordan while Dray was busy annoying Malory Grace? The door closed behind the pair, and Dray heard the echo of it like the death knell for her own unexpressed desires. Why hadn't she ever told Jordan how she felt? And now, as those two left with no impediment between them, it was too late.

She lowered herself into the water and under, letting the hot jets massage her head and neck. When she resurfaced, she saw Jenny sitting outside the tub, dangling her legs in the hot water.

"Problems?" Jenny asked.

"Probably not anymore," Dray said in despair.

Jenny jerked her head toward the exit. "You think something's going on between those two?"

"Don't you?"

Jenny laughed. "Red can't exactly mask his emotions, can he?"

"No, not much." Dray wallowed in her inner gloom. Her mind drew pictures of Red and Jordan together in ways that made her want to drown herself in the hot water and end her misery.

"Do you think Jordan likes him?" Jenny asked.

Dray sighed, trying to focus on reality instead of her self-pity. "I can't tell. I'm a little biased when it comes to her."

"Yeah, I can see that. I can see the way she looks at you sometimes, too. I'd say you're still in the running."

"Really?" Dray didn't try to hide the hope in her voice.

Jenny laughed. "Not that I'm any expert in this area. And thanks, by the way, with the Malory thing."

Dray smirked. "She didn't much like that, did she?"

Jenny looked down into the bubbling water. "No, I guess she didn't."

"Can I ask you something?" Dray stood up in the water, letting the jets beat at her sore leg muscles.

"Sure."

"Not that she's any gem or anything, but why did you leave her?"

Jenny kicked at the bubbles. "I didn't. She left me when she made lieutenant. I guess it didn't help her career mobility to be tied down to a cadet corporal."

It was left unsaid that the promotion shouldn't have caused the breakup. The military turned a blind eye toward commander/subordinate relationships as long as they didn't involve direct reports. Dray pulled herself out of the water and grabbed her towel. "If she left you, then why is she always dogging you?"

Jenny shrugged. "I wish I knew."

"Come on," Dray said, drying off. "Let's drown our girl troubles in some stout Terran beer."

Jenny stood up. "Make it Vintak spiced wine, and you're on."

Is everyone else multicultural in their tastes? Dray thought as she grabbed her towel. Dray knew she had to expand her cultural awareness when even Earth-born Jenny had more exposure than she had. She promised herself she would, if she had any chance left with Jordan.

"ARE THINGS WORKING out for you here?" Red asked as they walked down the hallway.

Jordan glanced back over her shoulder, but the hot tub area was out of sight. She didn't want to see it anyway. Not with Dray all but seducing Jenny in front of them all. Her jaw clenched. "I'm fine."

He looked at her sidelong. "It would be more believable if you said it without the frown."

Jordan turned away from him. "Sorry."

"Anything you would like to talk about?"

She resisted the urge to look back, again. "It's nothing. I'll get over it."

He folded his hands behind his back as they walked. Jordan could not match his long stride, but he kept his steps slow for her benefit. She looked up into his brilliant green eyes. A ripple of deeper orange swept over his face. She knew what that meant, but did not comment.

"May I hazard a guess at what is upsetting you?" he asked.

"You think you know?"

"Perhaps. One cannot help but notice a mutual attraction."

Was he referring to himself? she wondered. She was formulating a polite way to let him know she was not interested when he continued.

"You are fond of Dray, yes?"

Jordan's step faltered. Was she that obvious? "How did you know?"

He grinned, showing his sizable teeth. "The signs are there, to one who has reason to be observing them. And Dray likes you."

She held his arm to stop him. "How do you know that?"

"Let us just say she has made her interest in you obvious to any other potential suitor."

Jordan did not know what to say. She wanted to believe him. "Then what was all that, back in the hot tub?"

Red sighed. "That, my friend, is as much a mystery to me as it is to you. I can only say I believe Dray is very much interested in you, romantically."

He walked her to her quarters and left for his own. Jordan

entered the dark room and sat on the edge of her bed. She was relieved he hadn't pursued his interest in her during their walk. Maybe what he said about Dray was real. Or maybe it was just his way of finding out if she was attracted to him. The Tarquins were not the most straightforward culture. She got up and turned on a light, refusing to brood about what Dray might be doing with Jenny. She grabbed her bed clothes and headed for the bathroom. There was nothing she could do about it. Nothing at all.

Of course, it did not stop her from banging as many drawers as she could while she got ready for bed. Nor did it stop her from pausing beside Dray's empty bunk before flopping down on her own.

Chapter Three

BY THE TIME Dray dragged her exhausted self back to the dorm, most cadets were long since asleep. The door to her quarters slid open, and she stepped into the dark interior. Relief washed over her at the sight of just one body lying under the covers in Jordan's bed. She padded quietly into the bathroom to change for bed. When she came out, Jordan was sitting up, her bare arms wrapped around her knees. A small bedside lamp lent the room a soft, yellow glow.

"Hey," Dray said. "Sorry I woke you."

"It's okay. I only turned the lights out a few minutes ago."

"Oh." Dray's heart sank. Had Red been here all that time?

"How did your night with Jenny go?"

"We went for some drinks." Dray sat on the edge of Jordan's bed, unsure of herself, yet still craving to be close to Jordan. "How about you and Red?"

"No beers, but we talked a lot."

Dray nodded, unable to ask what they had to talk about and not wanting to know.

"So, did you kiss her?"

"What? Who?" Dray frowned, taken off guard by Jordan's odd question.

Jordan pulled her arms tight around her legs. "Jenny."

Dray's eyes widened. "No. Why would I?"

"Well, she's not really your mentor anymore, is she?"

Dray crossed her arms. "Well, Red's not your mentor anymore, either."

"So?"

"So, did you kiss him?"

"Red?" Jordan's cheeks reddened. "No, but I wasn't giving him back massages in the hot tub, either."

"Shoulder massage," Dray corrected with a grin. "And that was for the aggravation of one Lieutenant Malory Grace."

"You mean the woman in the next hot tub?" Jordan frowned.

"The very same. Seems she dumped Jenny when she made lieutenant but hasn't quite managed to let go yet."

Jordan's gaze held Dray's. "So you haven't been flirting with Jenny?"

"Only for Malory Grace's benefit, and Jenny knows that."

Jordan smiled. "You're evil sometimes, you know?"

"So I've been told." Dray ignored her fears and asked the question she'd been thinking about all night. "Are you and Red, you know?"

Jordan unwrapped herself and stretched her legs out behind Dray. "No, I don't know or I don't want to know what you've been thinking. And no, there's nothing between us."

Dray relaxed for the first time since entering the room. "Glad to hear it."

"Really," Jordan teased. "And why is that?"

"He's not right for you." Dray played with the edges of her gray sleep shorts.

Jordan shifted her legs, brushing her bare skin against Dray's back. The scent of Jordan's freshly washed body filled Dray's senses as her gaze moved up Jordan's long brown legs to the barest hint of skin peeking out from Jordan's top. Dray's hands shook, and she clenched them into tight fists to control herself.

"So who is right for me?" Jordan asked softly.

Dray blinked and refocused her attention from Jordan's stomach to her clear, brown eyes. She fumbled for something to say but words wouldn't come. Color flushed Jordan's cheeks and her gaze held Dray's for a moment. Jordan looked down. Dray's mind went blank as she struggled with how to answer Jordan's question without sounding like a lovesick teenager.

Her struggles faded when she felt the barest touch along the back of her clenched fist. Her gaze dropped to see Jordan's finger tracing the outline of Dray's hand. She relaxed her fist, opening to Jordan's tenuous touch. Her heartbeat pounded in her ears as Jordan's fingers caressed her palm. Dray's fingers touched the softness of Jordan's hand. Desire heated her cheeks, and a different heat focused below her stomach. She traced her fingers along Jordan's wrist and caressed Jordan's arm. She braved looking back into Jordan's face. Brown eyes, dilated by desire, stared back at her. Jordan bit her lower lip, a red, moist lip Dray wanted to feel with her tongue. She leaned closer, watching Jordan closely for any sign she might pull away from her. Dray closed her eyes just as she brushed her lips against Jordan's in the lightest kiss. She lifted her free hand to slip through Jordan's long black hair, its silky strands brushing along the back of her hand. Dray pulled Jordan closer, deepening their first kiss. She tugged Jordan's lower lip, hearing a soft moan escape from her.

Jordan pulled slowly out of their kiss, and Dray froze, fearing she'd gone too far. She opened her eyes to see Jordan's shy smile and relaxed. Resting her head on Jordan's shoulder, she caught Jordan's scent, indescribable and arousing. "You smell wonderful. What perfume are you wearing?"

Jordan tensed and pushed Dray off. She sat back, crossing her arms. "We should go to sleep. We've got N'Gollo's lecture first thing tomorrow, and I don't want to be too sleepy to follow her lesson."

Dray shifted back to her own bunk, confused and frustrated. Hadn't Jordan been a willing participant in that kiss? And now she was shoving Dray off with some lame excuse? "Fine," Dray said. But she didn't feel fine as she crawled under her covers and struggled to understand what had just happened.

JORDAN CURLED UP with her back to Dray, silent until she heard the soft sounds of Dray's snoring. Then she let the tears flow. The memory of Dray's lips on hers mingled with the sting of Dray's words. Of course Dray would sense Jordan's unique scent and question it. Jordan should feel lucky Dray didn't recognize it as a Novan scent. Jordan's pheromones weren't as strong as a full-blooded Novan's. She would have to be sitting right next to another Novan to be recognized, but Terrans always reacted to it. It was the curse that kept Jordan from trusting any relationship. In that moment, when Jordan pushed Dray away, she hated her father for the first time, and the Novan traits she inherited from him. If she was truly Terran, she wouldn't be crying in the dark. She'd be making love to a beautiful woman who wanted her. Instead, she was forced to isolate herself again. And how would Dray feel? She'd hate her, and Jordan couldn't do anything to stop it.

THE 28th SQUADRON stood outside the lecture hall, waiting for Instructor N'Gollo. Dray and Jordan stood by opposite walls in the crowded corridor. Dray's concentration was focused on Jordan, still wondering what she'd done wrong. She didn't hear Jenny and Red come up until Red tapped her on the shoulder.

"Oh, sorry," she said.

"You seem distracted this morning," Red said with a wink.

Dray looked up into his wide green eyes, puzzled, until Jenny whispered in her ear, "What do you think he and Jordan talked about last night?"

Dray couldn't hide her frustration and didn't try. Was Jordan just playing with her? First she confided who knows what to Red, then she ignored Dray all morning after they kissed the night before.

"Am I missing something?" Jenny asked.

"I know I am," Dray said. N'Gollo opening the lecture hall door ended their conversation. N'Gollo waited for the squadron to settle into their seats, then she flicked on the vid-screen. A Tamil-class troop transport illuminated the screen, superimposed over a planet Dray didn't recognize. A handful of groans from her squadron mates suggested some of them did recognize the planet, and not in a good way.

"Okay, as some of you already guessed, we are going on an excursion today," N'Gollo, said, standing to the side of the vid-screen. She pointed to the gray-brown planet. More groans emerged from the class. "We're going to Achilles-1. We'll take a Tamil-class transport and practice landfall and planetary take off. As you can imagine, this will take a few days. It's not the prettiest scenery, but you'll get no storm interference."

A short tremor rolled through the infrastructure of the classroom. Dray looked around, confused, as N'Gollo paused in her speech. The squadron sat in silence, as confused as Dray was. Two more tremors shook the classroom, rattling chairs and Dray's nerves. She heard a muffled rumble, like an engine starting, from somewhere above them.

N'Gollo marched to the door. "Cadet Corporal Baron, take over." She flicked on her personal com-link as the door slid shut behind her.

Red walked to the front of the class. His steady composure seemed in stark contrast to Dray's nervousness. Base stations didn't rattle, at least not in her experience.

Red stood in front of the vid-screen. "As Instructor N'Gollo was saying, we won't be leaving the transport during this exercise. The ship has already been loaded with food and supplies."

They all heard the echo of a remote explosion of some kind. Seconds later, the emergency alarm clanged in three rapid segments, paused, and repeated the alert while the classroom com-link roared into life.

"Station emergency. Initiate lockdown procedures. Repeat. Station emergency. Initiate lockdown procedures."

The message blared in a continual loop until Red turned down the volume. "Bello! Hold open that door until N'Gollo gets back in here!"

Bello jumped out of his seat and stood before the door, slapping his palm against the Chip-ID reader. When the automatic open did not trigger, he banged on the manual door open pad. "It's too late. We're stuck in here until this drill is over."

Red marched to the door and pushed against it in frustration. Another tremor rolled through the classroom. "This is no drill."

"What do we do now?" Dray asked.

Red returned to the front of the classroom. "We wait. Whatever the problem is, we're in lockdown. Every lecture hall has been automatically shut, and every major section of the station is in isolation by now. If it's a hull breach, we'll be released as soon as they isolate the section and verify the rest of the station."

Jordan moved to sit beside Dray. "And if it's not?"

Dray shrugged, masking her own nervousness. "Probably a cadet just blew a landing."

Another explosion rumbled somewhere above them, strong enough to throw the vid-screen out of focus. Half the squadron jumped out of their seats, pushing toward the locked door. Red hopped on top of the front desk.

"Back to your seats. That's an order." His voice boomed over the upset cadets. Most obeyed. A few stragglers waited until Red stood over them, his muscular orange bulk staring down at them until they shuffled back to their seats.

"There are over three thousand people on this station," he said. "Including two full fighting wings in active status." His words sent a wave of calm over the squadron. "Whatever is going on out there, they are more than capable of taking care of it, and we are better off right here, out of their way."

Within an hour, the squadron had relaxed into the monotony of their forced isolation. A group of cadets huddled around a game of electro-dice, while a handful of others pushed the desks to the side and practiced martial drills in the back of the room. Dray and Jordan sat with Jenny at one of the side tables. They kept away from Red, so they wouldn't detract from his status as de facto commander of the squadron. From time to time, Jenny went to talk to him.

At odd intervals, more explosions rattled through the base station.

"I wish it would stop." Jordan sat on the desk with her arms wrapped around her legs.

Dray looked at her, wanting to hold her to comfort her, but not daring to. "There's fewer of them now."

Jordan gave her a weak smile as another explosion shook the classroom.

Two more hours passed, accentuated by repeated, distant explosions, before the com-link changed the lockdown message. Jenny pointed out the change to Red, and he turned the volume back up.

"... ...systems failing. All personnel report to your evacuation launch point. Repeat—Buenos Aires has been compromised. Life support systems failing. All personnel... ..."

The door that Bello was leaning against slid open behind him, and he jumped back. Fear of the unknown gripped most of the squadron, no longer eager to leave the relative safety of the classroom. Bello leaned out of the door, then came back inside. "Two other rooms are marching double-time."

Red joined him at the door. "Any sign of N'Gollo?"

"Not that I can see."

Red turned back to the squad. "Okay, we've done this as a drill before. We stay as a squadron. The nearest evac pad for us will be launch bay 6-17D, one level above us."

The squadron lined up behind him in formation.

"We go two by two, double-time. Cadet Corporal Tomiko?"

"Yes, Sir," Jenny answered.

"You are in front with me. Bello, take the rear."

In military order, the 28th squadron trotted down the hallway with one other squadron trotting along side them. Dray kept pace with Jordan near the middle of the column of cadets as they made their way to the fire-safe stairwell leading up to the evacuation area. The 28th led the two squadrons up the stairs. The precise clang of boots on composite stairs gave Dray renewed confidence. They were trained for emergencies and would all come out of this together.

The column stopped. Word came down the line that debris blocked the stairwell above them, and they would have to use another evac site. Dray looked at the door below her. They would have to go down to Level 19D, where the fighter pilots stayed.

Red worked his way down the line and led them to the lower exit. "We don't know what's beyond this door, but obviously there's been a lot of damage to the station in this section. We'll go out in groups of six. Keep your eyes open and stay together."

Red opened the door and led the first group through. Dray and Jordan waited with Jenny, who would lead the second group. Dray scanned the staircase below them, where dusty steps were covered in debris. Composite rods protruded from fragments of the plasteen wall. She trotted down the steps and picked up a piece of the shattered plasteen wall.

"Jenny," she said, bringing the fragment back up. "The edges are melted."

Jenny examined the plasteen. "Looks like weapons fire."

"And we just sent Red and five others out there unarmed," Dray said.

Jordan examined the fractured wall leading down to Level

20D. "She's right. There are clear laser burns all the way down."

Dray looked at the wall fragment again. Laser guns? On an orbital space station? Whoever attacked the station was either insane or trying to destroy the entire station. One stray shot through the station hull and the area would become a vacuum. Dray hoped the automatic bulkheads were still functional.

"Okay," Jenny said. "Send word up the line. Tell them to go back to Level 18D and find an alternate route to the evac site on 19D."

Dray looked at Jenny. "What about you?"

Jenny turned to the door. "I'm going after Red."

"Not on your own," Dray said.

Jenny turned back. "I can't order you to come with me."

"And you can't order us to stay behind," Jordan said.

"Okay," Jenny said. "Warn the others the station is under attack. Tell them to arm themselves."

The two squadrons moved back up the stairs, with the alternate squad's leader in command. "Where's the nearest weapons cache to us?" Dray asked.

"The central store's depot on ring one. That's halfway across the station. Unless you want to go up a couple of levels," Jenny answered.

Dray stared at the closed door. She had no intention of deserting Red and the other cadets he'd taken with him. She wished they had hand weapons, at least. "Let's get going."

JORDAN'S HEART POUNDED as Jenny hit the "door open" button. The door slid back halfway before it stuck in its track. The three women squeezed through the opening and into the nearest dorm room. Dray examined the room's contents while Jordan scoped the activity down the hallway. A haze of smoke occluded her view, but she heard the distinct crackle of projectile weapons being fired in the distance. She saw no sign of Red and his group of cadets.

"Nothing useful in here," Dray said.

"Let's work our way down the hallway and check each room. These are officer's quarters and some of them must have weapons," Jenny said.

They trotted in and out of multiple rooms as they made their way down the deserted hallway. All they managed to pick up was a metal-tipped cane and an antique survival knife. An open doorway in front of them led to the shared common area. Jenny leaned through the opening.

"Anything?" Jordan asked.

"Something is burning. I can't see beyond that. No wait. There's a group huddled behind the counters on the near side."

"Red?" Dray asked.

"I can't tell, but some are wearing cadet uniforms." She ducked back into their hallway. "Are you ready? We're in an open area between here and the group. If there are enemy forces in there, we'll be easy targets."

Dray gripped the survival knife as sweat beaded on her forehead. They hadn't trained for weaponless combat. "Ready."

In a crouched position, they scrambled from their relative safety to the counters with the other group. No shots were fired in their crossing.

Red watched their approach. "Where are the others?"

"I sent them back up a level. We figured out the station was under attack." Jenny crouched next to Red.

"You should have gone with them."

Jenny smirked. "Yeah, and I'm happy to see you, too."

"We haven't seen the enemy yet, but we can't see much beyond that burning storage bin," he said. "I'm going for recon. If it's clear, I'll signal for the rest of you to follow."

"We should go back," Jenny said. "We can follow the rest of the squad to another evac site."

"I can't. Did you count? There's only five of us here. Paxton panicked and ran ahead. I have to get him back."

Jenny nodded. "Take this." She handed him the cane. "It's all we could find."

Red grinned. "Thanks, but it's not much help against projectile weapons."

He scrambled from their cover to the nearest overturned table. The smoke from the burning bin filled Jordan's nostrils as she tracked Red's progress through the common area. They should have sent someone smaller, she thought as she watched his bulky body through the haze. He zigzagged across the open space until he was even with the burning bin. As he scrambled out from his last cover, shots rang out, echoing through the near-empty area. Red fell to the ground.

"He's hit." Jenny ran out into the open before Jordan could grab her.

"What's she doing?" Jordan asked, panic rising in her voice. If anything happened to Jenny, they were leaderless. Jenny scrambled from table to table, following Red's path. Two more shots rang out as she ran from cover to cover. *Jenny will be an easy hit if she goes for Red*, Jordan thought. She turned to the other cadets huddled with them. Four were near panic. They wouldn't help. That left Venkata, a hulking, gray Gilgaran female wearing black protective eye covers and an air filter generating the atmospheric content of her home world.

"Venkata," Jordan said. The gray Gilgaran turned to her. "Can you make sounds like weapons fire?"

"What are you doing?" Dray asked.

"Gilgarans can imitate any sound they hear," Jordan explained.

Venkata looked down the smoky space separating them from where Jenny paused. "Just tell me when."

"When Jenny makes her move for Red, simulate an assault rifle," Jordan said.

"Make it sound like half a squad is laying down cover for her," Dray added.

Venkata nodded and pushed her way forward. With arms the size of thighs, there was no room for anyone else by the edge of the counter they hid behind besides Venkata. Jordan prayed the Gilgaran would come through. A heartbeat later, Venkata threw her head back and the sound of realistic projectile fire came forth from her massive lungs. The sound was enough to make the other cadets cover their ears. When Venkata stopped for a long breath from her air filter, Dray scrambled around her and looked down the hall.

"Yes! It worked. Jenny's got Red with her behind an overturned table," Dray said, slapping Venkata on the back.

"Now what?" Jordan asked. "If he's hurt, there's no way she can drag him all the way back here."

Jordan heard shouting coming from the hallway where they had first come into the common area. The distinctly female voice continued shouting and banging her way down the hallway. Whoever it was, if she continued making that noise, she'd be a sizable target for whoever was firing on them.

"I have to go shut that idiot up," Dray said.

Jordan grabbed Dray. She stared into Dray's blue eyes, regretting all that had and hadn't passed between them. She slid her hand down Dray's arm. "Please be careful," she whispered.

Dray lifted Jordan's hand to her lips and kissed it. "I'll be back soon. With that screaming idiot either in tow or unconscious."

Jordan let go reluctantly. Dray clutched the knife and sprinted back down the common area. Venkata sounded off another round of simulated fire to protect Dray's dash to the hallway.

Jordan's mind went numb as she watched Dray disappear through a doorway. Venkata's simulated noises ended, but the echo of weapons fire remained in Jordan's mind. What if the person was one of the enemy, she thought. And Dray just ran after them with nothing but a knife. Jordan shifted to a squatting position. "I'm going after her."

Venkata shot out a massive forearm, pinning Jordan to the spot. "No, you're not. We're supposed to be a unit, not a scrambling bunch of frightened rabbits."

Jordan pushed against Venkata's arm, but nothing was moving that bulk. "She could be hurt."

"Just listen."

Jordan tried. "I don't hear anything. It's gone quiet."

"Well, that's partly true," Venkata said. "The woman stopped hollering. Dray is talking to her."

"You can hear her?" Jordan relaxed. Dray hadn't run into a trap.

"I can't make out the words, but yes, it's definitely Dray's voice. The other voice sounds familiar, too."

Jordan did not care who the other woman was, so long as Dray came back safely.

DRAY SLID TO a stop just inside the dorm hallway. She could hear the woman clearly now, storming from room to room. Dray approached the nearest dorm room just as a familiar blond woman emerged, holding a real assault rifle aimed at Dray's chest.

"Easy! I'm Draybeck, from the 28th squadron!" Dray held up her hands, dropping her knife. The ammunition magazine in the rifle marked it as station-safe, but it would still tear a sizable hole in her chest. Dray saw movement to her left. To her surprise, Bello came out of another dorm room, holding a handgun. They'd obviously found a weapons cache. His eyes narrowed to slits when he saw her, broadcasting his anger. She didn't particularly welcome his presence either. "Why are you here?" Dray asked.

Lieutenant Malory Grace lowered her weapon. She grabbed Dray by the cuff of her collar. "Where is she? Where's Jenny?"

"She's safe." Dray was still wondering why Bello wasn't with the rest of their squadron.

Malory let out a low sigh. "I heard weapons fire."

Dray loosened Malory's grip on her clothes. "Most of that was simulated fire. Jenny's safe, but she's pinned down by a sniper, with Red. He's injured, but I don't know how badly."

"Take me to them." Malory pushed Dray forward.

Dray picked up her knife and trotted to the nearest cover from the hallway door. It was enough to set Venkata sounding off cover fire again. The other two hid back, but Dray grabbed Malory. "It's simulated weapons fire. We have to run fast before the Gilgaran gets out of breath."

The three sprinted to join the rest of Dray's group, ducking behind the counter just as Venkata ran out of air. Malory scanned the small group. She turned back to Dray, the panicked expression returning to her face. "She's not here."

"I know. She's trapped out there." Dray pointed down the open space between them and the overturned table where Jenny crouched with Red propped up beside her.

Malory's expression turned from fear to determination.

"What's your plan, Lieutenant Grace?" Jordan asked.

"Where's the sniper, do you know?" Malory asked.

"We're not sure. Somewhere on the other side of the fire," Jordan said.

"I'm going after them." She took her eyes off of Jenny for a moment, turning to Dray and Bello. "I need your help. If Red can't walk, I'll need you two to help Jenny get him back here, while I protect you from the sniper."

"With respect, Ma'am, I should stay here and cover your back." Bello held up his gun.

Jordan pushed her way forward. "I'll go."

Dray's heart flip-flopped at the thought of Jordan running across the open space. What if she got shot? Dray cursed Bello under her breath for being a coward, but she had no time to convince Jordan to stay behind. On Malory's signal, the three of them darted from their cover and scrambled from table to table until they joined Jenny and Red. Light red blood pooled by Red's side from a wound below his shoulder.

Malory grabbed Jenny and pulled her into a frantic hug.

"Glad you could join the party," Red said, shifting to a sitting position. The effort painted a grimace across his pale orange face. He had a dark red bruise on his forehead from where he'd hit the ground.

Jenny pushed Malory back. "Why didn't you evac with your own pilot squad?"

Malory sat back on her heels. She glanced at Dray. "Our launch bay was mined. Those of us who survived split up to help evac the cadets. When I ran into the rest of your squad, Bello told me you lot were up to something stupid." She looked around at their sparse shelter. "Obviously, I was right to make him lead me to you."

"Paxton's gone," Red said. "I don't know if he made it through or not."

"You did your best," Jenny said.

"Thanks," Red said. "Now, if we could move this happy reunion someplace else?"

"Yes," Dray said. "Someplace less in-the-line-of-fire?" They were still far too exposed, and she wanted Jordan safely off the station. Dray watched over her shoulder as Jordan examined Red's wound. The bleeding had stopped.

"Can you walk?" Jordan asked.

Red shifted to a crouch. His jaw tightened in pain. "Yes."

"Okay, you three go for it," Malory said. "Venkata should do her magic once she sees us on the move. I'll follow."

Dray and Jordan waited on either side of Red, with Jenny in front to set the pace. On Malory's signal, they moved out. With the sounds of Venkata's simulated fire mixing with Malory's real weapons fire, they moved from cover to cover. When they made the final distance to the rest of their small group, Red collapsed to the floor, fresh blood oozing from his wound.

"Not as bad as it looks," he said, holding his shoulder. His hand came away speckled in blood. "Tarquins heal fast."

"Okay, let's move out of here," Malory said. "What evac site were you headed for?"

"This one," Dray said. "But we're blocked from that now."

"Then we go down to the next evac on Level 21D and across to ring six," Malory said, leading the way.

Dray helped Red stand, hoping his was the last injury their party sustained.

JORDAN HURRIED WITH the rest of the group as they worked their way through the deserted Level 20D. In stark contrast to the level above, this level had no visible sign of attack or debris. Jordan didn't trust the eerie silence. Even the evacuation alert was silent.

"How are you doing?" she asked as she walked beside Red through the quiet hallway.

"The bleeding has stopped." He examined his shoulder. "Do you think everyone made it off from this level?"

Jordan looked around. "I think so, yes. Do you know what's going on?"

"Not much more than you. It looks like a full-fledged attack."

"Novans, I bet," Bello said.

Malory grabbed Bello's arm. "Did you see any of the enemy? Are they Novans?" The thought of Novans on the base station did not frighten Jordan as much as she thought it would. She knew she was in a mild state of shock already, as were most of her fellow cadets. She saw the signs of it in each of their faces. Some were just shy of panic. Except Bello. Jordan found the Aquaran's expression unreadable as he marched behind Dray.

"I don't know," Bello answered. "I wouldn't put it past them to attack a bunch of unarmed cadets, would you?"

Jordan ignored Bello's comment. When she first came to the

program, she flinched every time someone insulted Novans, but the bias was so pervasive she barely registered yet another jibe against her father's people. It just reinforced her determination to keep her heritage a secret.

They reached the stairwell on the far side of the common room after a successful foray into a small arms cache on ring one that Malory had clearance to unlock. Jordan picked out a handgun and shock grenades. Dray came up next to her, loaded down with her own selected weapons.

"Do you think we'll make it off the station?" Jordan asked.

Dray hoisted a burst-fire machine gun onto her shoulder. "Yeah, I think so," she said with a determined grin. In any other circumstance, Jordan would have laughed at Dray's ever-present bravado. Now, she just prayed Dray was right. Their weapons were all station-safe, but their attackers didn't seem to be worried about blowing a hole through the station's hull.

Chapter Four

MALORY SCOUTED AHEAD on the stairs as the rest of the group waited for her report. Dray glanced at Bello. He sat on his own, unusually quiet. None of his friends were in their small group. Dray tensed at the sound of boots stomping up the stairs below them. She remained alert when she saw Malory coming up the stairs.

"I found N'Gollo," she said, out of breath as she reached their level. "She's with a group of younger cadets, holding position outside the evac area."

Red stood up. "How many enemy combatants are there?"

Malory shrugged. "No idea."

They worked their way down the staircase to Level 21D, scrambling over debris blocking their path. Malory shouted her name and rank as she neared the hallway leading to the launch bay control room. Two young cadets came out of hiding to give the all-clear signal, letting the group proceed behind their makeshift barricade.

"You all stay here while I go talk to N'Gollo," Malory ordered.

Red squatted down beside the young cadets, favoring his injured shoulder. The rest of the group split up along the barricade for extra protection, but Dray left her machine gun behind and followed Malory into the control room. Not that she didn't trust her, but Dray wanted to be sure of an accurate account of N'Gollo's orders.

N'Gollo studied the holo-screens, the glow of their displays reflecting off her dark skin. Covered in dust and spots of dried blood, she looked far worse than most of their own group, except for Red.

N'Gollo turned to them as they entered. "Name and rank."

Malory stood at attention. "Malory Grace, Lieutenant."

Dray stood to the side, unsure if she should announce herself or keep quiet.

N'Gollo's black eyes scanned her up and down and turned

back to Malory. "How many in your party?"

"Ten, Ma'am. One wounded," Malory reported.

"Who and how badly?"

"Red Baron. A projectile wound on his shoulder. The bleeding has stopped," Malory said.

N'Gollo turned back to the holo-screens. "What are the ranks in your party?"

Malory thought a moment. "Seven cadet privates first class, three cadet corporals, and one lieutenant."

N'Gollo swore under her breath. "I've got one cadet corporal and fifteen cadet privates here." She looked back up. "You're second in command, Lieutenant Grace. You'd better be up to it."

"Yes, Ma'am."

Dray watched the color drain from Malory's face. She regretted forcing herself into this meeting with N'Gollo. Only recently promoted to cadet private first class herself, she was out of line.

Dray felt N'Gollo's stare as the instructor's attention turned to her. "Draybeck. Can I assume Bowers is here as well?"

"Yes, Ma'am." A trickle of sweat slipped down Dray's brow.

"Good. We need all the help we can get. Come here, both of you."

Dray and Malory joined N'Gollo at the holo-screens. To Dray's dismay, three of the four screens showed scenes of destruction. Twisted plasteen jutted out from billowing clouds of smoke and fire. Dray turned to the fourth screen. It took a while for her to make out the dark images displayed there. When she realized what she saw, she turned away in disgust.

"It gets worse," N'Gollo said. "That was a group of veterans trying to break through the blockade so our group of cadets could evacuate. The enemy had the corridor mined."

Dray closed her eyes, forcing the bile back down. "Is it Novans, Ma'am?"

N'Gollo's jaw tightened. "Yes, but the few I've seen are not in Novan military uniforms. They're most likely a terrorist cell. Who knows how long they've been operating on this station. Nothing officially sanctioned by the Novan government, I'm sure. They'll claim it was an independent attack." N'Gollo turned back to the holo-screen. "I can't tell how many there are left in this area. The damage to the station is extensive. It was a well-planned strike."

"Ma'am?" Dray interrupted.

"Yes?"

"Why here? Why this station?"

"Just a guess, but I'm thinking they were after the Recon section." She glanced back at the two of them. "It was classified, but I'm sure half the cadet wing tried to get a look at it anyway. We captured an intact Novan fighter two weeks ago. It was stored on this station, temporarily."

Dray remembered the day she ran into her brother, when she was one of those cadets sneaking a peek at the enemy ship. She was glad he was far from the station now. "But, Ma'am, we're pretty far away from where the ship was stored."

"Yes, but what better way to make it look like a random act than to blow up as many parts of the station as possible? I'm sure they were after that ship. It was the latest model, and we'd never captured one intact before."

"Did the others... Did anyone evac from this area?" Malory asked.

N'Gollo grimaced. "Not that I've seen. The Novans cut off external communications and vid-screens. We can't see how many evac ships made it off the station."

N'Gollo punched up a different holo-screen. This one displayed a map of a different region of the base station. She called Malory over. "Do you recognize this location?"

"Yes, Ma'am," Malory said, staring at the map. "The interior ring one maintenance bay."

"That's where we are heading. There's usually at least one ship in there, flight-ready. I'm hoping the Novans didn't think to take over those areas."

N'Gollo straightened up, wincing. "Are you all armed?"

"Assault rifles and shock grenades," Malory said.

"No stun launchers?"

"No, Ma'am."

N'Gollo shrugged. "It'll do. Let's move out."

JORDAN SAT BEHIND the barricade with Sahar, the only cadet corporal with N'Gollo's group. "How did you end up here?" she asked.

"I was tutoring a group of cadets when the Novans attacked. N'Gollo caught up with us and redirected us from a destroyed evac site."

Dray came out of N'Gollo's command center, her face pale. They were heading to the maintenance launch bay, their last hope to get off the station. With N'Gollo leading their combined group, they worked their way through three rings without incident. Red took up position as rear guard with Dray and Jordan. N'Gollo kept Malory at her side in the front, feeding her instructions along the route.

Jordan felt sorry for the young cadets, some of whom were not even adults yet. They marched through one long abandoned corridor after another. By the time they reached ring two, the group had regained some semblance of calm, though N'Gollo kept strict military order in the group. Even Jordan's tight-lipped concentration began to loosen as they marched on.

Shots rang out in the front of their group. Jordan reacted on instinct, pulling the nearest cadets into a maintenance closet for cover. She watched Red make his way silently up the corridor to investigate. Before he reached the front, Malory stepped into the corridor, giving the all-clear signal. Her face was ashen. Jordan and Dray trotted forward, catching up with Red as they joined Malory.

As the group of cadets parted, Jordan saw Jenny huddled over a body on the ground. Red leaned over her, then fell to his knees. Jordan pushed her way through and stood over the still form of Instructor N'Gollo. By the size of the hole in her chest, there was no doubt the older woman's death had been mercifully quick.

Red clenched his fists and let out a roar that could only be compared to that of a Terran lion. His face turned a deep red. "How?" he asked, staring at Malory, who backed up a step.

"There was a blast of laser fire and before we knew what was happening, she was down," Malory explained. "There was too much fire for one man, but all we found alive was him." She pointed beyond their group. Jordan turned and saw that Bello and Venkata held a straggly, bearded man in brown fatigues, bleeding from a wound in his leg. Next to him lay another body, dressed the same as the first man. Another Novan. Jordan took an involuntary step backward. Had he sensed her? She didn't think he was close enough.

Red growled and charged the prisoner, raking the man's chest with his claws before Venkata could pull him off.

"Leave him," Venkata said. "It won't bring N'Gollo back."

"He deserves to die," Red said, panting.

"We need him," Malory said, stepping away from N'Gollo's body to put a hand on Red's shoulder. "If he's down here, there could be more. Or they could have mined the maintenance launch bay as well."

Red pulled away from them and leaned against the wall. Jordan knelt by N'Gollo's body and performed the unpleasant task of stripping the instructor of her weapons and grenades, as well as her com-link. She unclipped one of N'Gollo's ID tags and stuffed it in her pocket.

"Why?" Dray asked in a whisper.

"In case something happens and we can't recover her body." Jordan looked at Dray with tears forming in her eyes. "I want to give something to her family to remember her by."

Jordan eyed the remaining terrorist. She could barely make out his unique scent, but it was enough to confirm that he was Novan. She backed further away from him, not daring to get close enough for him to mark her as Novan as well. She grabbed Dray's elbow. "What's Malory going to do with him?" she asked in a fierce whisper.

"Shoot him on the spot, I hope. He's Novan, and he killed N'Gollo."

Jordan blanched. Dray's words emphasized just how much danger Jordan was in. If they discovered her Novan origins, they'd turn on her as well.

"We need to keep going," Jenny said, turning to Malory.

Malory pushed her blond hair back, fear and uncertainty reflected in her blue eyes. "Yes, you're right." She clutched her weapon to her chest and looked back to N'Gollo one last time. "She wanted us to try the maintenance launch bay. We just need to find the right corridor."

"What about him?" Bello asked, shaking his prisoner.

Malory didn't answer right away.

Jordan panicked, squeezing Dray's arm. "Tell her to leave him behind. Lock him up or something."

Dray pulled her arm away and rubbed the spot where Jordan was holding her. "Are you okay?" she asked.

Jordan crossed her arms to hide how much she was shaking. In all her planning, she had never considered the possibility of meeting another Novan. Not on a Terran base station. She had to protect herself. "I'm fine. I just...I want to get out of here."

Malory turned back to their Novan prisoner and leveled her weapon at his temple. "Are the corridors to maintenance mined?"

His pale gray eyes glared back at her. "I'm not with the Novans. I was trying to protect your C.O. when this man fired." He pointed at the corpse on the ground behind him.

"And I should just believe you?" Malory asked.

The prisoner sighed. "Look, you're a pack of leaderless kids in more danger than you realize. I'm not your enemy."

"Then who are you?" Malory asked, her gun still pointed at his head.

"Captain Franklin, Terran Military Intel. I've been working under cover for the past two months."

Malory frowned and lowered her weapon.

"He's lying," Jordan said. He glared at her, but Jordan couldn't let him con his way into their group. "If he's a captain, let him prove it."

"We can do that in part, anyway," Malory said. "Maintenance bay requires military chip identification. If your chip-ID gains us access, we'll know you're Terran."

Jordan scrambled for some way to explain how she knew chip-IDs could be fooled. She couldn't come up with anything that didn't reveal why her own chip-ID identified her as Terran when she wasn't.

Franklin stared at his palm. "I can't." He glared at Malory. "I had my chip-ID disabled for this mission."

Malory barked out a harsh laugh. "Right. Convenient excuse, Franklin. If that's even your name. Back to the original question. Are the corridors mined down here?"

"Officially, I outrank you, Lieutenant," he said through clenched teeth. "There is a very special ship on this station, and we need to ensure the Novans don't get it."

Malory's eyes narrowed. "And you expect us to help you? Red? I need your assistance here."

Red pushed off the wall and walked to her side. Franklin shrank back.

Malory looked like she wanted to spit at Franklin. "Have you never met a Tarquin before?"

Franklin shook his head.

"Did you know they used to hunt each other? Cannibals is what we'd call it on Earth. You have a choice," Malory said. "You can cooperate, or you can become lunch for my friend here. Tarquin males have excellent canines for gnawing the flesh off bones."

Red took another step closer, baring his teeth.

"There's only one ship of value down here, and it's not a standard ADF ship." Franklin tried to take a step back. Bello and Venkata prevented him. "The details are classified, but it will get us off this station."

Jordan stood to the side, holding her fear back and sizing up the cadets around her. If she were exposed, who would turn against her? As she examined each face, she doubted each one, with the exception of Red and Venkata. Tarquins were only loosely associated with the ADF, and Gilgarans maintained strict neutrality. Venkata would be transferring to the Gilgaran Planetary Defense Force once she got her officer credentials. Jordan studied Dray last. Would Dray accept her, or would her prejudice prevent her from seeing anything in Jordan but the face of her enemy?

"Are there more of your kind down here?" Malory asked the prisoner.

Jordan wanted to scream at Malory to just leave him behind, but she'd drawn enough suspicion on herself already.

"No one is supposed to be down here," he said. " I just—" he stopped short, as if he were about to reveal something he shouldn't.

Malory sneered at him. "You deserted."

"I'm a Terran officer."

"With no way to prove it. Bello, find something to tie his hands together. " She turned away and marched back to the group with Red.

RED WALKED PAST them all to take up his position in the rear. Jordan followed him, but Dray hesitated. Malory Grace was leading their group, again. The prisoner was right. They were a bunch of lost cadets trying to find their way out of a situation they were never trained for. Malory's skills were focused on her own survival, but Dray didn't think it was enough to keep their entire group alive. She would have stayed in the front to keep an eye on Malory, but Jenny waved her off. Dray stood to the side as the group marched past her.

"The ship we need to take is on the other side of ring one," Franklin said.

"We keep with N'Gollo's plan." Malory pushed him in front of her with the business end of her gun. "Lead the way, mystery man."

"My name's Franklin."

"Just lead." Malory pushed him along. "If the Novans did put mines down here, you'll be the first to pop."

In single file, they followed Franklin and Malory down the final corridor. It ended in a pile of smoking debris. Dray sensed the rising panic in the group of cadets around her. They needed to find a way off this station.

Malory turned the group around and backtracked, past N'Gollo's body and down another corridor. They passed two more destroyed launch areas before they found one untouched by destruction. The section was listed as classified, but Malory blasted through the locked door. Inside, the launch bay was deserted except for one modified Tamil-class transport.

"It's not a standard Tamil ship, for sure." Malory turned to Franklin. "This is the ship you were after, isn't it?"

"Yes."

The ship was massive compared to the Cygna frigate Dray had piloted. It seemed like a lifetime ago. This ship had all sets of gun turrets removed, leaving bare silver panels in their place.

Jenny and Sahar trotted ahead and scanned the interior and exterior of the ship while the rest of the group remained on guard outside. Dray waited with the rest, fidgeting from foot to foot. She hated their position. They were in the open with nothing between them and any attackers entering the area. But at least no more explosions rattled the station.

Jenny poked her head out of the access ramp. "It's got a few days' provisions, but no weapons."

Sahar came around from the aft section. "The engines are modified, but I can't tell why."

Malory glared at Franklin. "You want to tell us what's up with this ship?"

"I told you, it's classified. If we're lucky, the Novans don't even know it's here."

"It's enough to get us off this station." Malory studied Franklin for a moment. "I don't know if you really are a Terran officer or not, so you come with us until we can prove who you are. Let's go."

The group trotted up the ramp and into the transport ship. The Tamil-class ship had ample room to hold their small group. Dray waited for Jordan, who walked up the ramp last. She seemed to keep as far from the Novan prisoner as possible, and Dray didn't blame her. Dray had never seen Jordan so rattled by anyone before, but they were all reacting to a frightening and dangerous situation.

By the time Dray boarded the ship, the rest of the group had moved into the interior, with Venkata taking control of the younger cadets. Jenny and Red sat in dual copilot seats, leaving the main command console open for Malory. Sahar and Bello sat on either side of the prisoner in the far crew seats, acting as his guards. Dray strapped into a spare crew seat next to Jordan.

Malory buckled into the ship's commander seat and swiveled her chair to face the group behind her. "N'Gollo said we should fly clear of the station, but stay within Buenos Aires perimeter until the rescue team arrives. There were over twenty evac ships on station. Some of them must have made it clear."

She turned back to the front, locked her chair in the forward position, and synced her command implant into the ship's controls. Dray realized how lucky they were to have Malory with them. Only a credentialed pilot with the right command authorization could launch this ship.

"Prepare for launch," Malory said.

Dray watched the long rampart fold up under the ship and the access doors seal shut. The engines rumbled beneath her boots as Jenny and Red worked their way through launch preparations.

"This nightmare's almost over," Dray said to Jordan, sitting next to her.

"Thank God." Jordan looked pale. She kept glancing back at the prisoner as if she expected him to escape.

"Don't worry, he's not going anywhere," Dray said.

"Malory should have left him behind."

Dray stared at the prisoner. "If he's with us, at least we know he's not telling the rest of his cronies what we're up to." The engines lifted them off the launch bay floor, returning Dray's attention to the command deck.

"Clear to launch," Red said.

"Engage launch engines." Malory stared at her holo display as she coordinated takeoff.

Dray looked out the ship's front view port at the black expanse of space beyond the launch bay. The transport rose and hovered over the launch bay a moment and moved toward the black open space. Dray let her eyes drift shut, relaxing into the smooth acceleration of the ship. They made it off the station.

"We're clear of the launch bay," Jenny said.

"Take us around to planet-side," Malory ordered. Dray opened her eyes and watched the expanse of empty space through the view port next to her. Pinpoints of light marked the distant stars, but she saw no evidence of other ships in the vicinity.

The ship turned to port and accelerated toward the far side of the base station. Dray studied the station as it passed by her view port. It looked the same as always, a metal behemoth in orbit around Achilles-5's largest moon. As Jenny steered the ship toward Achilles-5, the rest of the station came into view.

"Look," Jordan said. "That's where they blew out the launch bays."

Dray kept her eyes on the damaged station, unable to resist staring at the destruction. *How many people died in this attack?* she wondered. Craters marred the surface of the station, marking each bomb site. The Novans had primarily targeted the launch and maintenance bays. Their group was lucky the Novans hadn't reached the classified bay where they found this ship. She glanced at the prisoner, wondering if he was supposed to be the one to blow up this one. He made it clear this was the ship he'd been referring to when they first left N'Gollo. *Why insist on escaping in the ship if he was supposed to blow it up?*

"We've got debris." Red's hands flew over the ships controls.

Scraps of metal drifted across the front view port as Jenny and Red guided the ship through the debris field. "What do you think it's from?" Dray asked. Why were parts of Buenos Aries drifting this far out?

The perimeter alarm clanged, sending Dray's heart racing.

"We've got hostiles," Red said. "Anything at all for weapons?"

"Nothing," Malory said. "Whatever this ship's for, it's not combat-ready."

"We're not alone out here," Jenny said. "I'm picking up FX-27s." She turned to Malory. "A partial squadron is between us and the hostiles."

"What class are the enemy ships?" Malory asked.

"Novan fighters. Three of them." Jenny turned to face Malory, all color draining from her cheeks.

Malory leaned back. "Damn it. This wasn't some random terrorist attack. Give me full flight control. We'll see if we can intimidate the Novans with size."

Dray watched as Malory enabled her flight-reflex implants and steered the transport toward the Terran fighters, accelerating into the turn.

"Three hostiles heading for the FX-27s," Red declared.

Dray stretched in her restraints, trying to get a clear view through the front view port. She could make out the seven FX-27s in formation. They were in the shape of a half-V formation, like a wounded flock of birds. Still, seven against three were good odds for the ADF force.

Jenny scanned her display. "There is a cluster of evac ships on the far side of the station with a full wing of FX-27s protecting them."

And we came out in the middle of a battle, Dray thought. The Novan fighters were too small to see from a distance, but as Malory steered closer, Dray made out three ships approaching the FX-27s. The black space between Terran and Novan forces lit up with glowing trails of weapons fire. One of the Novan fighters transformed into a glowing ball and disappeared.

"Score one for the good guys," she said. Weapons fire traced across the black space again, but the two remaining Novan fighters avoided the attack, flying closer to the FX-27s.

"Have the hostiles fired any weapons?" Malory asked.

"Negative," Jenny said. "So far only our ships have fired."

Dray leaned forward. "What are they up to?"

The closest Novan fighter turned hard and spread what looked like elongated wings. The phantom wings separated an instant later into ten individual attack vessels. The second ship similarly transformed and the ADF squadron collapsed, with at least three fighters destroyed in less than a minute.

"They're Legion-class!" Jenny shouted.

The Tamil-class forward engines roared to life as Malory reversed direction. The ship turned hard to starboard. Dray's heart pounded as she watched the ruins of the lost fighters. She twisted in her seat, trying to see through her side view port. She saw Jordan's face in profile, tears tracing a path down her cheeks. She wanted to reach for her. Two more FX-27s exploded and dissipated into another debris field. Dray saw the unmistakable signs of four more Novan Legion fighters heading for their transport.

"Bringing up the hyper-engines," Malory said.

"We have no flight plan," Red replied.

Jenny swore. "Can we outrun them?"

"Not in this behemoth," Malory said.

Dray's heart pounded as two Novan fighters came in full view. She heard the high-pitched whine of the hyper-engines, but with no flight plan, they would be as good as dead if they jumped to hyperspace.

"Lieutenant Grace!" Franklin shouted. Malory looked at him over her shoulder. "Pull up the ship's travel log. Look for the last hyper-jump."

Malory glared at him for a heartbeat. "You heard him, Red. Find us a flight plan."

Red's orange hands tapped out commands on his console as Malory lurched the ship away from the nearest fighters.

"I've got one. Last used less than a week ago," Red said.

"Where to?" Malory asked.

"Not sure," Red studied his display. "An unmarked semi-habitable planet in an unclaimed zone."

Malory ran a hand through her disheveled hair. "Anything else?"

"No. It's the only hyper-jump in the log. It looks like a two week trip through hyperspace to get there."

"Well, that's where we go." Malory sat back in her seat. "Punch in the flight plan, and I'll take us out of here."

Bello squirmed in his seat, leaning forward. "Are you mad? It could be a Novan base for all we know."

Malory glared at him. "Keep silent, cadet. That's an order."

Dray watched the two closest Novan fighters heading toward their left flank. They were close enough to see each drone fighter as it launched. They were banking toward the Tamil ship for their final run. Dray gripped the arms of her seat as she watched.

"Flight plan ready," Red announced.

"Engines activated," Malory said.

Jordan grasped Dray's hand and held it as the hyper-engines roared. Dray hated the initial disorienting transition into hyperspace. It always left her nauseated for the rest of the day.

"Jump engaged," Malory said.

Dray's stomach lurched as the ship accelerated. Everything changed. Sight, sound, all senses faded, leaving her with the sensation of falling from an immense height. She couldn't feel the seat or her restraints, nor could she feel Jordan's hand in hers. The free-fall flooded her senses. Then it shifted into a complete lack of sensation. Dray fought a wave of panic. This was not hyper-jump. Something was very wrong.

Two panicking minutes later, she slammed into her restraints, feeling them stretch across her chest. Sight and sound returned as well, with a blast of sensation that sent her mind reeling. She blinked back tears. The ship decelerated as it approached a massive gray planet illuminated by a single star.

"You're hurting me," Jordan said.

"Oh, sorry." Dray let go of Jordan's hand, embarrassed at how tightly she had been clutching it. Jordan looked much more together than Dray.

Malory Grace sat slumped in her command chair. "What's wrong with Malory?" Dray asked.

Jenny turned and unbuckled herself. "She must have tried to stay in control of the ship through, well, through whatever the hell just happened." She lifted Malory's face in her hands. "Her reflex implants have gone into overdrive."

Malory slowly lifted her head, coming awake. She looked around in a daze and gave Jenny a half smile. "I'm okay." Relief washed Jenny's expression and she returned to her seat.

Red's hands flew over his controls as a frown spread across his wide features. "This is definitely not a standard Terran ship."

"Ship status?" Malory asked, disabling her link to the ship and holding her head in her hands.

Red frowned. "Near as I can tell, we are operational, but we've burned through most of our energy." He turned to Malory. "Whatever experimental engine we've got in this ship, it won't get us back to Buenos Aires."

"Great. So where are we?" Malory lifted her head. Dray didn't know what a reflex implant in overdrive felt like, but if Malory's pained expression was any indication, Dray hoped she never experienced it.

"We're just outside the planetary orbit of an unmarked giant-class planet," Jenny replied. "No sign of local technology or habitation."

"Planetary vitals?" Malory asked.

"Gravity is 1.1 Terran-standard. Atmosphere is borderline," Jenny said.

"How borderline?" Malory asked.

Red scanned the readout. "The air is breathable to Terrans but only for short periods. After three or more hours, the air will have detrimental effects. Terrans will be ship-bound most of the time."

"Is this the planet indicated by the hyper-jump flight plan?"

Red nodded. "It is a solitary giant-class planet in an F-class star system. And our two-week trip was condensed into a few minutes."

Malory leaned back. "Does this ship have a distress beacon?"

"We've got three," Jenny said.

"Good. Send off one with our situation and coordinates. Then take us planet-side."

JORDAN INTERRUPTED MALORY. "May I make a suggestion before you send off the probe?"

Malory glanced at her over her shoulder. "Well?"

"We don't want to send it back to Buenos Aires. The Novans might have access to our encryption codes by now." Jordan took a steadying breath. "I could reprogram the probe to use a special ambassador code." A map of jealousy was stamped on Malory's expression, just as Jordan expected. She ignored it. "It would keep our message from being intercepted. The Novans wouldn't be able to find us."

Malory waved her forward. "Who am I to stand in the way of the privileged?"

Jordan ignored the taunt. She'd spent most of her life under the jealous glare of others. As she keyed in one of her mother's ambassador codes, she hoped she wouldn't see the same look of envy on Dray's face. Getting rescued and away from the Novans was Jordan's top priority. And her mother had enough political clout to ensure the fastest rescue possible.

Jordan finished her entry. "Now you can add whatever you want to the message." She glanced at Dray, who was watching her approach. Was Dray envious? She shouldn't be, coming from a well-positioned military family. Jordan sat back down and buckled in as the ship's engines slowed.

"How will they decode that at Buenos Aires?" Dray asked in a whisper.

"It's not going to Buenos Aires," Jordan said. "It will be redirected to my mother, wherever she is."

Dray's eyebrows lifted. "Good thing you didn't say that to Malory. When you mentioned your special code, she looked like she'd just swallowed a cat. And it clawed its way down."

Jordan smiled and reached out to hold Dray's hand. "Thanks."

"For what?"

"For not making a big deal out of this."

Dray cocked her head to the side. "I could have done the same thing."

"Really?" Jordan stared at Dray, then realized she was being teased. "You have special access codes?"

"No, but I'm sure I could have come up with something to give Malory a similar case of envy-itis."

Jordan watched the planet surface reveal itself through the front view port. It looked gray in the dim light as Red skirted the shadow region between night and day on the planet. Jordan closed her eyes, less interested in the rock they would settle on than in calculating how long it would be before her mother reacted to her message. *More like overreact*, she thought. Her mother held considerable power within the Terran political structure, and Jordan knew she wouldn't bat an eye at directing that power toward a speedy rescue. Jordan hadn't played by the rules either, when she bypassed the probe's navigation to send her message to her mother. It was the first time she'd stepped out of her role as cadet and used her own political connections to get results. She opened her eyes and glanced at their prisoner. She'd be trapped on a planet with the Novan for some time, even with the strings she'd just pulled. She extracted her hand from Dray's and crossed her arms, trying not to stare at Franklin. She'd seen so much death in the last few hours, more than she'd ever imagined.

Chapter Five

LANDING THE SHIP took much longer without the aid of Malory's implants, but she couldn't risk another hookup until she was cleared by a med-tech. After they landed, Red and Venkata set up solar panels outside the ship, and Malory ordered a full system check. When night came, an icy nocturnal wind howled across the desolate landscape, forcing everyone inside the ship. Dray volunteered to double-check the ship's provisions. She walked down the long central corridor dividing the ship in half along its vertical axis. The layout afforded maximum capacity for transporting troops and material between military posts. Officers' solo sleep cubicles lined the start of the corridor on the top level. Dray found the food supplies on the lower level, adjacent to the dormitory-style bunk rooms and the empty cargo holds. The ship hadn't been flight-ready when they escaped. The food was all field rations, the kind that lasted for a century but tasted like recycled plastic. Worse still, the water tanks were less than a third full. They'd be recycling water after a few days.

Jordan was heading for one of the officer cubicles when Dray returned. She looked haggard, but when Dray approached her, Jordan brushed her off. Dray found another empty cubicle, but it was too early to sleep. Whenever she relaxed, she saw N'Gollo's body on the floor. She tossed in her bunk most of the night and woke with a dull headache. Dray slid off her cot, resolved to talk to Jordan. Jordan had played hot and cold with her, reaching for her in the crisis, and avoiding her when things settled down. She needed to know where she stood. And it gave her something to focus on beside the destruction of Buenos Aires and the long wait for a rescue ship.

Dray stepped into the officers' mess and greeted Jenny, who sat alone by the blank vid-screen. Wherever they were, they were out of range of the Terran news feeds. Dray looked around. "No coffee?"

Jenny nodded toward the opposite counter. "Mandatory water

rationing. Help yourself to a nice, cool cup of recycle."

"Where is everyone?" Dray poured herself a small ration of water, thinking Malory was overreacting by rationing so soon.

Jenny munched on a wafer. "Already out, most of them. The planetary scan we did before landing didn't show any major signs of water. Malory authorized exploration parties to see if there are any water sources that were too small for the ship's scanners to pick up."

"We have enough on board if we recycle, don't we?"

"Not with an Aquaran on board. Bello and Sahar are already working on converting one sleep cube to a more hospitable environment for Bello. It'll be a makeshift job and will waste more water than it recycles for sure."

"His implants must be working overtime to keep him from drying to a crisp. Do we have any land craft to explore the planet with?"

"Nothing. Whoever modified this ship stripped it of anything useful," Jenny said. "We're limited to foot patrol."

"Jordan left, too?"

Jenny nodded.

Dray felt a creeping sense of loneliness. Jordan hadn't woken her for the trip. "What about you? How come you're still here?" Dray asked as she bit into a dry wafer.

"I just got off guard duty for Franklin. He's an odd one."

Dray's shift wasn't until later in the day, but she didn't look forward to the boredom of sitting outside a locked room with nothing to do. "Do you want to go exploring?" she asked. The thought of sitting inside the ship for the day seemed unbearable, especially with Jordan already outside somewhere.

Jenny drained her drink. "Sure. I'll report our plans to Malory, then meet you in the supply room in ten minutes."

Dray watched Jenny leave and finished off her dull breakfast in a few quick bites. At least the ship had food. Maybe a trek planet-side would ease the ache in her head and her sense of loneliness.

Dray met Jenny in the supply room. "How long do we have?" she asked as she clipped on a com-link and strapped a water test unit over her shoulder.

Jenny handed her a remote reader which would pick up any water within a kilometer radius. She tightened the straps on her backpack. "Malory's keeping trips down to an hour, just to be on the safe side. Red and Venkata have already gone off on a longer trip, since the atmosphere doesn't affect them."

"How's his shoulder?"

"Scabbed over nicely. Tarquins heal even faster than Novans."

"Here's hoping they find water." Dray and Jenny left the ship through one of the side hatches and hiked along what looked like a dry riverbed. The rock-strewn path sliced a wide canyon between two short gray cliffs no more than fifteen meters high. The air blew warm across Dray's exposed face and hands as they scrambled over a series of boulders blocking the canyon path. It was already hot and by mid-day, they would want to be locked inside the simulated climate within the transport ship.

"Any news on a rescue?" Dray asked as she scanned her reader for signs of water.

"Nothing yet. We've got Jordan's encrypted distress signal going from the ship as well as the beacon we sent back to Buenos Aires before we landed. They'll come for us soon."

Dray didn't feel as optimistic. The beacon's signal would probably reach Ambassador Bowers within a day or two. How long would it take a rescue ship to reach them after that? Standard hyper-engine drive would take two weeks, and they didn't have water to last that long if Bello was bleeding off their supply. And that didn't account for the aftermath of the Buenos Aires attack. If other facilities were attacked, how long would it take before a rescue ship could be sent out for their small group? She brushed a dusty hand across her brow, trying to think of something better to talk about. "So, how's it going with you and Malory?"

Jenny frowned and looked away. "What do you mean?"

"Come on, she did the whole hero thing back on Buenos Aires. That's got to mean something."

"Yeah, I just wish I knew what."

Dray picked up a rock and tossed it along their path. "So, is she back to her old self?"

"No. She's been very kind to me, actually, but we haven't really talked."

"Hmm. Not that I'm taking her side or anything, because I'm not. She's not good enough for you."

Jenny laughed.

"Anyway, she's our C.O. for now. And the commanding officer can't exactly be romancing one of the troops, now can she?"

"I suppose you're right." Jenny sighed. "I'm not even sure I want her to anyway. I mean, how do I trust her again?"

Dray thought she saw a blip on her reader and stopped. She stared at the instrument, trying in vain to get it to show signs of water. "I thought it just read water-sign. Maybe I'm hallucinating," she said, handing the reader to Jenny.

"I don't think so." Jenny laughed. "We'd have to be out here another hour or more before the atmosphere starts playing with your mind."

"I'd start hallucinating?"

"Not right away. First you'd just get silly, like drinking too much alcohol. Then you'd hallucinate."

Dray stretched her back. "Then I'd drop dead?"

"If you're lucky. If not, you'd linger in a vegetative state for years, well into your old age."

"Nice," Dray said. "How long before we have to head back?"

"Another twenty minutes, maximum." Jenny handed the reader back to Dray. Twenty more minutes didn't seem like much time. Not when they were climbing over rocks and dry riverbeds. Dray hoped the other teams were having more luck locating a usable water source.

JENNY ENTERED THE ship in front of Dray. As they turned down the central hallway, they came face to face with Malory, who smiled at Jenny. Malory's gaze flicked to Dray, and her smile faded. Dray shrugged and walked past her in search of Jordan. So what if Malory didn't like her? The feeling was mutual.

Jordan wasn't in the officers' mess. Dray continued to the back of the transport where Franklin was locked up in a storage room. She found Jordan sitting outside his make-shift cell, sipping a cup of water.

"How long have you been on duty?" Dray asked. She was unsure of herself now that she was alone with Jordan.

Jordan pushed her bangs from her eyes and smiled. "I haven't been here too long."

"Anything interesting with the Novan?"

Jordan's smile faded, and her hands fell back into her lap.

"What's wrong?" Dray sensed Jordan's mood shift. What had she done wrong now?

Jordan stared at the black floor. "Nothing."

Dray put a hand on Jordan's shoulder. "Hello? That was a very unconvincing *nothing*." Dray dropped her hand. She still didn't know how Jordan felt about her and wouldn't push it.

Jordan's smile returned. "I just don't much like being here."

"On the planet?"

"No. Here with Franklin."

Dray clenched her fists. "Has he been bothering you?"

"No." Jordan brushed her hand along Dray's arm. "Nothing like that. I just don't like him being here."

"Me, either. We have enough problems without a Novan hanging around." Dray had a lifetime of hatred behind her. A Novan fleet took her mother from her when she was only four. She stepped to the door. "I want to talk to him."

"Are you mad? You can't go in there with him." Jordan laced her fingers over Dray's hand. "Just sit here with me, okay?"

Jordan's fingers trembled. Was she feeling the same heat Dray was? Or was she just frightened by the Novan? Dray gave Jordan's hand a squeeze, then slipped her hand free. "He's the first Novan I've ever seen. I want to see for myself what they're like." She stood facing the door, waiting for Jordan to open it.

"I won't go in there with you."

Dray's jaw tightened as she waited.

JORDAN PALMED THE door control, stepping aside as the door slid open. She glanced at the interior of the brightly lit room. A gray table and chair lined one wall, while the opposite wall had a makeshift bed on the floor. Franklin jerked up in his bed when the door slid open, his disheveled brown fatigues clinging to his tall, thin frame. Jordan's pulse quickened as Dray's arm brushed her when Dray stepped inside. She clenched her jaw, frustrated by her body's betrayal. She also knew enough about Novan physiology to know physical attraction heightened the ever-present pheromones. And she'd never been this attracted to anyone else. Would she broadcast her attraction enough for the Novan to sense her?

Jordan hung by the door, holding her pistol at chest height while she fought the urge to run, desperately trying not to shake. How close was too close? She could always sense Novans on Gilgar before they could detect her because her pheromones were weaker. But she had never been broadcasting her own attraction to someone else at the time.

"What have you got to say for yourself?" Dray's voice was harsh, and Jordan recoiled from the hatred she heard.

Franklin stood against the far wall, his eyes drifting from Dray to the weapon in Jordan's hand. "Why should I talk to you?"

Dray folded her arms across her chest. "I don't see anyone else volunteering to listen to your dribble, Novan."

"I'm not a Novan."

"You're lying," Jordan said. She could sense him from the doorway, but she couldn't tell Dray. "We saw your ships attacking Buenos Aires."

Dray glanced at her and back to Franklin. "If you've got something to say that'll convince me you're not a Novan, then let's hear it."

Franklin read her name tag. "Draybeck." His gray eyes studied Dray. "You look like Kelvin."

Dray took a step forward. "How do you know my brother?"

Franklin sank down on his messy bed. He relaxed, but his gaze still flicked between the two women. "You wouldn't believe me if I told you. Let's just say we work together."

Dray took a step closer. Jordan read the anger in her posture. "You're calling my brother a traitor?"

"No. I'm telling you I'm not Novan. I'm an undercover operative."

"Don't listen to him," Jordan said.

Franklin's gaze turned to Jordan. "You've got a lot to say for someone hiding in the hallway."

Jordan shrank back further, clutching her weapon. What would she do if he tried to reveal her secret? Could she shoot him, just to protect herself?

"Leave her out of it," Dray said, standing between him and Jordan.

"I was on a mission when the attack started," he said.

"With the Novans," Dray said.

"Yeah, Novans. I was sent to find out more about their elite ground troops. Did you notice them in your fine military education?"

"The Black March?"

Franklin snorted. "Yeah, them. I was delivering information about the so-called Black March."

Jordan pictured the massive, black hulks the Novan military incorporated in their news propaganda.

Franklin continued. "Funny how twenty years ago no one had ever heard of them. And now? They're in every news-vid about Novan military capabilities."

Dray leaned against a wall. "So why are they in those huge encounter suits? They're like moving tanks."

"We don't know for sure. They self-destruct if captured. They are the Novans' disposable troops."

Jordan stared at Franklin. "That's barbaric."

"We didn't treat the Aquarans much better, up until ten years ago," Franklin said. "They used to be the Terrans' disposable troops."

"Terrans didn't set up that tradition," Dray said. "*Genesis-II* did, and they weren't Terran."

Franklin shrugged. "The Genesis generation ships predate the Terra/Nova split, but some were just as Terran as you and I are. They enslaved the Aquarans, and Terrans continued the second-class status for centuries after we rediscovered the *Genesis-II* descendants and the totalitarian government they'd set up over the Aquarans."

"He's right," Jordan said. "The Novans are just repeating human history with their Black March, whoever they are beneath those encounter suits."

Franklin leaned forward. "If anything happens to me, you have to deliver this information to Kelvin. Only Kelvin. Do you understand?"

Jordan bit back the urge to warn Dray again, but she was just as eager as Dray to hear what he had to say. Dray nodded her agreement and Franklin continued.

"The Black March are the biggest genetic mistake the Novans have ever made."

Dray stared at him. "What do you mean?"

"The Black March aren't Novan anymore. They are a mixed bag of species wrapped into one package. Some of the neutral planets won't stay neutral when they find out the Novans stole genetic material from them to create the Black March." Franklin opened his mouth to continue, then froze. Someone approached Jordan from behind, and she turned in time to see Bello walk up beside her. His skin was mottled and his lips were cracked. Water rationing was taking its toll.

"Were you authorized to talk to the prisoner, cadet?" Bello asked.

Jordan's calm voice and icy stare were a mirror of her mother's when she was dealing with a stubborn diplomat. "Lieutenant Grace holds authority here."

"She's right, Bello. I don't have to explain my actions to you." Dray nodded to Jordan and the two of them stepped out of the room. Jordan closed and secured the door behind them, barring Bello from entering.

"I wouldn't waste my time with him, Draybeck," Bello said. "He should have been left at the station, if you ask me. I don't know what Malory was thinking, dragging him along."

Dray stiffened next to Jordan. "Our commanding officer made a logical choice during a hostile takeover."

Bello looked between the two of them. "I'd watch what company you keep, Bowers. Some trash aren't worth associating with." He might have been referring to the Novan, but he stared at Dray for a heartbeat before he turned to leave.

Jordan watched him march back down the empty hallway. "I don't trust him. He doesn't respect Malory's authority here."

Dray's hand pulled at her sleeve. "Don't let him get under your skin. He's just looking to stir up trouble."

Jordan knew it was more than that, but if Dray wasn't aware of the hostility toward her, Jordan wasn't going to be the one to point it out to her. They all had enough to worry about.

"Any news on the water situation?" Jordan asked.

"Red found a source about five kilometers away. Enough to

keep us on minimal rations for an extra four days, he estimates."

Jordan didn't want to think about what would happen after that. So far, Malory had been able to maintain order. She stared down the corridor after Bello, wondering how long before the group decided he was an unnecessary drain on their water supply. She shivered, hoping it wouldn't come to that.

"You're worried about what Franklin said?" Dray asked. "There's no way we can verify it until we get off this planet."

"I don't believe him, even if he does know your brother somehow," Jordan said. "He killed N'Gollo. I think it's more likely he's a Novan spy trying to pass himself off as Terran to save his skin."

"You're probably right."

Of course, she was right, but she didn't push it. She didn't have any explanation for why he knew Kelvin, but it didn't change his telltale Novan scent.

"How much longer do you have on duty?" Dray asked.

"Another hour."

Dray shuffled from foot to foot. "I wanted to talk to you."

Jordan looked into Dray's blue eyes and knew what was coming. "Can it wait? I'm still a bit frazzled."

Dray stuffed her hands in her pockets. "Yeah, sure." Neither spoke. Dray backed away. "I should get going."

Jordan wanted to say something to take away the sting of her words, but nothing came to her. She watched until Dray disappeared down a bend in the hallway. Jordan slumped in her chair, letting her head fall into her hands. What was she doing? She had someone who was interested in her, who'd stood by her throughout this crisis. No matter how much Jordan tried to distance herself from Dray, she couldn't deny her own feelings. Dray was brave and funny and caring. And just the sight of her freckled face sent Jordan's pulse racing. Maybe she was wrong. Maybe Dray did care for her more than just the pheromone attraction. Jordan wished she'd asked her mother how she knew her feelings for her Novan husband were more than biochemical.

Thinking of her parents and the love they shared gave Jordan the courage she needed. Dray's feelings for her might not be real, but pushing her away was no way for Jordan to find out for sure. A different strategy was in order, and Jordan had an hour of solitude to figure out what that strategy was.

DRAY SKULKED OFF down the corridor. She knew her face was red, but she didn't care if anyone saw her embarrassment. She should just accept that Jordan had no real interest in her and stop harassing the woman. *Get a spine, Draybeck,* she thought. Anger replaced self-doubt as she stomped through the ship. A couple of cadets ducked into their sleep cubicles to get out of her way.

Her path through the ship brought her to the officers' mess, where the thought of food woke her empty stomach. Dray stepped into the room with tangled emotions of how to deal with Jordan and nearly stumbled into Bello's back. She stopped short and scanned the scene around her. Bello and a few of the younger cadets stood on one side of the room. On the other side, Malory Grace sat alone at a table. Something about Bello's posture put Dray on the defensive. Keeping him in view, she pushed past his group of followers and walked to the water jug to pour her afternoon water ration.

"You're wrong, Malory," Bello said. His belligerent tone grated on Dray.

Malory looked up from her cup of water. "You'll address me by my rank, Cadet."

Bello's expression hardened. "As you wish, Lieutenant. Your decision to remain planet-side is wrong, and you are risking all our lives by staying here."

"I don't recall asking for opinions on my decisions." Malory wrapped long fingers around her cup and eyed him coolly across the small officers' mess.

Bello wasn't here just to question Malory's decision. Dray wasn't sure what else he had in mind, but she thought the numbers certainly weren't in Malory's favor. She didn't know if Malory even recognized the danger she might be in, if Bello had more in mind than simple insubordination. She decided not to wait and find out.

"Lieutenant Grace, Cadet Corporal Baron sent me to find you," Dray said. "He wants your approval on the new duty rosters."

It was a flat-out lie, and the look on Malory's face said she knew it. Luckily, Bello and company did not. Malory accepted Dray's excuse and left the room. Dray lingered, eyeing Bello over her cup of water. He walked over to her.

"So whose side are you on?" Bello asked, his arms crossed.

Dray sipped her cup before answering. "I'm not sure what education you received, Bello, but my military training clearly taught me to obey my C.O. and follow directions."

Bello snorted. "Figures. No spine."

He turned his back to Dray. Big mistake, she thought as her anger boiled to the surface. She grabbed the loose material at his collar and spun him around to face her. He had a handful of centimeters on her in height but the way his eyes bulged told her all she needed to know about his inherent bravery.

She leaned in and whispered, "Insubordination is one thing,

Bello, but leading others to mutiny during a military action is cause for summary execution. And I'd be first in line if our C.O. ordered your head on a platter."

She released his collar and addressed the group. "We're in a military emergency, and under the regulations you all agreed to follow when you joined the military, the highest-ranking officer is in command. She expects your obedience and so do the rest of us."

Dray saw the fear reflected in the younger cadets' expressions as they backed off, leaving Bello alone. Dray stared at him, waiting for his reaction.

His eyes narrowed to slits as his mottled face darkened. "You're quick to call someone else mutinous, for a traitor's daughter."

Dray was too stunned to react. She stood in silence as Bello stalked off. In the immediate aftermath of the Turin disaster, a small minority had been ready to declare her mother a traitor or possible spy. No evidence was found to corroborate either charge. How would Bello know the rumors and why would he care? She sat in the empty room, no longer registering her hunger as she struggled not to follow Bello down the corridor and beat the dry, chapped smirk off his Aquaran face.

JORDAN ENTERED THE officers' mess when her shift was over. Dray sat with her back to the door, clutching a cup. Jordan paused. This was her chance to talk things out. She rummaged through the food stores, grabbing a bag of dried fruit as she tried to figure out how to apologize. She was still puzzling it over when Dray got up without a word. If Jordan had any delusions Dray wasn't angry with her, they disappeared as fast as Dray's retreating back was about to. Jordan put down her bag and rushed after her.

"Hey," she said, placing a hand on Dray's elbow. "Sorry about earlier."

Dray paused and turned to Jordan. The sadness in her expression tore at Jordan's heart.

"Really, I'm so sorry," Jordan said. "I'm grossly incompetent when it comes to all this."

"All what?" Dray asked.

Jordan swallowed her fear. Do or die, she thought, and she leaned in to kiss Dray on the cheek. "All this," she whispered in Dray's ear. She kissed her neck. Dray leaned into her as she flicked her tongue along the tip of Dray's earlobe. It was so soft.

"Jordan," Dray said.

"Hmm." Jordan didn't want any interruptions as she nuzzled into Dray's neck.

"Jordan." Dray pushed her away with a gentle nudge. "The officers' mess is getting kind of busy."

Jordan opened her eyes and looked around. Four or five cadets had wandered past them without Jordan realizing it. And at least two stared at them with grins on their faces.

Jordan blushed. "What can I say, you're irresistible."

Dray's smile faded. "I was pretty resistible an hour ago."

"I was being foolish." Jordan took Dray's hand in hers, leading her out of the room and into the deserted hallway. "I'm sorry. I know I've been giving you mixed signals."

"Yeah, I noticed. What I don't know is why."

Jordan took a deep breath. "Because I've had some bad experiences in the past, where someone else's interest in me was only physical." It was a partial lie, since she'd never let anyone close enough to her to explore a mutual attraction, but the half-truth explained her inner fears well enough.

Dray brushed her fingers through Jordan's hair. "I'm not those other people, whoever they were. I care about Jordan the person. Jordan the pilot who can kick my ass. The only one who can," she added with a smile.

Jordan leaned into Dray's hand, suppressing a sigh. "I want to believe you."

"What can I do to prove it to you?"

Jordan looked at the floor. "Can we just take it slow?"

Dray lifted her chin. "Slow is good. Nothing too physical too fast. I can do that." Her crooked smile pulled at Jordan's heart. Dray placed a chaste kiss on Jordan's cheek. "See? I can do slow."

Jordan grabbed Dray's shirt and pulled her close, kissing her deeply. The heat of Dray's lips weakened her resolve. When the kiss ended, they both stood, breathing hard. "Not too slow," Jordan whispered.

DRAY JUMPED UP when Jordan entered the officers' mess the next morning. "How'd you sleep?" Dray asked, ignoring her own sleepy state.

Jordan placed a light kiss on Dray's lips. "Not as well as I used to on Buenos Aires."

Heat rushed to Dray's cheeks, then centered below her waist. "We don't have any major duties this morning. Want to go have some fun?"

Seeing deep crimson color Jordan's cheeks, Dray corrected herself. "I mean, outside the ship. You know, search for water?"

Red interrupted Jordan's reply when he entered the officers' mess. His face was a mask of frustration.

"What's wrong?" Jordan asked.

"No sign of a rescue ship or any other water. And now the foolish Aquaran has gone off-ship himself, to search."

"That's stupid," Dray said. "He'll lose more moisture off-ship."

"I could not convince him of that," Red said. "And Malory would not order him to stay on board. I think she hopes he falls in a pit somewhere and does not return."

Dray smirked, silently agreeing with Malory. "Jordan and I were about to go off-ship ourselves. Is there any area we haven't scanned for water yet?"

Red slumped into a chair. "We've searched everything within Terran walking distance. Venkata and I are heading out again later to extend our search range."

Dray recognized the source of Red's exhaustion. He and Venkata must have been jogging out and back multiple times a day, searching beyond the distance anyone else on the ship could go. She placed a hand on his shoulder. "You've already given us a safety cushion with the water source you've found. Someone's got to come for us before the water runs out."

"Yes, you are right. The ADF must have a ship coming for us by now," he said.

Dray left the officers' mess and packed their equipment, including a hydroprobe which could detect water deeper in the ground than the hand sensors they had been using. Once outside the ship, they walked along the canal of a dry riverbed. When they came to the end, she shifted her backpack and pushed herself up over the edge of the canal, onto a rock shelf. She turned back to offer a hand to Jordan. They rested, back to back, catching their breath while Dray took in their new surroundings. The flat surface around them was not more than three meters wide. The terrain split into a jagged series of dry canals spotted with rocky caves and scattered dry brush. Some moisture must be feeding the plant life, she thought.

"Where to next?" Jordan asked.

Dray opened her tracking locator. "Red's map puts the water source outside a set of caves twenty meters south and another two kilometers down inside the canal."

Jordan checked her watch. "We've got a little under ten minutes before we have to head back."

"Okay, let's get into the right canal and start searching."

Dray led the way along the flat shelf for twenty meters, then checked the locator again. "Down here."

She sat on the edge of the shelf and lowered herself down. The loose footing made her go slowly down the rocky surface as gravel slipped beneath her feet. Dray paused at the bottom to brush herself off as Jordan followed her down. The canal floor was cluttered with boulders and piles of gravel that had tumbled from the walls. A light wind blew through the canal, creating an eerie whistling noise as they walked. The dark entrances of caves pitted the canal walls around them.

Dray opened her backpack and pulled out the hydroprobe.

"What do you think we'll find?" Jordan asked.

"I'm hoping Red's water source is fed by something underground."

Jordan helped her set up the probe, their shoulders brushing as they worked. Dray surreptitiously inhaled Jordan's unique scent. She'd learned not to be obvious with her attraction because it made Jordan uncomfortable. It didn't stop her from stepping just a little bit closer so she could feel Jordan next to her. Jordan's gaze locked on hers and an exquisite heat ignited inside Dray. She gave a nervous grin and stepped away before Jordan did.

Dray lifted the probe and pushed it into the dirt. "Might as well try our first reading here."

Jordan played with the instrument panel while Dray pulled out her binoculars and scanned the visible portions of the canal walls. Seeing nothing of interest, she gave the binoculars to Jordan and watched the data being measured by the hydroprobe. No sign of water.

Movement along the horizon caught her attention. "What's that?"

Jordan looked up. "A ship, maybe?" She focused the binoculars on the light spot streaking toward them. "Oh, dear God," she whispered. "It's Novan."

Dray grabbed the binoculars. She saw the erratic approach of a small vessel with the unmistakable markings of a Novan vessel. "It's civilian, at least," she said. "And in serious trouble." She put down the binoculars. The vessel was heading toward the Tamil-class ship, but it wasn't going to make it. They were close enough to hear the sounds of impact when it crashed.

Dray pulled the com-link out of her backpack and connected to the Tamil ship. "We are approximately 200 meters from a civilian Novan vessel that appears to have crashed."

Malory was on communications duty. "Do you have weapons?"

"No, Ma'am."

"I'm sending out a team. Do an initial recon and report back. Do not engage."

Dray shut down the link and scrambled to repack their equipment. "We've been ordered to do recon."

Jordan hesitated, her face pale. Dray strapped on the backpack and took Jordan's hand. "It's definitely a civilian ship. And there could be survivors."

Jordan's lips thinned and she nodded. They climbed up the slope.

DRAY CREPT FORWARD, and Jordan followed, though her mind screamed for her to go back. It was crazy for her to approach a Novan ship, but she couldn't ignore a direct order, nor could she ignore someone in need. Silently she prayed the Novans would be unconscious, if they had survived the crash. The wind was blowing most of the smoke from the crash away from them, but she could still smell burnt plastic. Jordan moved to a large boulder and peered around the side. To her surprise, she saw a small, frightened child. His clothes were torn, and his eyes were glassy with shock.

Jordan kneeled down and signaled Dray to follow. The boy was no more than three or four. He watched them but didn't move. "Did you bring any snacks?" she asked Dray.

Dray pulled off her pack and took out some dry crackers. Jordan took them and held out the crackers. The boy stared at her with oversized eyes, then inched closer. Picking up the cracker from her hand, he sniffed it, and a small tongue flicked out and licked the cracker. The boy talked in unrecognizable baby babble and took a bite of the cracker.

Jordan smiled as she moved closer. The boy watched her for a moment, shuffled up, and sat beside her. She stroked his light brown hair while checking for serious injury.

"Figures," Dray said. "You could charm anything. You think he's Novan?"

"Probably," Jordan said. She knew he was. His scent was already altering to register that he'd recognized her as Novan as well.

"Can he talk?"

Jordan glanced at Dray. "Would it matter? I doubt he'd speak Terran Standard if he did." She looked back at the child. "Besides, I think he's too young to know how to talk anyway. Novans don't learn speech until they're four or five."

"You know a lot about them," Dray said.

Jordan froze, her hand shaking on the young boy's shoulder. "Gilgar is neutral, remember? I met a few Novan families there."

The wind shifted, bringing with it voices from the crash site. The boy trembled and babbled faster, looking to Jordan for protection. Dray signaled for Jordan to be quiet, and she made her way around the boulders toward the voices. Jordan picked up the boy and followed. If there were adult Novans alive, she needed to know. As she neared, she realized the voices were speaking Terran Standard, and she relaxed. She considered walking back when she recognized Bello's distinct voice.

"We should finish them off," Bello said, his voice pitched high and shaky.

Jordan and Dray moved closer to the voices. Jordan lay flat on the ground and peered around the edge of a rocky outcrop. The Novan ship was still burning from the tail section. It was a small vessel, probably a personal travel ship. The access doors were open but the interior looked empty. Bello and Sahar were in front of the nearest door, standing over the corpse of an adult Novan. Hovering over the still form was another Novan child.

"It's just a baby," Sahar said.

Bello pointed an assault rifle at the child. "It's a Novan baby." His hands shook.

Dray stood up from her hiding spot. "Bello!"

Bello swung his rifle toward her and fired. She dove behind the boulder, her heartbeat pounding in her ears. "Grab the boy and run!"

Jordan scooped up the frightened boy and raced along the canal. Dray caught up with her and pulled her through an opening in the canal wall that joined it with a different path. They scrambled through dry, heavy brush as the boy cried in Jordan's arms. They ran until the sounds of Bello's shouts faded in the distance. Dray gasped for air, looking back along their path. Jordan scanned the canal walls around them, searching for a possible defensive position. If Bello and Sahar climbed up to higher ground, they would be easy targets in the narrow canal.

"Head for that cave," Jordan said, pointing at a dark opening ten meters ahead.

Dray hadn't yet caught her breath from running, but she scrambled up the loose gravel leading to the cave opening. She took Jordan's free hand and pulled her up the slope, sliding once and muffling a curse. They crawled into the dark cave, Jordan and the boy huddling in the back while Dray took up a position at the cave opening.

WHY HADN'T SHE taken the com-link with her? Dray thought. She could picture exactly where she left it and her backpack when she'd run from Bello. So far they hadn't been followed, but they were overexposed to the planet's air. She watched for signs of Bello or Sahar and tried to calculated how far she was from the ship. She could hear the Novan boy crying in the back, but didn't risk a backward glance for fear of missing Bello. The bastard tried to shoot her. She couldn't believe it.

Dray sat at the cave opening until a sense of calm slowly settled over her. She knew she was still in danger, but it was a small voice in the back of her head, easily ignored. She crawled to the back of the cave to join Jordan. "I can't see or hear anyone," she said.

"Do you think they'll kill the other child?" Jordan's brown eyes mesmerized Dray. She didn't respond right away.

"I don't know," she said eventually. "I didn't hear any other weapons fire after he shot at me."

Jordan held the boy closer. Dray didn't remember when he had stopped crying. She looked down to see his eyes closed, his small hands clinging to Jordan's dusty shirt.

"You do have a way with kids," Dray said with a smile.

"Don't start thinking I'm all maternal now."

Dray stifled a laugh. She felt silly, sitting in a dark cave with a little Novan boy. Something nagged at the back of her mind saying they were still in danger, but that made no sense. She crawled back to the cave front and pulled out her binoculars. Still no sign of the other two cadets. She leaned back against the cave wall, watching for any sign of movement. Her thoughts drifted.

Had she fallen asleep? She wasn't sure how long she'd sat there before Jordan joined her.

"Where's the boy?" Dray asked.

"Sound asleep in the back."

Jordan ran her fingers through Dray's short hair. "You're quite the hero, you know."

Dray chuckled. "Not really. Mostly, I just stood up and painted a bulls-eye on my chest."

Jordan laughed. "Very smooth."

"That's me, smooth." Dray put down her binoculars and slipped a hand behind Jordan's head, pulling her closer. "I'm persistent, too."

Jordan leaned into her. Dray's pulse quickened when Jordan's warm lips pressed against hers. She wrapped an arm around Jordan's back and lowered them both down onto the cave's dirt floor. Something in the back of her thoughts screamed they were moving too fast, but she felt oddly free, and she wanted this. Dray sighed as Jordan's body pressed down on top of her. Jordan's strong legs intertwined with hers.

Jordan lowered her head and traced her lips along Dray's jaw, ending with a nip at Dray's ear. A bolt of desire electrified Dray. She pushed her leg between Jordan's thighs and Jordan pressed against her. She pulled at Jordan's shirt until she could slide a hand under it, feeling Jordan's warm skin under her fingers.

Jordan moaned as Dray caressed her back. Dray rolled them over, positioning herself on top. She lowered her head to brush her lips along the edge of Jordan's collar. She lifted a trembling hand to cup Jordan's firm breast beneath the thin material. Jordan pulled her closer, thrusting her hips into Dray's thigh. Dray pressed her own throbbing need hard against Jordan.

"Touch me," Jordan whispered, stroking Dray's arm and lowering Dray's hand.

Dray shifted her leg from between Jordan's thighs and replaced it with her hand. Jordan arched up to meet her, pressing herself against Dray's palm.

"Harder," Jordan moaned.

Jordan wanted it, wanted her, and Dray wouldn't deny Jordan anything. Dray pushed against her, feeling Jordan's heat through the fabric of her pants. Jordan's building excitement filled her, drawing her own desire along with it. She rocked against Jordan's thigh as her fingers circled hard against Jordan. Jordan kissed Dray's neck and moaned louder as her body trembled under Dray's urgent fingers. Dray's desire rose in time with Jordan's, their two bodies working together, rising together to peak in an explosive climax.

Dray collapsed beside Jordan, her heart pounding, and her breath coming in short rasps. She felt strange, lightheaded. Jordan curled up and draped her arm across Dray's stomach.

"Thank you," she said, her eyes closed and a soft smile curving her lips.

"My pleasure," Dray said, grinning. Jordan's scent surrounded her, filling her with awareness of the body next to her. Her head was fuzzy. She yawned.

"Hmm. Time for a nap?" Jordan asked.

"I'm not sure we should." Dray's eyes drifted shut. She felt like she'd drunk too much alcohol. Maybe Jordan just had that effect on her, she thought as she drifted off to sleep.

Chapter Six

DRAY ACHED. HER eyes stung and pain radiated from her shoulders when she tried to lift her arm. Where was she? She couldn't focus on anything but her sore body. She wanted to go back to sleep and escape the pain, but the throbbing in her head wouldn't allow that. She forced her eyes open.

Venkata hovered over her, the Gilgaran's black eye-covers reflecting Dray's pale face. "You are awake," Venkata said, leaning back in her chair.

"Where am I?" Dray asked, her voice raspy.

"Still on the Tamil ship in the middle of nowhere. How are you feeling?"

"Not so good."

Venkata leaned closer. "What can you remember?"

Dray concentrated. "We were in a cave, I think." The sensations of Jordan in her arms flooded back to her, and she blushed.

"Excellent. That's good, considering you were outside at least three hours past your limit."

"I don't understand."

"When the Novan ship crashed, Red and I went searching for it. We found Bello and Sahar, but it took longer to find you two."

Dray wanted to say something about Bello, something important, but her mind wouldn't focus. "What about Jordan?"

"She is doing well. She woke up a few hours ago. Those children you brought in do not leave her side."

Dray struggled to remember how they'd found them. "I only remember one boy."

Venkata patted her arm. The large gray hand felt like a stinging slap against Dray's tender flesh. "You were over-exposed by three hours and hallucinating by the time we found you," Venkata said. "You'll probably experience some memory loss, but you should not suffer any permanent damage."

Dray rolled away from Venkata. *Memory loss?* She clearly

remembered only one Novan child in the back of the cave when she fell asleep in Jordan's arms. Did she hallucinate that? If it was real, what would Jordan be thinking now, when Dray'd promised not to get physical too soon?

Hours later, Dray pulled herself out of bed. Her head still throbbed, but her other aches had subsided. She needed to see for herself that Jordan was okay. She stepped out of her room and leaned against the cool composite wall, waiting for a wave of dizziness to end. She walked down the corridor to Jordan's room but found it empty. Her head pounded, but she continued down the corridor, following the sound of voices coming from the officers' mess. She squinted as she came into the brightly lit room. Jenny and Jordan sat on the floor, two small children playing between them.

Jordan looked up and smiled at her. "Finally waking up, sleepy?"

Dray tried to smile in return, but the effort made her head ache. Something in Dray's face must have startled Jordan, because she jumped up, frightening the children and sending them scuttling to Jenny. She came over to Dray and wrapped an arm around her waist. Dray leaned on her and let Jordan lead her to a chair.

"You should still be in bed," Jordan admonished, studying Dray's face.

"I feel better than I look."

"You're a bad liar." Jordan leaned down and picked up the boy clinging to her leg. "This one is Apollo, and she's Artemis."

"You named them?" Dray asked.

Jordan blushed. "It was Jenny's idea."

Jenny poured a small cup of water and handed to Dray. "Well, it was easier than saying this one and the other one."

"Why Apollo and Artemis?"

Jenny scooped up the girl. "They look the same age, so I figured they're twins. So why not the ancient Greek twins?"

Dray laughed. Jordan looked good. In fact, she looked great. "How come I feel like a used-up ammo cartridge, and you look fine?"

Jordan wrapped Dray's hand in her own. "I've been awake longer." She leaned in and placed warm lips on Dray's, lingering just long enough to stir Dray's desire. "You'll feel better soon, I promise."

"I feel better already," Dray said. She studied Jordan, not trusting her own memories. "Do you remember what happened in the cave?"

Jordan frowned. "Not much. Do you?"

Uncertainty seemed to wash over Jordan's face. How could

Dray find out if they'd made love without embarrassing herself?

"I don't remember much before then, but I remember hiding in the cave from something. I'm not sure what else happened, though." Maybe Jordan would bring up the topic for her.

"You don't remember before that?" Jordan asked.

Dray swallowed. Did something important happen between them before the cave? She lowered her head into her hands, trying to force the memories back. "No, I can't really remember. I'm sorry."

"You don't remember meeting Bello and Sahar?" Jenny asked.

"No. We didn't leave with them, did we?" Dray asked.

Jenny whistled. "That's unfortunate."

"Why?" Dray asked. Bello's name brought up a strong sense of disgust, but nothing solid.

Jordan hugged her. "Don't worry. Sahar and I witnessed it as well."

"What happened?" Dray asked.

"Bello fired his weapon at you. He claims it was a mistake and he thought you were another survivor from the crash," Jordan said.

Dray couldn't remember, and that bothered her, though not as deeply as her uncertainty over whether she and Jordan had made love or not.

"If you're up for it, you should report to Malory. She'll want to know anything you can remember, for the record," Jenny said.

Dray stood up, ignoring the wave of dizziness threatening to unbalance her. "I can't tell much, but I'll give my report anyway."

Dray caught up with Malory outside Franklin's makeshift prison. By the expression on Malory's face, the meeting hadn't gone well. Dray realized Franklin might know if they were on a Novan world or not. From Malory's look, maybe they were.

"Glad you're awake," Malory said, though her expression didn't match her words. "Are you ready to give your report?"

"Yes, Ma'am," Dray said.

Malory led her to the communications room she used as her office. Malory didn't sit down, but leaned against the back of a console table. Dray's dizziness returned. She hoped she was standing still and not swaying to match her spinning head.

"Tell me about your trip," Malory said.

"I don't remember much. Jordan and I went for a hike, looking for a deeper source of water. I don't remember meeting up with Bello at all."

Malory's voice remained calm, dispassionate. "There was evidence of weapons fire. Do you recall how that happened?"

"No, Ma'am."

"Okay, what else do you remember?"

Dray's pulse quickened as she thought about her time with Jordan. How much should she tell if she was no longer sure it was even real? "Jordan and I were in a cave. We had only one Novan child with us, I'm sure of that. I, I might have hallucinated some things."

"The other child was found with Sahar and Bello at the crash site." Malory's voice wavered enough for Dray to know she and Jordan must have been found in each other's arms.

"I don't remember anything else that would be useful."

Malory clenched the edge of the console. "One last thing, Draybeck. Off the record."

Dray raised her eyebrows. "Yes?"

Malory stepped forward. "I don't know what game you are playing, and officially, I can't say or do anything about it. But if you hurt Jenny, I'll be on your tail like a bad afterburner."

"Jenny?" Dray asked, amused by the implication. "Off the record, Malory, you are the only one on this ship who's hurt Jenny."

"I know I have no chance with her now, but I won't sit by and watch you dance between her and Jordan Bowers. As your C.O., I can't do anything about it right now. Once we are off this rock, I can and will."

The fire in Malory's eyes took Dray by surprise. "You still love her, don't you?" she asked.

Malory nodded, then looked away.

"Not that you have a right to know," Dray began, "but Jenny and I are just friends. We've never been anything more."

Malory studied her. "Nothing between you and Jenny?"

"Nothing," Dray repeated, with a smile. "Jenny's still in love with someone else."

A wave of hope washed over Malory's face.

Dray closed the gap between her and Malory. Malory was taller, but Dray stared at her as if they were equals. "And since we're talking off the record, if you hurt Jenny again, I'll stuff your sad, blond ass out an airlock."

To Dray's surprise, Malory laughed so hard she had to wipe tears from her eyes. When she finally calmed down, she seemed more relaxed than Dray had ever seen her.

"If you weren't so damned arrogant, Draybeck, I'd almost like you. Now get your butt back to bed before you pass out."

She wanted to take Malory up on the offer to go back to sleep, but she had one more task to perform. "I'd like to talk to Franklin first."

Malory gave her authorization, and Dray walked back down the corridor. She reported her orders to the two cadets on duty outside Franklin's room and let herself in. The disheveled prisoner glanced at her from his bed and returned to staring up at the ceiling.

"Don't you get tired of poking sticks at the prisoner?" he said.

"Is this a Novan planet?" she asked.

"I haven't a clue where we are. I told your lieutenant all I know."

Dray slouched into the lone chair, fighting her exhaustion. "Will somebody come for the children?"

Franklin sat up. "What are you getting at?"

"Just that Novans are dedicated to family, aren't they? Answer the question." Dray's head pounded as she focused on Franklin. She had no idea how he knew her brother, or if he really worked for the Military Intelligence Division. Maybe he was working for the Terrans. She was sure the ADF hired Novans who were willing to spy on their own kind, for a fee.

"My, my," Franklin said with a smirk. "A military brat who can see beyond the tip of her own nose. Are you sure you aren't in the wrong branch? We could use another sharp mind in Military Intel. Yes, someone will come for them. Pray to your god of choice they search for the children before blowing this ship to bits."

How long would it take for a rescue ship to come for the Novan survivors, she wondered. She reported Franklin's comments to Malory and stumbed back to her own room. She found Jordan asleep on her bunk, with the two Novan children asleep on a bed of pillows and blankets on the floor. Too tired to wonder at the implications, she curled up next to Jordan on the small bunk and fell asleep.

JORDAN WOKE UP as Dray settled on the bed beside her. She froze, wondering if she should say something. Within moments, a light snore told her Dray was fast asleep. She shouldn't be in Dray's room, but she couldn't stay away. And of course, the Novan children wouldn't leave her alone. The rest of the ship was calling her Mama Bowers, thinking she had a special way with children. Jordan knew they had recognized her as Novan and would never leave her side, but neither of the children were old enough to talk and reveal her secret. She sent up a silent prayer of thanks that Novan children took longer to learn full speech than Terran children.

She closed her eyes as she nuzzled Dray's hair. She smelled Dray's unique scent, mingled with the dirt from the cave. The memory of Dray's touch on her body thrilled her. She wanted to feel that closeness again. Had it been real on Dray's part? Or was it just the combination of the planet's poisonous air quality and

Jordan's Novan chemistry that brought Dray to her? Jordan desperately wanted Dray's feelings for her to be real. She curled around Dray's body, determined to discover the truth somehow. Doubts gnawed at her resolve as she drifted off into a fitful sleep.

THE POUNDING NOISE in Dray's dream became reality when she opened her eyes and realized someone was knocking on her door. She tried to uncoil herself from around Jordan. When she moved, Jordan groaned and rolled to the other side, then fell off the small bed. Jordan ended in a surprised clump on the floor, just missing the two sleeping children.

"Sorry," Dray said, smiling. "All the bunks on this ship are singles."

Jordan rubbed her sore backside. "If you were sorry, you wouldn't be smiling."

The incessant knocking on the door kept Dray from inviting Jordan back to bed. She opened the door to see Red standing outside, grinning.

"About time you two woke up," he said.

Jordan scrambled up off the floor, looking embarrassed. "Not so loud, please, they're still sleeping." She pointed at the bundles on the floor and Red whispered an apology.

"What's the big emergency?" Dray asked, her voice barely above a whisper.

"We just got a signal on the ADF security band. Looks like we will be rescued sometime today."

"That's great news," Dray said.

"Lieutenant Grace has ordered everyone to make preparations for departure. That's why I had to interrupt you love pigeons."

Dray groaned as she saw Jordan pulling on her boots. "Excuse me," Jordan said as she squirmed her way out of the small room.

"You don't have to go," Dray said. There was still so much she wanted to talk to Jordan about, but not with Red standing between them now, glancing from face to face in confusion.

Jordan's embarrassed expression softened. "I'll meet you in the front. The children should sleep for a while longer." She walked off, stomping her feet occasionally to finish putting her boots on as she went.

"I am sorry for upsetting your girlfriend," Red said.

Dray scratched at her dirty hair, wishing for a way to get clean. "It wasn't your fault. She and I just need to talk a few things out."

"Well, you should have plenty of time for that on our return trip. I do not imagine our rescue ship will be equipped with whatever experimental drive this ship has."

Dray sat back on the bed, looking around for her own boots. "By the way," she said as she rammed the first boot on. "It's lovebirds, not pigeons."

"Ah, I see. And pigeons are not romantic in Terran society?"

Dray pictured the greasy gray birds that had managed to migrate to every Terran planet or space station she'd ever visited. "No, not really. "

Dray and Jordan joined the rest of the crew outside the ship. Malory ordered full preparations for departure and that meant dismantling the temporary processing stations they'd set up since landing. They joined Venkata at the solar converters stretching out in a wide pattern behind the ship. The portable energy panels required two people on either end to retract them into storage bins. By the time they finished the task, the rest of the external stations had been stowed for takeoff.

"Any sign of the rescue ship?" Dray asked as she stepped into the command deck, followed by Jordan.

"Not yet," Jenny said. She sat at the com-station with more patience than Dray would have managed.

"Where's everyone else?" Jordan asked.

Jenny pulled off her communications ear piece. "Malory sent most below to scrub down the storage bays. It'll keep them from loitering around here, waiting for news."

Dray took the empty copilot's seat. "You mean like us?"

Jenny smiled and shrugged. "If the space gear fits..."

"Okay, we can take a hint," Dray said as she stood up. A signal whistled from the console behind her. "I didn't touch anything, I swear."

Jenny left her post to scan the console by Dray. She frowned as she typed in a series of commands, one of which turned off the signal.

"It's the proximity detector. It's showing we've got one incoming vessel," she said.

"That's great." Jordan leaned over Jenny's shoulder to read the report.

"I'm not so sure," Jenny said. "If it was our rescue ship, why wouldn't they have communicated with us by now?"

"Can you identify the ship?" Jordan asked.

"Not until it gets closer."

Dray stood up, Franklin's warning echoing in her mind. "Where's Malory?"

Jenny turned to her. "She's outside, doing a final inspection of the ship before we take off. We're supposed to meet the rescue ship in orbit and be towed back to Buenos Aires air-space."

Dray spun around and left the ship in search of Malory. If

something other than the ADF ship was landing, then the C.O. had some hard decisions to make. She ran around the back of the ship and found Malory with Red, examining the rear thrusters.

"We've got an unknown ship heading our way," Dray said, coming to a stop next to Red.

Malory stood up too quickly, hitting her head on the composite casing surrounding the thrusters. "Can you identify the vessel type?" she asked, rubbing her scalp.

"Not yet," Dray said. "Jenny and Jordan are working on it."

The three ran into the ship to the command deck. Jordan and Jenny were seated in the copilot chairs.

"Status," Malory ordered as she took the commander's seat and turned up the readouts.

"Incoming vessel has landing gear down, heading for our position." Jordan turned to them, her face pale. "It's Novan, assault strike-class."

Malory cursed and turned on the ship's intercom. "Prepare for emergency takeoff. Repeat, prepare for emergency takeoff."

She turned off the intercom. "Red, go down to the bays and make sure those kids are strapped in. Copilots, start the forward engines."

Just as Dray strapped into the seat, an explosion rocked the ship, sending Jordan sprawling across the floor.

"Report!" Malory ordered.

"They've hit the rear thrusters," Jenny said. "We're grounded."

Malory swung out of her commander's seat. "Draybeck, get whatever weapons we have and arm whoever you find. Get Red and Venkata to stay in the rear with the unarmed cadets. Jenny and Jordan, find us the emergency com-station and oxygen tanks in case we need to evacuate."

Dray ran down the central corridor, her heart pounding as she pushed her way through the dazed cadets standing around. "Strap on whatever weapons you've got and meet up in the front. We're under attack."

She paused by the door to her room, hearing the cries of the two children. "I'll come back for you," she promised as she ran on. She found Red in the rear crew deck. "I need your help," Dray said. "The rest of the cadets are armed and ready. Malory wants you and Venkata to stay back here with the unarmed cadets."

"Okay," Red said. "What are you doing?"

"Getting a baby-sitter for the children."

Dray ran back to the central corridor and down the hallway leading to Franklin's prison. She rounded the corner to Franklin's room. As expected, his guard had already left. Dray palmed the lock panel and the door slid open. Franklin sat in a ball under the table in his room.

"What the hell is going on?" he asked, recognizing Dray.

"Get your boots on, Franklin. The ship's under attack."

He scrambled out of his hiding place and shoved on his boots. "How bad is the damage?"

Dray led the way down the hallway. "So far, only one hit to keep us on the ground."

Franklin grabbed Dray's arm. "Did you ID the attacker?"

"It's Novan."

Dray skidded to a stop outside her room. When she opened the door, the two children ran out and wrapped themselves around Franklin's legs. Recognized one of their own, she guessed. "They're your responsibility, you understand?"

He nodded, picking up Apollo, the boy. "This might not be all they're after, you know that, right?"

"What do you mean?"

"This ship. It's a classified Terran experiment. You can't let the Novans get hold of it."

Dray nodded as she turned to the girl clinging to Franklin's legs. Her mind wanted to reject the idea that these were her enemy. "They seem so normal."

"They are. There are fewer differences between them and us than you think."

Dray scooped up Artemis, the girl. "Come on."

Franklin hesitated. "You trust your lieutenant? If the Novans try to take this vessel, you'll have to destroy it."

Dray held Artemis to her chest. "Yes, I trust Malory. Let's go." She didn't want to think about how she'd destroy a ship as massive as a Tamil-class transport. But something told her Franklin would know how.

Dray led them up the corridor to where the rest of the crew waited. She pushed through the crowd, hearing grumbles behind her as they recognized Franklin and the Novan children. She didn't have time to deal with sensitivities and prejudices.

"Malory," she said in a quiet voice. "There's something you need to know about the attackers."

"Now?" Malory asked. "And why is he here?"

Dray passed Artemis off to Jordan as she pulled Malory back into the pilot area where Jenny sat, still scanning the incoming vessel. She called Franklin forward. Jordan grabbed the girl and rushed off the command deck, her brown eyes boring into Franklin, but he ignored her.

"I don't want him on my command deck, Draybeck," Malory said.

"He thinks they may have come for this ship."

Malory leaned on the back of Jenny's seat. "And you believe him?"

"Makes sense. If they wanted us dead, they could have blown this ship to bits by now. They want something, and that something is inside this ship."

"Where's the Novan ship now?" Malory asked.

Jenny returned to her console. "It landed about two hundred meters away."

"Can you get a visual?" Franklin asked.

Jenny turned to Malory, who gave a nod in agreement. Jenny focused the external viewers and piped the video to her console. The Novan ship shimmered from the heat of its landing engines. Franklin leaned in, studying the ship. "This is bad."

As they watched, a contingent of dark, tank-like figures emerged, the Black March troops. Their massive black encounter suits seemed to swallow the surrounding light as they marched in formation down the ship's ramp. Dray's stomach turned to cold lead. Facing a contingent of Novans would be bad enough, but facing their shock troops? At this point, Franklin's secret about the Black March didn't matter. Formerly human or not, the Black March troops were known to kill everything in sight.

Jenny looked up. "Lieutenant Grace, the crew is awaiting your orders."

Dray turned to scan the faces of her fellow cadets. Fear and sweat hung in the air in the crowded main cabin. Grim-faced cadets held their weapons in white-knuckled grasps. And yet none but a handful of them on the command deck knew what awaited them outside.

"Suggestions?" Malory asked in a low voice.

"I recommend splitting the group," Jenny said. "Half to the rear exit of the ship with Red and the others. Then we wait and see what the Novans do. If they attack, we hold them here while the rest escape from the back."

"The fewer people who know the Black March are outside, the better," Dray said.

"Okay," Malory said. "Jenny, you're going back with Red."

"No way." Jenny jumped out of her chair to face Malory. "Respectfully, Ma'am. I belong here."

Malory grasped Jenny's thin hands in her own. "Please. I need to know you're safe."

Jenny took a step closer. "I'm not leaving you."

Dray interrupted them. "We need to act before the Black March come into view."

Malory dropped Jenny's hand and turned to face the crew.

"Our attackers are approaching on foot, possibly to negotiate." She designated which cadets would remain and which would take the remote com-station and join Red in the back.

Only Dray, Jenny, and Malory remained on the command deck with Franklin. The children had given him up in favor of Jordan, who stood on the far side of the main cabin. The small group waited in silence around the main vid-screen where Jenny piped the images of the Black March approaching. Dray counted at least twenty hulking figures kicking up a dust cloud that distorted the electronic images. "Does anybody know how the Black March communicate?" Dray asked.

No one said anything at first. Then, Franklin spoke, looking more in command than the rest of the team, even in his scraggly beard and clothes. "They don't communicate," he said. "At least not that anyone's ever recorded."

"Great," Malory said.

He continued, "Their encounter suits are resistant to projectile fire, but if you can detonate a shock-grenade near them, it may trigger a systems malfunction in their suits. Not enough to kill, but it could give you the chance to run like hell."

Jordan spoke up from the seat she'd taken near the far wall, with both children in her lap. "Nothing personal, but I wouldn't take the word of a Novan spy on how to disrupt their death troops. For all we know, it would just trip them into a killing frenzy."

Franklin's expression darkened. "I've explained this before. I am a Terran officer under the command of Captain Kelvin Draybeck." He reiterated his rank and mission to the small group. "I am no more Novan than the rest of you. And just as interested in keeping myself alive."

Dray studied him, still unsure what to believe. "How come the Novan children ran to you when they were frightened?"

"Novans have a unique chemical scent." He rolled up his sleeves, showing a small, white scar on his upper arm. "I have biotech implants that mimic the scent. But you see they didn't stick with me, did they? Because I don't have the ability to alter my scent like a true Novan would when they come in physical contact with another. They'd rather stick with Cadet Bowers than a Novan stranger who doesn't react properly to them."

"DO YOU HAVE implants to detect Novans as well?" Jordan asked. Her heart pounded, wondering if she should believe him.

"No. We've measured and duplicated the scent, but not how to detect it ourselves. We'd ferret out a lot more Novan spies if we could."

Jordan stood up, fear making her hands shake. She knew she alone of the crew could prove or disprove his words. The children followed her as she walked forward. Using Artemis as an excuse to get close, she lifted the girl up and handed her to Franklin.

"We don't have time for this." He took the child, and Jordan covered his hand with hers. She kept it there for a moment, pretending to help hold the girl. She prayed no one would see through her ruse as she waited. Nothing happened. His scent never altered.

She took a step back and Artemis reached out for her. She scooped the girl up. "I believe him." She let out a long, unsteady breath. He at least, couldn't reveal her secret.

Jordan looked back to the view screen. She prayed no one in Red's party decided to open the back hatch while the Black March marched past. Sweat trickled down between her shoulder blades as she waited. A wave of dread engulfed her and the rest of their small party when the first of the Black March came into view in front of their ship.

The enemy formed a wide arc around the front hatch, twenty paces from the closed ramp. They stood, black and unmoving. No one could break the lock of fear permeating the main cabin, but Dray's warm presence beside Jordan comforted her raw nerves.

Something moved within the Black March wall, a subtle parting of the black-clad troops. Jordan leaned closer to the view port as one lone figure emerged from the wall of shock troops, smaller in stature, wearing a simplified steel gray flight suit. A Novan officer. Jordan's heart pounded. There was no doubt the figure in front of them would know her as a half-breed Novan. The officer walked a few paces in front of the Black March and made a show of taking out his weapons, placing them on the ground, and walking away from them, closer to the Tamil-class.

"Nice show," Malory said. "But what about the wall of death behind him?"

"We've got an incoming transmission," Jenny said. "The ADF rescue ship has detected the Novan vessel." She turned away from her console to look up at Malory. "They're coming in fully armed."

"They won't get here in time," Franklin said.

"He's right," Jordan said. "We don't know if they are after the children or this ship. But if we send out the Novan children, that might distract them long enough for the ADF ship to get in target range."

Malory watched the lone figure waiting outside their ship. "I won't order anyone outside this ship."

"You won't need to," Dray said. "I'll take them out."

"You could end up dead," Malory said.

Malory's words shocked Jordan more than the wall of troops in front of them. She couldn't let Dray face that. "I'm the one who should take them," she said.

Dray's face paled.

"You know it has to be me," Jordan said. "The children trust me. And I'm the only one who can speak some of the Novan language. Unless you want to send Franklin."

Franklin stared at her. "How do you know Novan?"

"I am the daughter of the Gilgaran Ambassador. Do you think she would let me get away with not learning all the major languages on Gilgar?" It was a believable lie they'd worked out to cover her fluency in her father's primary language, and her friends believed it.

"All right," Malory sighed. "Take a couple of shock grenades. Jenny, where's the ADF ship?"

"In low orbit. ETA in fifteen minutes."

"Make this fast, Bowers," Malory ordered.

"Yes, Ma'am."

Jordan waited by the front exit ramp, holding the children. Dray stuffed Jordan's pockets with grenades and scooped up Apollo.

"Let me come with you," Dray said.

Jordan saw the sadness in Dray's eyes, but she couldn't give into it. If she faced the Novan, she had to do it alone. "I'll be fine," she said. "I promise."

"Ready?" Malory asked.

Jordan nodded. Dray palmed the door lock, and they watched the long metal ramp lower to the ground. Dray put the boy down, and he clung to Jordan's hand as they walked down the ramp and onto the dusty ground. Jordan wondered if Malory would close the ramp once they were clear, but she didn't. Her return path waited, in case she needed to make a run for it. Facing the wall of Black March troops at ground level, Jordan prayed she would not have to make a hasty retreat.

Once clear of the ship, she walked slowly toward the lone Novan. He met her halfway between the Tamil-class ship and the rest of his troops. Jordan glanced past him to the black behemoths, holding her fear at bay. The hulks each carried two heavy blasters strapped across front shield armor, but none held their weapons in a firing position. She kept her own hands clear of the grenades in her pockets as she stopped a few paces before the Novan. He stood a head-span taller than Jordan, watching her. Sweat dripped down her neck as she waited.

The Novan unhooked the gray helmet, taking it off to reveal a dark face covered in a thick, curling beard. Jordan stared at clear black eyes, inhaling his scent as it adapted to hers. She went down on one knee, keeping her eye on him as she put Artemis on the ground. The two children ran to the tall Novan, who hugged each one.

"Where is their mother?" he asked.

"She died in the crash." Jordan stood still as the Novan studied her, praying he would not expose her secret.

"You are half-bred," he said. "You speak our language well."

"My father taught me." She willed herself not to shake.

He glanced at her name tag. "Bowers." His gaze bore into hers. "It is not a Novan name."

"He took my mother's name. Now please, you have to go," she said.

The unmistakable sound of a spaceship engine whined from the distance. Jordan glanced up to see the ADF vessel approaching.

The Novan looked up at the vessel, but did not move. "You should be with your own kind. Do you wish to come with me?"

"I am with my own kind. I am Terran, too. Now go," Jordan urged. For the first time, she thought he might force her to join him. Dray and the others wouldn't let that happen, but looking at the wall of Novan troops, Jordan knew they would all die, and the Novan would still take her if he wanted to. "Please. My father is dead. All I have is my Terran heritage now."

He stared at Jordan a moment longer, emitting a low series of sounds to pacify his children. "I am Colonel Hadro Nassien, from the New China system. For saving my children, I offer you a place in my family." He put his helmet back on and scooped up the two children in his long arms. He glanced back at the Tamil ship. "When they reject you, come to us."

His words gripped the cold place in her heart that feared rejection. He studied her for a moment longer, then turned and walked back to his troops. The black wall absorbed the gray-clad figure once again, and they marched back toward their own ship. Jordan trotted back to the Tamil ship with a lightheaded sense of relief that she'd survived as the ramp closed behind her.

Chapter Seven

DRAY WATCHED THE control monitor as the Novan ship took flight. The speed of its escape surpassed the speed of the approaching ADF ship, which was a Tarquin short-range Baeron-class attack frigate. *Armed and ready*, she thought as she scanned the readouts for the approaching vessel. The fact it was armed and Tarquin didn't surprise her. After all, the Tarquin government provided the fastest and strongest armada in the ADF fleet. But a Baeron-class? It meant two things in Dray's mind: The ten mega-ton Baeron mother ship must be close—and they were in deep trouble.

Baeron destroyers were the elite of the ADF force, and the Baeron drive was an order of magnitude faster than Terran jump drives. It explained how the Baeron ship got there so fast, but not why. They weren't sent on routine search and rescue missions. Dray punched up the planet coordinates again, verifying they were not in Novan space, though they weren't in Terran territory either. They were in one of the many unclaimed zones.

"So who has friends in high places?" Jenny joked from the copilot's chair. She obviously recognized their unusual rescue ship as well.

Jordan leaned into Dray and whispered, "This is my fault."

Dray frowned at her.

"I sent the rescue beacon off to my mother. I guess she overreacted."

Malory's face paled as she saw the frigate open its aft doors. A row of heavily armed Tarquins emerged, marching double-time to surround the Tamil-class transport. She flicked on her com-link. "Red, get up here, now."

By the time Red trotted into the command deck, the armed greeting party was clearly visible from all external view ports. Red's orange skin color rippled in pale stripes as he nodded his greeting to Dray.

The inter-ship communication link lit up under Jordan's gaze, and she clipped on her headset to listen. After a moment, she turned to Malory. "They're insisting we enable ship-wide broadcast for them."

"Okay," Malory said. "Do it."

A moment later, the speakers throughout the ship came to life, creating an odd echo as the dispassionate voice of the Tarquin commander spoke. "Your vessel is now under the control of Tarquin Security. You will remain in your vessel and cooperate fully with the containment team when they board. All external ship communications have been terminated. All internal communications are being monitored. Your cooperation under the ADF Inter Space Code 13004 is mandatory. That is all."

Dray turned to Red. "Any idea what this is all about?"

Red shrugged, but even his casual personality could not make light of their current situation. "Tarquin Security does not usually make its presence known."

"They're Black Ops," Franklin said, crossing his arms as he stared out the front view port. "They specialize in two things. Uncovering enemy secrets and making things disappear."

Jordan turned to Dray and mouthed the word "disappear." Dray would have done anything to mollify Jordan's fears, but at that moment, the inter-ship communications came to life again.

"This is Major Jenak. Open your rear cargo doors."

Jenny started to reply, but Malory cut her off.

"This is Lieutenant Grace from Base Station Buenos Aires. Please redirect your team to the forward command doors."

"This was not a request, Grace," Jenak said, his voice showing his annoyance. "Cargo doors, now."

"I don't recommend that you ignore them," Red said. "Tarquin Security considers any life forms destroyed during a mission as collateral damage."

"So don't piss them off, is what you're telling me." Malory turned to Jenny. "Warn Venkata and the others of what's coming and then open the cargo hatch."

As Jenny complied, Dray tapped her fingers across her console keyboard, typing in a search for the Baeron-class ship. What came up gave very vague details about its crew capacity, fire power, and purpose. Not enough to answer her questions. "Red, can the Baeron-class frigate scan us internally?"

"You mean detect how many of us there are on board? Probably. This is an old ship and the Baeron is equipped with the latest technology. No one can hide, if that is what you are thinking," he added.

"I was thinking they can detect the concentration of our crew in the back of the ship, and they are going after them first," Dray said.

Malory stood up, brushing back her long blond hair with a heavy sigh. "Whatever scheme you're cooking up, Draybeck, just forget about it. They're ADF troops and we're finally getting off this planet."

Jordan stood up to lean against Dray's chair, her hand resting on Dray's shoulder. "Why all the bravado? We're a lost ship of cadets with one lieutenant. It's not like we're the ones who attacked Buenos Aires."

Dray gazed into Jordan's eyes. She saw the look of guilt and confusion. She wanted to tell Jordan this wasn't her fault. Jordan's mother could not have enough Terran political muscle to redirect a Black Ops mission to rescue a group of cadets. So what else was going on?

"They're after this ship, the experimental drive that got us here so fast," Franklin said.

"How do you know?" Dray asked.

He looked at her. "What other ships do you know that can travel as fast?"

Baeron ships, Dray thought. "How did a Terran ship get a Baeron engine?"

Franklin didn't answer.

The control deck settled into a tense silence. Jenny flipped on the vid-monitors for the cargo bay and everyone clustered around her. Frustration washed over Dray as the containment team aimed their weapons at the huddled group of younger cadets standing behind the gray bulk of Venkata and the two others. Jenny played with a few controls, but could not bring up audio, so they watched the silent proceedings with a growing sense of dread. As a group, the rest of the cadets dropped to their knees. Venkata stood like a sentinel before them, holding her ground until an unknown projectile weapon brought her to the ground. Red growled behind Dray, but she couldn't spare him a glance. The sight on the vid-screen held all her focus.

"She'll be all right," Jordan said as Venkata pulled herself back up from the ground, but stayed in a passive position.

The ship-to-ship communications clicked on. "Open the Command hatch," Jenak ordered.

The group stood as one, with Franklin in the back, and faced the hatch as Jenny flicked the control to open it. The steel bulk split in two as the upper half rose to form overhead protection and the lower half became an entrance ramp. Ten Tarquin security guards trotted up the ramp and targeted Dray and the others. Behind them came a lone Tarquin male, wearing the insignia of his rank, the double-width gold bars of a major, on the shoulders of his black uniform. *Jenak*, Dray thought. Her stomach clenched and she fought the urge to look away when Jenak's deep green eyes scanned her.

"Who is in command?" he asked.

Malory stepped forward. "Lieutenant Grace, Sir."

"Grace, I want your team assembled outside this vessel."

"Sir, what about the other cadets? The ones in the cargo bay?" she asked.

"They are no longer your responsibility, Lieutenant."

"Sir, we also have a prisoner who claims to be a Terran officer."

"Bring him as well." Jenak turned away, walking down the main corridor.

Malory led their small team past the gauntlet of armed guards and out onto the flat expanse between their ship and the Baeron frigate. Dray peered around the back of the ship but saw no sign of the rest of their party. Four of the guards split off from the rest and formed a loose square around Dray's group, keeping them under armed guard.

Franklin stood beside her, fidgeting from foot to foot. "Don't answer questions about this ship," he said in a harsh whisper.

Dray frowned. "Why?"

Franklin leaned in closer. "It has a modified Baeron-class engine, a Terran prototype built from stolen Tarquin specs."

Dray pushed him back. "Why would we steal from our own allies?"

He smirked. "Welcome to interstellar politics. They'll be pissed to find out we've got their technology now. Don't give them an excuse to take it out on you."

Jordan pulled Dray away from Franklin. "These are ADF forces, no matter what. And we're ADF military just like they are. The ship records have already tracked everything that's gone on here."

Franklin shrugged and walked a few paces away. Dray watched him purposefully turn away from her. Jordan was right, though. They hadn't committed any crimes.

Footsteps clanked down the command ramp. Dray looked up as Jenak came out, followed by three guards who still barely managed to surround the sluggishly walking Venkata. Red stepped to the front of the group, at eye level with the nearest Tarquin guard. Dray noticed the guard was Tarquin female, her full figure wrapped in the same black uniform Jenak wore. The guard eyed Red up and down in a manner that bespoke only one intention. Red seemed immune to the Tarquin female's appraising stare, until she emitted an odd hissing sound. Red's eyes widened, and he growled back at her. She laughed and stepped to the side as Venkata separated from her guards and stumbled into their small group.

Red held Venkata up and half carried her to the others.

"How bad are you hurt?" he asked.

Venkata breathed in deeply from her inhaler. "Not as bad as it looks. Just a small penetration to each leg."

Dray gazed down to see the wet, silvery streaks along Venkata's lower calf. "What did they say to you?" she asked.

Jenak strode over to them, silencing any further conversation. "You have a prisoner in your party."

Malory paced to where Franklin stood. Her manner suggested she was more than happy to give him over to the security guards. Franklin walked passively to Jenak, but his eyes stayed on the far horizon. *Some method to control his fear?* Dray wondered. Jenak waved two guards over, and Franklin disappeared into the Tarquin ship. Jordan slipped her hand into Dray's and held it tightly as they waited to hear what Jenak would say.

"Your ship has been confiscated." He turned to the female Tarquin guard next to him. "Sergeant Rusa, escort them to a holding cell." He turned around and left without another word.

"Single file," Rusa ordered, directing the group with the tip of her gun. Jordan let go of Dray's hand and lined up behind Red. Dray followed, keeping as close to Jordan as she could without disobeying Rusa's orders. The thought of spending time in a holding cell frustrated her. They'd return to Buenos Aires space in the belly of the Baeron mother ship in orbit.

Dray's curiosity took over as she stepped inside the short-range vessel. At a tenth the size of the Tamil transport, the frigate felt small and cramped as they were marched through a narrow corridor. The ship's crew, what little Dray saw of it, seemed disinterested in her group, with few even noticing them march past. They ended their march in a small room, furnished with uninviting cots attached to the walls and a small partitioned-off area for toilet facilities. Rusa left them, using an electronic key pad to lock the door after her. Obviously, Tarquin Security didn't use chip-IDs like the rest of the ADF. Even non-Terrans like Red were implanted with identifying chips in their palms when they joined the ADF.

"What now?" Jenny asked.

"We wait," Red said, looking uncomfortable but trying to hide it from the group. Dray didn't think he fooled anyone. Of all of them, Red seemed the most uncomfortable on the Tarquin ship, his skin rippling a deeper red than normal.

Dray nudged Jenny, who sat on a cot next to her. "What's up with him?" she asked in a low voice.

Jenny watched Red pacing by the door. "Rusa is in heat, and she's scented Red."

"Really? When, or how?" Dray asked.

"When he faced her down over Venkata, I think. It's hard for a non-Tarquin to see it happen, but Red's reaction seems pretty consistent with a marked Tarquin male."

Jordan sat down next to Dray. "So does this mean they're going to—you know?"

Jenny shook her head. "That's the problem. She marked him and took off, locking him in here."

"So she's a flirt and a tease," Dray said.

"Worse," Jenny said. "Once marked, a Tarquin male must mate or he risks, well, he may never get to mate again, let's put it that way."

"Will she come back for him?" Jordan asked.

"I doubt it. She's a ranking Tarquin female, and he's a prisoner."

The prisoner status silenced their conversation for a time. The notion of being a prisoner didn't sit well with Dray, who got up and paced the small area around their cots. When the ship's engines roared to life, she sat back down, bracing herself for take-off. She was amazed the room had no safety restraints for take-off and landing, but realized after a few moments that it didn't need them. Another Tarquin advancement the Terrans didn't have. The ship traveled smoothly for a long enough time that she realized they must be free of the planet's gravity by now.

By the time they reached what she assumed was the mother ship, Dray had watched Red's agitated pacing for long enough to realize he was getting worse. *With a ship full of Tarquins, someone's got to notice his condition*, she thought. Assuming anyone came for them soon. Their Spartan quarters left no room for privacy, except for the small toilet facility, and the group showed signs of stress. Malory leaned against the far wall, staring at nothing. Jenny sat with Dray, watching Red struggle against his growing frustration, and Jordan moved off to chat with Venkata and see to her wounds.

The door to the room slid open on silent rails. Jenak entered, with three other Tarquins, including Rusa. Jenny jumped out of her seat, but too late to prevent Red from lunging for Rusa. Two guards held him pinned to the wall as Rusa stood idly to the side.

"It's her fault," Jenny shouted, pointing to Rusa.

Jenak ignored her and paced to Malory. "Your team will be interrogated individually. Choose the first three."

Malory kept her gaze averted from the rest of them. "Two of our party need medical attention."

Jenak scanned the group and turned back to Malory. "Choose, Lieutenant," he said, seeming to dismiss Venkata's injuries and Red's distress.

"No," Malory said. "You are not authorized to interrogate us under the ADF Prisoner Accord without proper medical attention first."

Jenak's orange hand slammed into Malory's stomach, doubling her over. Jenny cried out. Dray jumped to Malory's aid and got the firing end of Rusa's gun pointed at her head. She gritted her teeth and held her ground as Jenak waited for Malory to rise. When she did, she stared at Jenak with pure hatred.

"Choose," he ordered again.

"Take me," she said. "If you want more, choose them yourself."

The beginnings of a smile curled Jenak's thin lips. "Proceed, Lieutenant," he said, directing Malory to the door. As Malory walked out in stoic silence, Jenak turned to Rusa. "Take her as well," he said, pointing to Dray.

Rusa pushed the gun into Dray's ribs. Dray looked one last time at Jordan, who was being held back by Venkata. There was so much she wanted to say, but Rusa pushed her again, propelling Dray forward, away from Jordan. Taking her cue from the stiff form of Malory in front of her, Dray walked past Rusa and marched out the door.

JORDAN PULLED AWAY from Venkata's grasp as the doors to their makeshift prison shut. She ran to the door and pounded on it until Jenny came to her.

"They'll be all right," Jenny said, wrapping an arm around Jordan.

Jordan pushed her arm off. "You don't know that. None of us know what's even going on here." Why had they singled out Dray? Jordan hated to see Malory get hurt, but there was more to Jenak's behavior than just being a brute, Jordan was sure of it.

"We're still ADF military personnel," Venkata said from where she rested on the floor. Her silvery blood had congealed on her leg, no longer streaking her uniform or the floor.

Red paced back and forth in front of the door. "Tarquin Security doesn't operate by the same rules we do," he growled.

Jordan stepped away from the door, uncomfortably aware of Red's state and their own helplessness in dealing with it. "Is there any chance Jenak is not aware of your condition?" she asked.

Red's skin darkened as he spoke. "He knows. They all know."

"They've done it on purpose," Jordan concluded. When all eyes focused on her, she continued. "Systematic weakening of our unit. They want to poke at us without actually breaking any serious rules to see where our weakest points are."

"I wouldn't call shooting me in the knees not breaking any ADF rules," Venkata said.

"Video footage would show you resisting the order from a superior officer on a questionable ship," Jordan said.

"Why poke at us?" Jenny asked.

Jordan shook her head. "I don't know why. They incapacitated our two strongest, Venkata and Red. Then they took away the two people with the most leadership abilities."

Why they'd go through all that, Jordan hadn't figured out yet. Obviously, they knew about the modified Tamil, and the Novan ship. But why didn't they stop the Novan vessel? A Baeron-class frigate could have caught up with it. Unless the modified Tamil was more important.

"I think it's safe to assume we're under suspicion for either the Buenos Aires attack or the modified Tamil ship, probably both," Jordan said.

"There are enough cadets on our ship to vouch we were escaping Buenos Aires," Venkata said.

"True, and that's likely the lesser of the two problems we face right now." Jordan sat on a cot and tried to focus her thoughts. She pushed back unwelcome fears of what the Tarquin guards might do to Dray, especially if Dray didn't calm down and cooperate. *Like she ever backs away from a fight*, Jordan thought. She pushed back her thoughts as she concentrated on their situation. "We can assume they know most of what occurred with the Novan ship. If they don't have their own recordings, they have whatever we recorded on the Tamil transport."

"We gave up potential assets to save ourselves," Jenny added.

"We did what was necessary," Red said. The conversation seemed to give him something to focus on. Jordan wondered how long he could last, and what would happen to him as time passed if he didn't get help. That's what Jenak wanted, for them each to turn against the other in fear or mistrust. They'd have to deal with Red's problem, but for the moment anyway, he seemed in control.

"You make us sound like cowards," Venkata grumbled.

Jordan looked at their small group. "We need to choose our words more carefully. We were responsible for a group of young cadets, none of whom were trained for battle." She put up her hands. "No one here is trained for what we encountered, except Malory."

When Jenny paled, Jordan added, "I'm not blaming her in any way, but if we don't figure a good way out of our problem, Malory may end up taking the fall for all of us."

"Assuming Jenak is playing by the rules," Red added.

Jordan nodded. "Yes, but so far, he hasn't crossed any major boundaries. Yes, we're locked up, but you could easily say we are on a classified vessel, and he kept us isolated for that reason."

"So we used the Novan children as bargaining chips to save ourselves," Jenny said. Her voice didn't sound like she was convinced their story would hold up.

"Not just that. We had no weapons," Jordan said. "Our ship will prove that, and we were grounded with no immediate assistance." The ADF ship had been close, but had they chosen to fight the Novans, it was a good bet most or all of them would be dead. A handful of rifles and some shock grenades wouldn't have lasted against the Black March. "As for the modified Tamil, it was our only option to get off Buenos Aires. None of us knew anything about the modifications until we turned on the jump engines."

"And if that isn't enough to clear us?" Venkata asked.

"It has to be. It's the truth." And Jordan prayed Dray was telling them the truth, wherever they'd taken her.

RUSA SHOVED DRAY into a stark white room on the mother ship. Dray barely had time to realize the room had only one metal chair in the middle before Rusa stepped out and shut the door. Dray saw a small door in the back of the room open.

As the door slid to a stop, Dray heard the hum of a small engine just before she saw an awkwardly shaped droid glide into the room. The droid had six independent arms which unfolded as it circled around the chair and stopped to one side of it. Its flexing movements reminded Dray of an insect. *A very unpleasant insect*, she thought as she noticed that three of the six arms ended in mechanical pincers holding medical instruments. She recognized the interrogation droid, and the realization of what she was about to endure made her break out in a cold sweat. Why was Tarquin Security treating them like prisoners or traitors? They hadn't done anything wrong. Even giving over the Novan children was not strictly breaking any civil or military law.

"Please sit down," the droid said.

Dray ignored the request. "I am a Terran military cadet, training in the ADF. I request you return me and my fellow cadets to Base Station Buenos Aires."

"You are required to sit," the droid said. The main doors to the room slid open behind Dray, and two security guards entered. They grabbed her arms, and forced her into the metal seat, holding her there until the droid triggered hidden restraints to strap her wrists and ankles to the chair. Dray sat passively in the chair as the guards left. She knew she had no hope of release and wouldn't waste her energy. The chair was the only metal in an otherwise composite ship, and Dray knew that fact wouldn't work in her favor. As the droid approached her again, she had a feeling she'd need every ounce of strength she had.

"Your cooperation is required," the droid said. "Please state your name."

"Draybeck, Helena. Cadet private first class, based on Buenos Aires."

"Explain your mission."

Dray shook her head. "We have no mission."

Dray's body tingled uncomfortably wherever it made contact with the chair as an electric pulse ran through the metal. Sweat formed on her upper lip, but with no free hand, she couldn't brush it off. It was the least of her worries.

"That is level zero on the electronic pain inducer attached to your chair," the droid said. "Please comply by answering the questions appropriately. You were in a rendezvous with a Novan vessel on an unregistered planet, while in possession of stolen Tarquin technology. I repeat, what was your mission?"

"I told you, we have no mission. We escaped from the attack on Buenos Aires."

The droid ignored her. "You are the daughter of Katherine Draybeck. Did she arrange for you to work with the Novans before she died?"

Dray closed her eyes. *So they've accessed my personnel file.* "My mother was not a traitor. I am not a traitor." Her thoughts were shattered an instant later as a stronger pulse shot through her. She fought to slow her breathing as her head tipped forward. Was that a level one or had the droid skipped a few levels to speed things up? She didn't want to ask, for fear it was only one level up from the last. This was not going well for her.

Chapter Eight

JORDAN WAS LEFT with Red in the isolation room. The others had been taken away one at a time. No one returned. As Jordan watched Red pacing, she wondered whether she'd have been better off if they hadn't left her behind. Jenny was taken out hours ago, and Venkata shortly after. Jordan had forced herself to stay awake, not entirely trusting what might happen to Red if she fell asleep. He was in great pain, and his skin glowed a deep red she'd never seen before.

"How much longer can you hold out?" she asked.

Red didn't answer her.

Jordan went over the conversations she'd had with Jenny and Venkata before they were taken and made up her mind. Seeing Red suffer was bad enough, but she knew how bad it would get for both of them if she didn't act soon. As she walked over to him, she prayed she was making the right decision.

"Red," she said when she was within a meter of him. He refused to look at her, adjusting his path to avoid her as much as possible, but she trapped him in a corner of the room. She grabbed his arm to get his attention. The face that turned to her was a mask of rage. In an instant, he picked her smaller form up and slammed her against the wall. Pain radiated across her shoulder blades as he pinned her with one arm. His breath came is short gasps as he sniffed at her.

She stared into his deep green eyes. "Do it," she said through clenched teeth. His eyes flickered a moment, as if coming up from a deep well of isolation. "Do it now, before you do it later in a rage anyway!"

Venkata had been very clear. If Red didn't relieve himself sexually, his self-control would eventually snap, and he'd rape any available female. This way is better, Jordan told herself. This way, she offered herself to him. As he leaned into her, she repeated that mantra to herself.

The doors slid open and three sizable guards rushed in to

separate them. Jordan dropped to the floor, too exhausted to put up a fight. Red turned on the guards in a fury. Baring his canines, he attacked the two guards holding him, breaking the arm of one guard in the process. The third guard who had been standing over Jordan joined the battle to incapacitate Red.

Jordan saw her opportunity and darted for the open door. She entered a narrow corridor and ran for half the length of it before a burning pain hit her back and shot down through her legs. Her knees buckled as she lost control of her legs and crumpled to the floor. Her body convulsed with the excess electric current running through it. By the time she could move of her own volition again, two female Tarquin guards towered over her. She'd been hit with a shock gun, she thought. Her mouth tasted metallic, and she realized she'd bitten her own tongue at some point.

One guard bent down and hauled Jordan to her feet. "Your turn," she said as she pushed Jordan further along the corridor, away from the isolation room.

The guard jabbed Jordan to direct her through a hatchway and onto the mother ship. They traveled along the twists and turns of a multitude of corridors. Jordan took her time, observing as much of the ship as she could along their route. Her boots clanked along the grating that formed the floor to the corridor. They passed two open doors where Jordan peered inside until the guard jabbed her in the back to move her forward. Her observations did little to help her situation. She saw no one but Tarquin security personnel in each room.

The guard grabbed Jordan's shoulder, stopping her in front of a closed gray door panel. The guard punched in an access code and the doors slid open, revealing a paneled office with a faux-wood desk and three cushioned chairs. But what dominated the room was the expansive holo-screen behind the desk that revealed the silver cylinder of Base Station Buenos Aires. Some of the tension between Jordan's shoulder blades eased as the guard directed her to take one of the chairs and wait for someone to arrive. Jordan sat in one of the two chairs facing the screen, drinking in the image of home as it hovered in its stationary orbit around Achilles-5.

"Beautiful sight, isn't it?" said a deep, but decidedly female voice. Jordan turned to see a tall, dark-skinned woman enter the room. Jordan assumed the woman was human until she saw the brilliant violet eyes staring back at her. "My name is Therese," said the woman, holding out her hand.

Jordan stood and shook the offered hand, amazed at the coolness of the long, tapered fingers as they wrapped around her hand. She let go in what she hoped was a polite manner. "Cadet Private First Class Jordan Bowers, Ma'am," she said, remembering she was on a military ship. Regardless of Therese's civilian-looking off-white blouse and skirt, the woman was probably military personnel and out-ranked Jordan.

"Nice to meet you, Jordan. Please, take a seat." Therese took the seat next to Jordan, ignoring the chair on the opposite side of the desk. "You don't mind if I sit here, do you? I like to think once we pass the threshold into my office, we leave behind the confines of military protocol." Therese placed a vid-pad on the desk and smoothed her skirt over her knees.

Jordan smiled, unsure how to react to Therese. "May I ask why I'm here?"

"Of course. And I apologize for the lack of hospitality on this vessel. Tarquin Security just isn't equipped for hosting cadets." Therese leaned forward as she spoke. "I think you all have taken them quite off guard. And believe me, it's not something they are used to."

"Where is the rest of my group?" Jordan asked. She wanted to blurt out Dray's name, but held back. Something was just too smooth about this woman, for all she was attempting to make Jordan feel at ease. *She's trying too hard*, Jordan thought.

"They are each being debriefed," Therese said. "And I suppose we should get started ourselves. Now, we have the records from the attack on Buenos Aires. That was such an unfortunate event."

Jordan nodded. The memory of N'Gollo's body invaded her thoughts. So much had happened since then. Would N'Gollo have been proud of them for surviving?

"I'm sure she would have," Therese said, placing her cool hand on Jordan's knee. Jordan flinched, and Therese withdrew her hand. "I'm sorry, I should have properly introduced myself," Therese said. "You probably noticed I'm not quite human."

"Yes, Ma'am." Jordan's sense of ease disappeared, replaced with a wariness of the other woman.

"My primary father was Benthali, though my secondary father was Terran."

Jordan nodded as her mind raced to remember what she'd read about Benthalis. She knew they were used in both civil and military interrogations, but she also knew there were limits to what they could read from another's mind. They hooked into strong emotions, so Jordan would have to remain alert and focused.

"Anyway, to continue," Therese said. "You ended up on VT-115. That was under whose orders?"

"I don't recall the designation of the planet we were rescued from, Ma'am. We escaped Buenos Aires on what we thought was a training ship. There was only one navigation plan in the ship's database. We used it to escape the Novan attack vessels surrounding Buenos Aires air space."

"Who authorized taking the modified Tamil-class?"

Jordan stared into the cold eyes of her interrogator. "The situation on Buenos Aires left us without any direct commanding officer. By ADF regulations, Lieutenant Malory Grace assumed command of our cadet group."

Therese nodded. "Yes, that makes sense. And once you were on VT-115, you met up with a Novan military vessel. What can you tell me about that?"

Jordan folded her hands on her lap, concentrating on the base facts. Her career depended on avoiding thoughts of her own Novan background. "There were two children, survivors of a crashed Novan civilian vessel. The Tamil has full records of whatever we learned."

"I see," Therese said, showing more interest in the vid-pad she'd left on the desk. Was that how she concentrated to read Jordan's thoughts?

Jordan relaxed her shoulders, focusing on her meditation techniques to calm her emotions. When Therese frowned and put down the vid-pad, Jordan knew it was working.

"What can you tell me of your fellow cadets?" Therese asked.

"I didn't know many of the cadets who escaped with us," Jordan said.

Therese looked at her vid-pad. "You know Cadet Draybeck."

Jordan blushed. "Yes, Ma'am. We were bunk-mates on Buenos Aires."

"Yes, and you were together when you found the Novan children." It was a statement, not a question. Therese leaned closer to Jordan. "What did you give to the Novan military vessel?"

It was the question Jordan was waiting for, and likely what the interrogator was searching for. She chose her words carefully. "We returned the Novan children. It was a stalling tactic, Ma'am. We knew the ADF ship could not rescue us in time from the Novans after they landed."

"You chose not to defend yourselves against them. Why?"

"We had no significant weaponry on board. The Tamil transport had no defensive or offensive capabilities." Jordan kept her thoughts under firm control, studying the faint wrinkles on Therese's brow. The other woman was older than Jordan had originally thought.

"I see. So the Novans just happen to appear on the same planet as a prototype Terran ship, piloted by supposedly innocent cadets. It is rather an improbable string of coincidences, don't you think?"

Jordan concentrated, trying to fit the pieces together. "The Novan officer who took the children was likely related to them. I would assume he followed the flight pattern of the civilian ship to find survivors."

"Did the Novans board your vessel or in any way receive information about the modified Tamil-class?"

"No, Ma'am."

"Were you aware the Tamil drive engines were based on stolen Tarquin technology?"

"Not until your vessel landed on the planet. "

Therese sat back, as if disappointed in Jordan's answer. Jordan kept a steady focus on her meditation training. She had no real proof her efforts were working, but when Therese stood up, she was relieved the interrogation might be over. She let her thoughts drift to Red, wondering what was happening to him.

"You will be reunited with the Tarquin male cadet soon," Therese said, once again breaking into Jordan's thoughts. Jordan congratulated herself on giving up only inconsequential information.

"Well, I will give my report to Jenak," Therese said as she walked toward the door. Jordan stood up, but Therese held out her hand. "Please stay seated, Cadet Bowers. Security personnel will come by to get you shortly."

"One last thing, Ma'am," Jordan said. She pulled N'Gollo's ID tag from her pocket. "This belonged to our lead instructor on Buenos Aires. Please see that her family gets it."

Therese accepted the ID tag and typed a code into the door control panel. The door slid open. Jordan saw one orange-toned guard outside the door, but could make little else out before the door slid shut again. She had no option but to wait until they came for her. She sat, facing the image of Buenos Aires and hoping Dray's interrogation went as smoothly.

DRAY MUST HAVE passed out at some point. Her mind slowly drifted back to reality, escaping a series of bizarre dreams, haunted by images of her mother. Only when she became fully awake and aware of the hard metal chair she was still strapped into did she realize her dreams were reflections of the interrogation she'd endured. Dray looked around the stark white room, searching for the droid that had caused her so much pain. She moved her head too fast, causing a dizzy spell that threatened to sink her back into unconsciousness. Fighting against the nausea in her stomach, she scanned her surroundings more slowly. There was no sign of the droid, nothing but the empty room and harsh overhead lights. She closed her eyes and focused on her body, tensing and releasing each major muscle, searching for signs of injury. To her surprise, she found nothing significantly hurt. Of course the droid had used electric shock for most of the questions Dray refused to answer. Dray's own clenching reactions to the shock had caused most of her current muscle aches. No permanent damage, she thought. ADF policy was vague about any interrogation techniques that didn't leave physical evidence. Dray realized now just how fine a line there was between allowed and not-allowed levels of torture.

She'd learned enough from the interrogation questions to know someone had stolen key technology from the Tarquins, and she pitied whoever did it if the Tarquins caught up with them. She slowly moved her head, trying to relax strained muscles. She remembered the droid grilling her over her mother. They were especially concerned about whether the Novans had accessed any information on the modified Tamil-class.

Her thoughts settled on Jordan. Had she gone through the same interrogation? Dray pushed against her restraints. The metal cut into her wrists and ankles. She still couldn't move. A sense of uselessness overcame her and she lowered her head, fighting against her own fears for Jordan's safety. In the end, Dray had done nothing to protect Jordan. She'd failed. And now Jordan was probably strapped to a similar chair, enduring who knew what.

The sight of the door opening interrupted Dray's thoughts. Two Tarquins entered. The first, the taller of the two and female, stopped at the side of the door and triggered a hidden control panel. She punched a few keys and the straps holding Dray down retracted back into the chair. Dray rubbed her wrists as she stood slowly, not sure she wouldn't collapse back down into the chair. Her legs obeyed her, but her vision swam.

"Follow me," ordered the female Tarquin. Dray took a step and lost her balance, pitching forward onto the hard floor. The second Tarquin was at her side, pulling her up. Dray feared some kind of retribution for not cooperating, but the Tarquin guard only held her up, waiting for her to walk. Dray complied, walking toward the open door while the guard supported her whenever she stumbled.

She walked mechanically through a busy corridor, jostled by Tarquin soldiers nearly twice her size. Her guards kept to her side, leading her past multiple intersections where Dray saw more corridors alive with activity. The ship's velocity had changed, and she assumed they must be nearing their destination, wherever that was. The guards steered her down an intersection and they finally stopped outside a door. One of the guards keyed it open. As the door moved, it revealed a view that lifted Dray's spirits. She saw Base Station Buenos Aires in orbit through a holo-screen behind a desk. Dray's gaze drifted from the view to a tall, dark-skinned woman seated behind the desk. The female guard nudged Dray forward. Dray took one last look at her Tarquin captors and thought she saw a faint smile lift the corners of the guard's expansive lips. Was that a good sign or not? Dray wondered.

Dray stepped into the room. The woman behind the desk looked up at her and motioned for Dray to take one of the two seats in front of the desk. As she lowered herself into the chair, the woman triggered some control behind the desk, and the view of Buenos Aires disappeared. *A faked holo-display*, thought Dray. Her hope dwindled.

"You are correct, Cadet Draybeck," the woman said. "We are nowhere near Buenos Aires." The woman folded her hands on her lap. "I am assistant interrogator Therese Ramone."

"Cadet Private First Class Draybeck, Base Station Buenos Aires, Ma'am," Dray droned.

Therese waved her hand. "I've heard that far too many times from you already, Draybeck."

Dray studied the cool face in front of her. The eyes gave her away as a Benthali telepath, but how strong was she? And what was the purpose of replacing a droid interrogation with a Benthali telepath?

"While you proved particularly stubborn for my droid, your colleagues were more cooperative. I thought a face-to-face questioning might be more revealing of the truth."

Dray's thoughts went straight to Jordan, and her jaw tightened. Therese must have controlled the interrogation droid. *If this woman tortured Jordan...*

"No worries, Cadet. Your lover is quite safe. And, I might add, far more adept at deflecting a telepathic probe than you are."

Dray forced herself not to reach over and beat the smug grin off the other woman's face. When Therese paled and pushed away from the desk, Dray smiled. "There are benefits to being an open book to a telepath."

"There are two Tarquin guards outside that door. You wouldn't reach me in time."

"And I don't need to be a telepath to realize you don't believe that." Dray sat still, but the tension in her body reflected her readiness to strike, and she knew Therese knew it.

"Threatening a superior officer is grounds for criminal charges, Cadet."

Dray shrugged. "I haven't said or done anything, Ma'am."

Therese seemed to sense she was being toyed with, and a frown affixed itself to her dark features. "To the matter at hand, Cadet. You've been accused of aiding in the theft of stolen technology and in cooperating with an enemy of the ADF."

"I had nothing to do with the choice of vessels when we left Buenos Aires. And what enemy did I cooperate with?"

Therese lifted a sheet and read off it. "Two days ago, Terran Military declared war against the Novans. They are requesting full support of the ADF."

Dray registered the words with a cold detachment. War with the Novans seemed distant from her current situation. "Is this about Franklin?" *Did he set us up for this?*

"No, not Franklin. Your own classmate gave testimony against you, claiming you were involved in both the crash of the Novan ship and the decision to deal with the Novan attack ship."

Dray struggled to figure out who would turn on her like this. One name came to mind: Bello.

"Very observant of you, Cadet," Therese said. "It is now your word against his. Unlike you, he comes from a consistently loyal family, one who sacrificed many in the last Novan war."

Dray stared at the telepath. "You can determine the truth. Probe my thoughts. You won't find anything."

"You realize anything I learn can be incorporated in a case against you?"

"Just do it." Dray's patience had run out. She was tired of the accusations against her and her mother. She sat still while Therese came around the desk and placed her cool hands on Dray's shoulders.

"You will sense me within your thoughts. I recommend you don't resist as that can end in unpleasant sensations. I am oath-bound to only seek the information requested. Now, concentrate on the events of the past week."

Dray focused her thoughts, starting with the attack on the base station. At some point, Therese took over, leading Dray's memories from one event to another, until they had progressed to the present. Therese dropped her hands and walked back to her side of the desk. "You are cleared of these accusations."

Dray felt vindicated, but she couldn't relax. "Did you probe Bello as well?"

"No. Tarquin Security released him along with the other cadets. They have already been redeployed."

"Why did he lie about me?"

"Given your background and his, I think his doubts about you were misplaced, but understandable."

Dray had no idea what Bello's background was, but if he was spreading lies, she wanted to know why.

"The Buenos Aries officer training program is no longer operational. Those of your group who do not have the option to purchase a substitution are being reassigned to another suitable facility."

"What's a substitution?"

Therese smirked. "Your contract with Terran Military gives you the option to buy your way out of military duty in the event of war. Consider yourself lucky. Most of your group have no such convenient options."

Dray didn't remember anything like that when she signed up to be a pilot like her mother. Following her mother's footsteps was her primary focus. Her father must have made sure she had that option included in her contract. The thought that he would assume she'd run and hide in the face of real military action frustrated her.

"You have two options," Therese said. "You can choose to accept reassignment to another training facility, or you can purchase a drafted substitute to take your place in this war."

Dray's first thoughts went to Jordan. Would Jordan have chosen to buy out her contract? She was sure Jordan's mother would insist on it, but if Jordan had the choice, which way would she go? Dray wanted to believe Jordan would face the prospect of active duty with the same tense anticipation as she did. What if Jordan chose to return to civilian life? Could Dray follow her?

"What is your decision, Draybeck?" Therese folded her hands on the desk, waiting for Dray to answer.

In the end, there was little to debate. Dray's whole life was focused on being a pilot and proving she, like her mother, was a loyal Terran officer. "Reassignment."

Therese's broad smile held no warmth. "Excellent choice." She leaned forward, as if relishing her power over Dray's future. "One other thing. Active military duty doesn't recognize your external contacts. You won't be floating on your father's reputation anymore."

Dray bit back her response. The grin on Therese's face told her the other woman had read her thoughts anyway. Not that it mattered. Dray's thoughts turned to Jordan, and the realization she might never see her again.

"If you will follow me, please." Therese stood up and smoothed out her skirt, then circled around the desk and opened the door. Dray followed her with a heavy sense of duty settling on her as Therese led her down a labyrinth of corridors. The fog in her brain started to lift as they walked, and Dray realized the ship's engines had quieted to a dull hum. They were docked. She hadn't noticed the docking maneuvers and final connection, but her mind hadn't fully recovered from the interrogation procedures. She wondered how far she'd have to get in the military before she could hunt down and beat the crap out of whoever had ordered the shock therapy.

"Tarquin Security works under its own authority," Therese

said. "They wanted that ship and now they have it. And when they find whoever stole the plans and created the ship, that poor soul will disappear into the bowels of one of these Baeron ships and never surface again."

Dray didn't care who the person was. They emerged from the corridors to an open exit ramp. They were leaving the ship. She wanted to ask Therese again where Jordan was, but she knew she'd get no answer. Instead, she settled on a series of unpleasant fantasies involving Therese and the interrogation droid. Dray pushed a hand through her hair, satisfied when Therese took on a decidedly stiff posture as she clicked down the ramp in her non-military glossy black boots.

Dray did not recognize the heavily guarded receiving station they'd just entered, with its bare white walls and columns of personnel scanners. She followed Therese through the scanners and down another long corridor, every step taking her further away from Jordan, further from exploring what she thought might some day have matured into love. They'd never had a chance to see where their attraction would lead, and now, there was a good chance they never would. Jordan might already be on her way back to Gilgar, and Dray was going who knew where.

"We are docked in a military transfer station. Your final destination is in the Entari system."

Dray clamped down on her thoughts again, focusing on what little she knew of the Entari system. The entire star system was classified space, and now Dray had a better idea why. If it was where the active duty officers were trained, they'd need to isolate it from any outside surveillance. Dray's thoughts drifted back to Jordan. If Jordan had chosen substitution, Dray would be alone again.

Therese paused in front of a double-wide door at the end of the corridor. "And in just moments, you'll find out. Did you make the right choice?"

Therese's sardonic tone grated on Dray. "Piss off," Dray said.

"May I remind you I still outrank you, Draybeck. And insulting a senior officer is not acceptable behavior." Therese pushed the release on the doors; they slid open behind her. Dray ignored the cold smirk on Therese's face and pushed past her. The corridor opened into a waiting area. It was empty except for a few faces that Dray recognized. She focused on the one face she thought she might never see again: Jordan's.

Chapter Nine

"DRAY!" JORDAN JUMPED up from the cushioned chair, startling Malory and Jenny. She ran to Dray and hugged her close. The fog remaining from Dray's interrogation disappeared in Jordan's arms. Dray closed her eyes and buried her face in Jordan's soft, black hair, inhaling her unique scent.

Leaning back, she stared into Jordan's dark eyes and cupped her face in shaking hands. "Did they hurt you?" Dray asked, her voice betraying the pent-up anger that threatened to take control if Jordan had been mistreated.

"No," Jordan said. "I'm okay." She waved at the others. "We're all fine." Jordan slipped her hand in Dray's and led her to the rest of the group. The relief that flooded Dray weakened her, and she sought out an empty seat. Jordan sat on the arm of her chair, stroking the back of Dray's neck. Dray wanted to just lay her head in Jordan's lap and sleep, but she didn't want the others to know the heavy toll their situation had taken on her. Instead, she sought the stories of what had happened to each of them.

Jenny spoke first. "Mine wasn't much of an interrogation. They wanted me to blame Malory for taking the modified ship."

"But you didn't," Malory said.

"No. It was our only option to get off the station."

"So, what's your story?" Dray asked as she turned to Malory. Dray saw the muscles in Malory's jaw clench.

"Just a basic interrogation: why did I make the decisions I made; was anyone influencing those decisions. In the end, they gave me the choice of taking an open spot in another pilot squad that's protecting Buenos Aires while they rebuild, or joining an active flight wing out of Entari." Malory's expression darkened. Dray wondered if Malory had experienced the same interrogation drone she had.

"You should have chosen Buenos Aires," Jenny said. "You'd be safer there."

Malory studied her hands. "But you'd be at Entari."

Dray was going to ask Red next, but the bulky Tarquin had taken himself off to the corner of the room to stare out the space port.

"WHAT'S UP WITH him?" Dray asked.

"He just needs some space," Jordan said. She'd noticed Red's increasing agitation as Dray had asked one person after the other for their story. She wasn't surprised when he moved off before Dray could question him. From the time she'd entered the waiting lobby, he had avoided all contact with her, refusing to speak unless spoken to and not making eye contact with anyone else. The others probably assumed he was still recovering from their ordeal, but Jordan knew better. She also felt the stigma of what nearly happened between her and Red and had no intention of discussing it with their entire group.

Jordan deflected Dray's attention. "You haven't told us your story, yet."

"You first," Dray said, smiling up at Jordan.

"I had a heart-to-heart with that same telepath who led you in here." Jordan left out the fear and frustration she'd felt during the interview, knowing any mental slip-up would reveal her Novan secret. Her mother had prepared her for a psi probe, as she had prepared her for most situations. *Except falling in love.* She slipped her hand away from Dray's, uncomfortable with keeping her secret from the object of her love. She'd have to tell Dray, but how? Especially now that they were at war with the Novans.

Jordan couldn't assimilate that they were at war with her father's people. She'd seen so many Novan families on Gilgar. They weren't any different from Terrans. Jordan wouldn't accept the anti-Novan propaganda spilling across the news-vids now. She knew better.

"She interrogated me, too," Malory said, interrupting Jordan's thoughts.

"Therese," Dray said.

Jordan nodded, pushing back her doubts about the war. "Seems like maybe we all had a visit from our friendly neighborhood mind-spook. I have to say, I don't find her techniques entirely ethical. For the most part, it sounds like I had the same treatment as Malory. Questions about how we ended up on that planet and what we knew about the ship and the Novans."

"That's it? Just questions from Therese?" Dray asked.

"Just Therese," Jordan said. "What about you? What happened?"

Dray shifted in her seat. "Same thing. Lots of questions. And the option to get out of the war." Something in Dray's voice suggested she'd experienced more.

"Get out? How?" Malory asked.

Jordan shared Dray's discomfort, knowing if Malory hadn't been given the option of substitution, it was because she was from an unconnected family. Relieving Dray from the burden of answering, Jordan explained the contract option of subsidizing a drafted Terran instead of serving in the war themselves.

Malory's expression hardened. "I see. So you could have bought me or Jenny to save your own hides."

"But we didn't," Dray said, glaring at Malory. "I didn't ask for the contract option, I didn't even know it existed. I turned it down."

Malory didn't answer, but Jordan recognized the anger seething in her. Jordan was very glad they would not be reporting to Malory on Entari.

"I'm surprised Venkata isn't here," Jenny said.

Jordan shrugged. "Gilgaran neutrality. It's one thing to train at an ADF facility, but I'm sure she was under no obligation to sign on in a war between Terrans and Novans." Jordan wasn't obligated to serve, either. She had postponed her decision, knowing the contract gave her the option to resign at a later time. She needed her mother's advice first. And she couldn't have resigned until she knew whether Dray resigned or not.

"Why is Red here?" Dray asked. "Tarquins normally serve in their own military squads."

The side door where Red was standing opened up. An older man wearing the insignia of a staff sergeant approached Red and spoke quietly with him for a moment. Red walked back to Jordan and the others. "We have another long flight to the Entari system. The staff sergeant has made room for us on his supply ship." Red returned to the side door and the others followed quietly behind.

The supply ship had no spare facilities for traveling personnel. Dray and Jordan managed to find a storage room on the second level near the rear loading platform and the only toilets in the back of the ship. After managing a dreary meal in a tiny common room, Dray and Jordan walked back to the storage room they'd commandeered. They had two fire safety blankets and a series of flat packing foam mats for a bed, but Jordan didn't mind. When Dray crawled into their makeshift bed, Jordan was too shy to react. She tried to ignore the little voice inside her saying Dray knew she was hiding something. Jordan wanted to confess it, but fear swallowed the words before she could speak. And there was another, more sinister voice inside saying Dray didn't want her anymore, after they'd made love in the cave. Jordan's Novan physiology ensured she hadn't gotten as sick from the atmosphere as Dray had been. She remembered everything, but it had been her first time with anyone, and she was certain she'd messed things up entirely. That, combined with worrying about her future in a war, kept Jordan awake for hours.

DRAY FINALLY WOKE up and found Jordan sitting on the bare floor, studying a portable reader. Dray stretched, loosening stiff muscles, and sat up. "Any idea what time it is? "

"Ten o'clock," Jordan said. "But that's still Buenos Aires time."

"Past breakfast," Dray said, listening to the grumblings in her stomach.

Jordan stood up and pulled open a dull, gray sack. "Because I knew your stomach would be the first part of you to wake up."

She handed Dray a mini-microwave. "Great, thanks," Dray said, pressing the heat button on the silver case. A moment later, the case beeped once and slid open. Steam rose from a plate of warm cereal and a mug of hot tea. Dray devoured the food, burning her tongue twice in the process. The food tasted good, warming her inside and erasing the cloud of sleep from her mind. It wasn't until she'd finished completely that she thought to ask if Jordan had wanted any.

"No, thanks," Jordan said with a laugh. "I've learned not to get between you and your first meal of the day. I ate before you woke up." She pointed to the trash chute.

Dray got up and pushed her case into the chute, listening to it recycle the disposable microwave unit. "So, where is everyone?"

"No one else was around when I went foraging for food."

An awkward silence developed between them. Dray wanted to invite Jordan back to bed, but the lingering fear that their first time together had been nothing more than a hallucination stopped her. Could she just outright ask? Sensing Jordan's shyness, she thought not. Maybe Dray should just act as if it hadn't happened. After all, they had another two full days on this ship, with nothing much to do besides be alone together. Surely, Dray could work up the nerve to make love to Jordan again in that time? Feeling her hands start to shake, Dray shoved them in the pockets of her dirty cadet uniform. She looked down at the layer of dirt and dry sweat covering her and doubted Jordan found her the least bit appealing at the moment. Of course, the same layer of dirt on Jordan gave a rugged edge to her feminine features that Dray found gorgeous.

More like maddening, Dray thought, if she didn't know where she stood with Jordan. She clenched her fists in her pockets. "Any chance you found someplace to clean up around here? I feel like a human dirt-ball." And maybe a shower would kick-start her confidence.

Jordan shook her head. "Sorry, not much besides the hand sanitizer in the toilet."

Dray sank down onto their makeshift mattress. Two more days of feeling cruddy and shy wasn't so appealing. She tried to think of ways to broach the subject of their time in the cave. "So, how are you feeling?" she began.

"Better for having slept. How about you?"

"Okay, I guess." Dray ran a hand through her dirty hair and regretted it. How did Jordan manage to still look so beautiful when neither of them had showered in days? She ignored the dirt, focusing on her mission to discover whether her memories were real or hallucination. "I think I'm still feeling the effects of our exposure, you know, back in the cave?"

Jordan was at her side in an instant, feeling Dray's head as she studied Dray's face. Her exaggerated look of concern would have been comical in any other situation. "Do you think you're still sick? I'm sure this ship has only the basics for emergency first aid equipment."

Dray clasped Jordan's hands in her own. "No, I don't feel bad. Just a bit, you know, foggy about what happened." There, she'd said it. Now maybe Jordan would tell her what really happened.

JORDAN'S HEART SANK. *This is it*, she thought. Dray would tell her what a bad time it all was, what a mistake. Jordan bit her lip, fighting the urge to cry. She didn't think she could cope with the let's-be-friends speech. Not after all they'd been through together, and all they faced when they landed at their destination. Maybe it was Dray's way of distancing herself before they both faced active duty in a war. "I'm sorry," she mumbled.

Jordan looked up into Dray's blue eyes, then looked back down, unable to bear the intensity in Dray's gaze. "I mean, if it was, you know. The wrong thing to do."

"What was the wrong thing to do?"

Jordan felt the tension in Dray's body and gently pulled her hands away. This was going all wrong. She wanted to curl up in a corner, but she had to face what had happened. Maybe Dray would be willing to work through her lack of talent. Glancing back up, Jordan prayed that would be the case. Even with a layer of dirt and sweat, Dray was the most gorgeous person Jordan had ever met. Everything about Dray excited her. She couldn't let that go. She wouldn't without a fight. "I'm sorry if I was a disappointing lover," she blurted out. "I can get better, if you give me a chance."

Dray sat there, blinking rapidly for so long Jordan was sure her gamble had failed and Dray would just walk away, disgusted. To her surprise, Dray stroked her hair and pulled her closer. Jordan closed her eyes as Dray's lips touched hers. Her body thrilled to the touch of remembered sensations of Dray caressing other parts of her. She didn't want the kiss to end, but Dray pulled away after a moment.

"You are a fantastic lover," Dray said. "What we did in the cave was so fantastic, I thought maybe I'd just hallucinated it all." A smile pulled at the corners of Dray's mouth.

Jordan smiled in return. "Did you really think it was all just a dream?"

Color flooded Dray's pale cheeks. "Well, I'd been wanting you for so long, it just seemed too good to be true."

Lifting Dray's chin in her hands, Jordan kissed her again, lingering so long this time that they were both breathless at the end. She leaned back on the foam mattress, pulling Dray down with her.

A knock on the door interrupted them. Dray shouted at them to go away, but Jenny shouted back that Malory Grace was threatening to pull rank on them if they didn't join them to discuss their future.

"It doesn't matter," Dray whispered. "Malory won't be our commanding officer once we land."

Jordan laughed, but pushed Dray gently off her. "She is for now." Jordan helped Dray up off the mattress and kissed her once again. "We still have two nights here alone." Jordan's shyness melted away with the look of anticipation on Dray's face. Malory Grace could manipulate their days, but not their nights.

They joined Malory and Red in the empty storage room. With no chairs, they used plastic containers for seats and a broad, flat transport slab for a table. Red's bloodshot eyes turned away from Jordan when she entered. She clenched her jaw, determined to clear the air with him before they landed.

"We've got two more days of travel through space," Malory said. "These are your last two days before joining the war. As your C.O., I got briefed on what happens to you next." She paused, waiting for everyone to sit. "Like I said, your cadet days are over. You'll be joining an active boot camp on Entari and training as more than just fighter pilots. You'll be trained for search and rescue, tactical, and navigation, as well as a continuance of your flight training. Your skills will be assessed and you'll be given final assignment options based on your assessment scores."

"How long will it last?" Jenny asked. "Before we're deployed for active duty?"

"Eight weeks. Terran Military is ramping up fast for this war."

The news shocked Jordan. In two months, they could be facing a real battle, against her father's kind. When she joined the military, she thought she was prepared to fight against Novans. Now she wasn't so sure. She glanced at Dray, but whatever her girlfriend was feeling inside, all she showed was a lust for action.

"What about Venkata and the others?" Dray asked.

"Venkata resigned. The Tarquins released the rest earlier and they've been sent on to their posts by now."

"What about you?" Jenny asked.

"I'll have two weeks drill training with my new squad, then I'm active," Malory said. "The Entari system has a number of key assets we will protect against attack." She looked at Jenny. "It's a defensive flight squad. I should be able to come visit you on downtime."

Jordan saw the worry in Jenny's eyes, but it was something they were all facing now. Eight weeks wasn't very long, and then they'd be given a choice of assignments like Malory. Jordan had until then to determine what she wanted her role to be in this war.

JORDAN SEARCHED THE entire ship the next day, determined to talk to Red. She found him lying on a crate outside the crew quarters. She should have realized he'd seek out someone to chat with, even if he was isolating himself from his fellow cadets. He glanced at her as she approached, and abruptly stood up.

"You're not leaving," she said.

"I do not wish to disturb you with my presence."

"We need to talk. Please. What happened wasn't all your fault."

"I could not control my own base cravings."

Jordan knew why he had such a hard time controlling his attraction to her. She'd seen it many times before and managed to hide the real reasons for it. This time, she couldn't let him blame himself for something that was her fault. She clenched her fists and said what she had never told another soul. "I'm part Novan."

Red stared at her, speechless for once.

Jordan used his silence to continue before she lost courage. "My father was Novan. I inherited some of his Novan genetics, including pheromones that draw people to me who would not otherwise find me attractive."

Red would realize that her parents' marriage was illegal in Terran society. And as a child of an illegal union, Jordan had no basis for the Terran citizenship she claimed. She would have been safe on Gilgar, a neutral world, but her parents raised her as

Terran, and she wanted to be accepted by her own kind.

Red's skin rippled deeper orange as his gaze swept over her. It seemed to aggravate him more. He turned away. "You see? I have no control over myself."

"Maybe you're too hard on yourself. You were born into a warrior culture."

"I am an initiate in the Flame. I chose a different path."

She reached out to him, but he stepped away.

"I am honored you entrusted this to me. It must be a heavy burden for you, and if there is any way I can help you, know I am here for you. What happened on the Baeron ship was not related to your Novan origins. I am the one who was not strong enough. I bear the shame of what happened."

He stepped around her and walked away. She'd taken a risk by telling him she was part Novan. She should have confessed to Dray instead, but that confession would be much harder. She knew Red would not reject her for who she was. She wasn't as sure about Dray.

TWO DAYS WITH nothing to do and no responsibilities nearly drove Dray insane. The nights with Jordan made up for some of that time. Jenny teased her about the wide smile and sleepy look Dray had every morning, but she didn't mind. She'd have teased Jenny back, but she wasn't sure what was going on between Jenny and Malory. As for Red, she hadn't seen him since their meeting on the first day. Dray spent as much free time as possible in physical training. She did push-ups, sit-ups, and even found a spot in the cargo hold for chin-ups.

When the ship finally landed on a planet in the Entari system, they were led by a sentry through the loading area, a walk of nearly a kilometer. They reached the end of the massive dome of the loading area and passed through a security checkpoint to gain access to the rest of the facility. The next long corridor they walked through ended at yet another, more intensive, security scrutiny before they were allowed to proceed. *Paranoia runs high around here*, Dray thought. She remembered they were in a state of war. Maybe all ADF facilities acted like this now.

Malory was led off to a separate area, where, presumably, she'd join her fighter squad. Jenny's pale face and shaking hands expressed how difficult the separation was for her. The uncertainty of their futures weighed heavily on all of them. After another long walk past more checkpoints and a vast complex of glass-encased offices, they walked into an empty classroom. A tall Aquaran entered the room from the opposite door. He was a pale silver color, with a crop of what looked like white moss atop his wide, flat face. His smile looked toothless, his small teeth not visible beneath his thick lips.

"I am Major Sakai Duli, and I will be your C.O. and instructor during your final training." He looked down at the sheet in his hand. "Baron and Bowers, you are part of Zeta squad. Draybeck and Tomiko, you will be added to Alpha squad."

Jordan slipped her hand into Dray's and held it tightly. Dray felt the tension in her lover, and knew she shared her frustration. She hadn't considered the possibility that they'd be separated. Would they be able to share quarters as they had on Buenos Aires? How would they still see each other? The thought of being separated from Jordan distracted her, and she missed some of Major Duli's instructions.

"Your teams have been in training for a few days already, so you will have some catching up to do. Since you all came with high recommendations, I don't believe that will be a problem. Now, are there any questions?"

Red asked the only question. "Did everyone else from our group choose substitution?"

"No," Duli said. "Most weren't given the option. Tarquin Security released the other cadets days ago, but you should see some of your fellow cadets today, those that have been reassigned here." His pupils narrowed to barely discernible slits in his red eyes. "Don't mistake this facility for an extension of your officer training. You are training to fight in a war that has already proven to be bloody and unpredictable. You've only got eight weeks. Make the most of it."

Duli spoke quietly into his com-link. The conference door slid open and two young men entered, Bello and Sahar. Bello saluted Duli. Dray's jaw tightened as she stared at him. His lies had sent her into an interrogation chamber. And who knew how much of what the others went through was because of their association with Dray?

Duli introduced the two men. "These are your squad leaders. Cadet Corporal Jent Bello is Alpha squad leader. Draybeck and Tomiko, you will be joining his squad."

Dray refused to flinch as Bello's yellow eyes bore down on her. His pupils narrowed to horizontal slits. "Draybeck." He turned to Jenny. "Welcome to Alpha squad."

Sahar's broad, welcoming smile eased some of Dray's tension. At least Jordan had a respectable leader. And with Red in her group, she should be well taken care of. Duli dismissed them all. Bello signaled them all to follow him and marched out of the conference room. Dray wavered, unwilling to leave Jordan just yet, but Sahar seemed to sense her indecision. "We're all going to the same place," he told her as he walked to the door.

Bello led them down two levels and into a long tunnel. He ignored the trail of people behind him, marching as if he were alone. Sahar took the time during their walk to explain what he had learned about the training facility they were going to. It was built in a vast complex of enclosed biospheres that simulated multiple planetary environments. Their dormitories, cafeteria, and lecture halls were built into a three-story underground building.

"Which planet are we on?" Jenny asked.

"We're on Entari-Prime," Sahar said. "Most of our training outside the biospheres occurs here and on the second and third moons of Nebisius. You have a complete lesson on the Entari system waiting for you in the dorm. No one expects you to know anything about this area yet."

Bello turned on his heel. "No one is going to cater to your ignorance, either. You're already behind the rest of us." He marched ahead at the same quick pace. Dray would have to put up with his arrogance and manipulations for all of their final training. Jordan squeezed her hand, and gave her a look that said, "Don't be a troublemaker." Dray smiled in return, holding Jordan's hand until they emerged from the tunnel, where Bello lined them up in formation.

He glanced between Dray and Jordan, and his lips peeled back in an emotionless grin. "Alpha squad uses communal dorm number seven."

"Is that really necessary, Bello?" Sahar asked. "The rest of the squads are using single and double-bunk rooms."

"You can do what you like with your rabble, but Alpha has been getting top marks since I moved us to communal quarters. I'm not changing that for these two."

Bello's smile faded as he studied Dray and Jenny. "Remember this. Alpha team is top. Keep up with the squad, and you'll do fine. Fall behind, and I'll grind you into a pulp."

"Inspirational," Sahar muttered. "Anyway, it's past hours, so we all need to turn in for the night. You'll meet again at 0500 for drills before breakfast." He turned to lead his team members away. Jordan brushed her fingers along Dray's cheek and smiled before turning to follow her squad leader.

"This way," Bello barked as he turned down a different corridor. Dray marched in step behind him, with Jenny following. Bello keyed open the door. "Pass-key is 56554 and changes every five days. If you forget it, you sleep on the floor out here until the next pass-key change, understood?"

Dray nodded. She couldn't think of why he used a pass-key

entry instead of the standard chip-ID reader the rest of the facility used. Except, of course, he was a control freak and it gave him more power over his entire unit. It could be a long eight weeks, she thought as he led them into a dark room. Dray noticed the overbearing stink of body odor and the sounds of snoring. As her eyes grew accustomed to the dark, she made out the shapes of ten or more bunk beds lining both sides of the open room, with a narrow aisle down the middle. Bello led them part way down the aisle and stopped.

"Toilet facilities are at the far end. Your uniforms are in the trunks under the bottom bed," Bello whispered. "Questions?"

"No, Sir," Jenny said, saluting.

"Good. Be up at 0500 and in the meeting area where we split off from your friends." He turned and left the open room, closing the door.

"Why does he sleep somewhere else?" Jenny asked.

Someone from the top of the neighboring bunk answered. "Aquarans need specialized climate control to remoisturize. Trust me, you don't want to see Bello shed his skin. He's an ugly enough bastard as it is."

Dray stifled a laugh, remembering what he'd looked like the last few days on the Tamil-class.

Another squad member hissed at them from the next bunk. "Our squad leader deserves more respect than that. And the rest of us deserve some sleep."

Dray couldn't make out much about the owner of the voice in the dark. She was female, but something about her hair color seemed off.

Dray turned back to Jenny. "You want top or bottom?"

Jenny shrugged. "Bottom, I guess. Less to fall out of in a few hours."

Dray rummaged in the trunk and pulled out sleep clothes, then made her way to the showers. At least she'd be clean again. When she was finished showering and lay on her top bunk, sleep refused to come. Her thoughts drifted to Jordan, hoping her lover was having an easier time adjusting to their separation than Dray.

Chapter Ten

JORDAN STOOD BESIDE Dray in the meeting area. Both wore the standard dark blue-gray uniform, while Jenny and Red had the same uniform with one bar, signifying their rank as cadet corporal. Multiple squads mingled together, waiting for instructions.

"So, how did you sleep last night?" Dray asked.

Looking at the dark circles under Dray's eyes, Jordan realized she wasn't alone in having spent a restless night. She pressed her lips to Dray's, then pulled back. "Not as well as when we're together." Dray's tired smile seemed such a contrast to her usual intensity, but Jordan didn't have time to question what else might be bothering Dray. Major Duli entered the meeting area, flanked by four technicians, all in black uniforms.

Bello entered the room. Behind him came a woman with pale yellow skin and long blue hair, wearing a tight uniform that left nothing to the imagination.

"She's beautiful," Jordan whispered.

Dray turned to Jordan. "Excuse me?"

"Oh, don't give me the jealous face. Just look around you. Every eye is on her."

The woman scanned the room, and her gaze locked on Dray. Jordan felt a twinge of jealousy, and she took a step closer to Dray. She thought she might be imagining the faint curve of a smile on the woman's face as she continued across the room to stand with Bello.

Dray turned to Jordan. "She's not all that."

Jordan rolled her eyes. She didn't know if Dray was pretending not to be affected by the woman's attention, or if she really was oblivious to someone everyone else in the room was staring at.

Duli stepped to the center area, surrounded on four sides by silent rows of cadets. His red eyes scanned the squads as he spoke. "Today's exercise will be in the White-Out biosphere. Most of you have been in this situation before, but for the newcomers, you will be wearing fully shielded encounter suits in a simulated white-out atmosphere. You'll be entirely dependent on the readouts in your suit to survive. This is a timed mission to find the hidden weapons cache and destroy it. You'll pilot individual cloud skippers. Each squad is assigned their own cache, and you are competing for the best time."

Duli pointed to the four techs who stood with him. "These people are on standby should any incidents occur within the biosphere. If you screw up your flight pattern, they'll initiate an emergency override and fly you back to base. Otherwise, you are on your own in there. Squad leaders, prepare your teams."

BELLO RAN HIS squad down the connection tunnel to the biosphere. The clanking of heavy boots on the hard floor echoed in Dray's helmet as she kept pace with the others. Jenny struggled beside her, the weight of the heavy suit showing in her strained features behind the helmet screen. When they were lined up in front of the entrance, one of the technicians locked their helmets to VR-mode, and Dray's world took a dizzying shift to the unreal. Sight and sound were replaced by the virtual reality feeds on their helmets. She was off-balance as the door opened, and her team stepped into the biosphere. Dray relied on her vision to guide her, even during flight training missions. To be cut off from all normal input left her in a momentary panic. Her automatic reactions kept her in close proximity to her teammates, but her disorientation became obvious to Jenny and the others as they entered their cloud skippers.

"Get a grip, Draybeck," Bello said over her helmet com. "If you screw up this mission on me, you'll have a lot worse to deal with than just a VR headache."

Bello's words shifted Dray's emotions from panic to anger. The effect heightened her ability to function with the VR readouts as she launched her cloud skipper into the atmosphere. She tried to concentrate harder on her readouts so she could fly faster, but the effort blurred her vision. Gritting her teeth, she adjusted the display, dimming out some of the extraneous information so she could focus on the forward visual.

Her mistake became obvious when they were within visual range of their target. Dray had blocked out all backward-facing information, and it cost her. When the attack drone plane approached from her blind spot, Dray was defenseless. A painful jolt struck Dray when the drone zapped her plane with an electric pulse. The hit advanced her mission clock by two minutes, and Dray heard Bello curse. She turned her helmet's rear cameras back on.

The combination of the front and rear cameras made her head throb by the time the squad flew back to the biosphere entrance and the mission clock froze. The techs turned off white-out mode as soon as each pilot landed.

Jenny came over to Dray to commiserate. "Think it will fry the electronics if I throw up in my helmet?" she asked.

Dray laughed. "Probably not, but you won't find a buddy to help you out of the suit with that kind of mess waiting inside."

"I feel like a farm tractor plowing through permafrost in this suit. I must have added twenty seconds to our mission clock," Jenny said. "How'd it go for you?"

"Worse than that. I got hit," Dray frowned.

Jenny put her gloved hand on Dray's shoulder. "Welcome to being the newbies, eh?"

The rest of the team did not speak to them during the journey back to the training center until they were all stripped out of their encounter suits. Bello called them all together, and the squad formed a circle of sweating bodies around him, wearing only undergarments.

"Draybeck and Tomiko!" Bello shouted.

Dray and Jenny pushed through the circle to stand in the middle, under the taunts of the squad.

"Tomiko slowed down the mission, but Draybeck cost us the win by getting a drone hit." Bello's yellow gaze bore down on Dray as his lips curled into a sneer. He turned to the squad. "What do we do with dead weight?" he asked.

"Leave it behind!" the squad chanted. Dray heard the amusement in many voices, but one or two faces in the group seemed to recoil from Bello's taunting. Dray wondered if they were of a friendlier persuasion, or if they'd been subjected to his derision in the past. She stood still under the onslaught, but their jeers sunk into her. She had let down the team, something that had not happened to her in a long time. Whatever hazing they doled out, she would accept without complaint. Her father used to quote some ancient historical figure who said whatever did not break her, would make her stronger. She held onto that as Bello pronounced her fate.

"Since you're our dead wood, Draybeck, we'll be leaving you behind tonight," Bello said, enjoying his role as punisher. "You'll be locked out of the dorm until 0400."

"Yes, Sir." Dray kept her eyes focused on a space just beyond the gaggle of faces in front of her. Now his control of the pass-key made more sense. He couldn't randomly lock out personnel if they'd used a chip-ID reader.

"As for you, Tomiko," Bello continued. "You can spend the

next hour jogging the hallway in your encounter suit. Maybe the next mission, you won't fall behind."

After Bello finished, the squad wandered back to their lockers to gather clothes. Most took showers, but Jenny sat on a bench, catching her breath before getting back in the suit.

"I'll come with you," Dray offered.

"You don't have to. You weren't falling behind the way I was."

"No, but I was stumbling blind half the time. I need the practice with white-out mode." Dray felt like a pariah as the rest of the team avoided her. She did get one smile from the attractive, blue-haired Chameleon, who introduced herself as Dai Chittal, but she left as soon as Bello called for her. Dray recognized her voice as the woman who'd defended Bello the night before. Dray didn't expect any real friendship coming from that direction.

JORDAN SAT IN the communications room, watching a news-vid. Buenos Aires was the rallying call to war, with images of young cadets in body bags. The news-vid didn't mention the Baeron prototype transport or the captured Novan ship. Some of the news was propaganda, but Jordan couldn't ignore the death toll the Novans were inflicting on the Terrans.

Jordan heard someone outside and found Malory searching through the training section. "They're not back yet," Jordan said. "Alpha squad always takes longer on the drills than the rest of us."

Malory's expression clouded. "I guess I'll come back later."

"How are you and Jenny doing?" Jordan asked.

Malory hesitated, letting out a sigh. "I don't know. It's not the same. I wish I could figure it out, but something's just not right."

"Give yourselves some time," Jordan said, resting a hand on Malory's shoulder. "You went from hating each other to dating again in a very short time. And a lot has happened in that time, to all of us."

Malory looked up at her. "I never hated Jenny."

"Maybe you need to talk some things out." Jordan's words reflected her own thoughts about Red. He was still isolating himself. Maybe she could get Malory to help.

But first, while she had the free time and authorization, she needed to contact her mother. When Malory left, Jordan walked back into the communications room and turned off the news-vid. It took longer than normal to establish an encrypted, private link to her mother, but after a minute, the vid came to life.

"Jordan. Where are you?" Her mother looked tired. "Are you heading back to Gilgar?"

"I'm in the Entari system."

"Have you resigned yet?"

The question took Jordan by surprise. "No. I'm in boot camp."

Her mother leaned closer. "You can't mean to stay, not with the declaration of war."

Jordan's mind flipped to the images on the news-vid. "The Novans started this war. I was there, remember?"

"Do you know what would happen to you if you are discovered? At peace, you'd have been dishonorably discharged and sent home. In war, you could be tried for treason."

Treason? Jordan hadn't considered that possibility. "This is still my career," she said, ignoring the seed of doubt her mother had so deftly planted.

"And you think it's worth it with this risk looming over your head?"

"We all make sacrifices for our careers. You taught me that." The bitterness in Jordan's words had the expected effect.

Her mother crossed her arms. "That is not a fair comparison. I loved your father. We both agreed on the course we took to hide his and your background."

"And now I have to decide my own course. And for now, that's the military career I've been working so hard for."

Her mother relented. It was only a temporary truce, but the argument had focused Jordan's thoughts. She knew she was making the right decision. Her future was here, not back on Gilgar, hiding on a neutral world. She still wanted her military career.

ON THEIR FIRST day off in over a week, Jordan wandered into the common room, looking for Dray. Instead, she found Red, sitting on his own with his head in his hands. She marched up to him, determined to break him out of his isolation.

Something in her face must have revealed her intentions. Red looked up at her, his eyes bloodshot and rimmed in darkness. "Is it your turn now?" he asked.

His words confused Jordan. "What do you mean?"

He dropped his hands into his lap. "Malory just shouted at me. I assume you want to have a go at it next."

"So you'll just sit there and let someone else start shouting at you?"

He looked down at his hands. "It is a just punishment."

Jordan let out a long, slow breath. "Do Tarquins have some sort of martyr complex?"

"It is all a test of the Flame." He must have sensed Jordan's confusion. "You remember the tattoo I have over my heart? It marks me as an initiate of the Flame. It demands a life balanced between the physical and spiritual." He paused, clenching his hands together. "What happened on the Baeron ship... I became unbalanced. The Flame within me should have returned me to balance before I was any threat to you. It did not. I was too weak. And so, I must accept the punishment."

Jordan drew a hand through her hair, pushing the long strands back. "I don't know about this Flame of yours, but it sounds unrealistic and unfair."

"Once you accept it, the Flame dwells within you, guiding you and sustaining you. My faith was weak, and I failed. Now, I must regain the balance I lost."

"What a load of tripe," Malory said as she came into the room. "Whatever happened between you two, and yes, I do want details, it has nothing to do with failing this Flame of yours, Red."

To Jordan's surprise, Red took no offense at Malory's declaration. In fact, he looked almost glad to see her.

Malory stepped between them. "I'm not your commanding officer anymore, but humor me. Jordan, get your butt over to the gym and get your girlfriend."

"I haven't told her about this," Jordan said.

"You have until the next meal. After that, we all meet in Conference room C. Jenny's reserving the room for us now." Malory put a hand on Red. "You've been quiet for too long about what happened on the Baeron ship. We get it all out tonight."

DRAY FINISHED HER last form of Ti-Daken, the martial arts training she'd found in the gym's video archive. She was surprised to see Jordan watching her from the doorway. "Congratulate me. I just got first place for targeting and navigation," Dray said, pulling Jordan to her.

"Nothing personal," Jordan said, pushing Dray back. "But you're in desperate need of a shower."

Dray sniffed her own body and grabbed a towel to wipe the sweat off her face and neck. "Want to join me in that shower?"

"I actually had something I needed to talk to you about."

The hesitancy in Jordan's voice caught Dray's full attention. "What's wrong? Did something happen?"

"Nothing's wrong. I just needed to talk to you about what happened on the Baeron ship."

Dray grabbed Jordan's arm, "I knew it. They tortured you as well, didn't they? With the interrogation droid."

Jordan frowned. "No. Nothing like that. It has to do with why Red has isolated himself from the rest of us. It's kind of my fault."

Dray let go of Jordan, embarrassed by her overreaction. "How so?"

"I haven't told you the full story about what happened on the Tarquin ship. Do you remember how the Tarquin female scented Red?"

Dray nodded.

"Well, most of us didn't realize, but once a Tarquin is, well, sexually stimulated, he has to, um..."

"I get it. Why didn't he just hide in a corner and masturbate?"

"It's biologically impossible for a Tarquin. You noticed how his skin changes when he's attracted to someone? Tarquins require skin to skin contact with another person."

"So, he was aroused with no way to handle it?" Dray asked.

"Yes, and no." Tears formed in Jordan's brown eyes. "They left us alone."

Dray took Jordan's hands, unsure where this was leading, but knowing Jordan had been deeply affected by Red's problem, and fearing the worst. "Were there others with you?"

"No. Just me and Red." Jordan waited a heartbeat, then added, "Nothing happened."

Dray relaxed. Jordan hadn't been hurt after all. "You had me worried there."

Jordan lowered her head. "Something might have happened, but Red wouldn't let it."

"What? I don't understand."

Jordan's words came tumbling out. "Venkata said if he didn't relieve himself, he'd eventually go mad. He'd end up raping me."

Dray cursed. What had that bastard done? "Did he lay a hand on you?"

"I offered myself to him," Jordan said, barely above a whisper.

Dray struggled to comprehend. "You were going to have sex with Red?" The faint flicker of her old jealousies came back, and she struggled to control them.

"He wouldn't let it happen, and the Tarquin guards separated us at that point." Jordan lifted her head and held Dray's focus. "But, yes, if it would have solved his problem, I would have had sex with him."

Dray let go of Jordan and walked to a weight bench to sit. "Why are you telling me this now?"

"Because Malory is insisting we all meet to help Red."

"Malory? She has no authority anymore."

"Still, it's something I need to do. And I wanted you to understand what happened before we meet."

"Are you attracted to him?" Dray hated herself for the insecurity in her voice, but she had to know.

Jordan knelt beside her, cupping Dray's face in her warm hands. "No. And I didn't do it for any real noble purpose. I did it to save myself."

Dray studied Jordan's face, seeing in it a reflection of the fear Dray had experienced when she thought he might have raped Jordan. She pulled Jordan closer, kissing her head. "You did the right thing."

Jordan held her for a moment, then let go. "So what's this about an interrogation droid?"

Dray let out a sigh and prepared to tell her own story, but only to Jordan. The others didn't need to know.

MALORY ANNOUNCED IT was time to hear Red's story. The somber Tarquin had sat with them without saying a word. Dray was not sure he would talk at all, but Malory's influence seemed to ease him into opening up.

"My family background ensured I was never under investigation while on the Tarquin ship. My sister is a Tarquin delegate. I do not think what happened to me with Rusa was planned."

Malory kicked his foot to get him to continue.

"Mine was a fundamental test of faith. For a Tarquin who has accepted the Eternal Flame, I am bound by its main directive, the balance of physical, spiritual, and emotional." His voice was quiet, but no one made a sound to disturb him as he continued. "When Rusa scented me, I had a choice to make. I could restrain myself and suffer the consequences, or I could force myself on another to fulfill what she had started." He stared at his hands as if they held some fascination for him. "I was too weak. I failed myself and my duty as an initiate of the Flame."

Malory barked a laugh that shattered the silence following Red's words. "Is every initiate so melodramatic?" She leaned closer to him, placing her hand on his shoulder. "Tell them the rest."

His green eyes looked at her for a long time. As if reaching a decision, he turned to the rest of them. "Malory is right, there was more to my test. Before I matured, while I was still a young girl, I was taken against my will by a recently matured male."

Dray saw the color drain out of Jordan's face, and she understood now why the events had such a strong impact on Red. To turn from being attacked to being the attacker—she couldn't even guess what that would be like.

Jordan stood up and walked to Red. "I'm sorry," she said. "But it didn't happen. Nothing happened."

He looked up at her. "It would have happened if they hadn't

stopped it."

Jenny asked the question the rest of them had been thinking. "What happened after they separated you from Jordan? Did they cure you in time?"

A sardonic smile marred Red's somber expression. "I am not sterile, if that is what you are asking. There are medical interventions to prevent that. When Jordan left, I was given a tranquilizer to restrain me. I was cured, as you say. Though I still bear the weight of what I nearly did to a friend."

"I don't believe you were responsible for what happened, but either way," Malory said. "It's all in the past."

"It is not that easy," Red said. "I have become what I hated most. I cannot just forget that."

Malory turned to him. "Start with forgiveness. Isn't that what your faith teaches you?"

Red smiled. "I think you are confusing it with one of your Terran religions."

Malory threw up her hands. "They're all alike, aren't they? Forgive and forget? Isn't there some kind of cleansing ritual you can do?"

"Yes." He stood up, his massive body all but surrounding Jordan. "It is something which requires Jordan's participation. I have no right to ask."

"I'll do it," Jordan said. "Whatever it is, I'll do it."

RED INVITED THEM all to witness the ritual he would share with Jordan. It took him two days to gain permission for it from Duli. On the designated day, they joined him in one of the more temperate biospheres. The atmosphere was too nitrogen-rich, requiring them all to wear breathing regulators. Jordan looked down at her own freshly pressed uniform, hoping she had not made the creases on her pants too rigid or the collar of her top too stiff. She stood alone as Red had directed, in the middle of a grove of white snow trees. Her polished boots sank into the wet ground.

Jordan felt the urge to bite her nails, something she hadn't done in ages. She clenched her fists at her sides, waiting. Malory, Jenny, and Dray stood behind her, standing just beyond the edges of the grove. The sound of heavy footfalls brought Jordan's focus to the corridor of snow trees in front of her. Red emerged a moment later, dressed not in uniform, but in a pair of loose-fitting pants. He wore no top, and the tattoo of a blue flame seemed to glow and flicker on his chest as he breathed. Jordan swallowed hard and took the required three steps to meet him in the middle of the grove.

They bowed to each other. Overhead, some birds chirped a

melody. Red knelt in the mud in front of Jordan. He spoke quietly in his own language, but Jordan knew the meaning behind his words. It was a litany of sorrow and pain, his and hers. When his words finished, she knelt next. The coolness of the mud seeped through the knees of her pants. She spoke her part of the ritual, the Tarquin words coming in halting phrases she was sure were unrecognizable to a native speaker. Red had given her the option to speak in Terran Standard, but she refused. Even with her inability to pronounce some phrases, it meant more to her to say it all in Red's native language.

When the words ended, they remained kneeling in silence. Red would be meditating, but Jordan's mind drifted until her gaze focused on the blue flame on Red's hairless chest. It seemed again to flicker as he breathed. An illusion, she knew, yet it drew her deeper into the ritual. She found she could let go of the pain and shame of the past days. She wanted to look back at Dray, to see how her lover was reacting, but she stayed still. She and Dray had worked through some of their own problems already. It would take time for them to regain their own balance, just as it would still take time for Jordan and Red to rebuild the friendship they'd shared.

The ritual, as it drew to a close, was just the beginning, a way to start healing. And it gave Jordan the courage she needed. She had to tell Dray the truth about herself — and soon.

JORDAN SAT AT the surveillance console, leaving the piloting of their recon shuttle to Red. Their main transport, a Zapara cruiser, sat in orbit high above the planet they were investigating, NL-021.

"We've got the sector eleven longitudinal slice, running pole to pole," Red said. "Are your instruments ready?"

Jordan looked at her console. "Atmospheric data and life-form analysis is already running. Telemetry and video go on once we are in our sector." The planet had been divided up into sections, and Zeta squad teams were scanning the entire planet surface.

"Do you know what you are looking for?" Red asked as he maneuvered their shuttle to the right coordinates.

"Suitability for landfall and planetary investigation by a follow-on team." Jordan had memorized their mission instructions. Her curiosity drove her to delve further into the planet's background.

"We're in our sector now." Red slowed the shuttle as he began their first fly-over.

Jordan turned on her remaining controls, then launched the first of a handful of remote probes that would sink into the planet's surface and return data on what they found. She watched as the data on the planet came in. It wasn't the most challenging of assignments, but this was the site of their final mission, and they were responsible for their own mission preparations. Early recon, they called it. She let the ship's analysis program churn through the data as they flew. "Did you do any investigation on this planet before we left?" she asked.

Red glanced at her and back to his flight console. "No, why?"

"It was one of the first planets the Terrans liberated at the start of the last Novan war."

"So it has strategic importance?"

"Only for what's left on it. It has an automated defense system which the ADF will re-enable for our final training mission."

Red eyes widened. "Just for us."

Jordan glanced at the graphs being displayed by the analysis program. She pointed at one graph. "Plenty of vegetation. Surface temperature is frigid by Terran standards, and according to the ground probes, the landmass we are flying over is mineral-rich." The ground temperature would not be a problem for Novans. Their altered physiology allowed them to colonize borderline planets Terrans would have bypassed.

"It doesn't tell us much about what our final mission will be."

"True." Their squad was flying within the planet's disabled defensive perimeter, but Jordan saw the mesh network of defensive orbital stations blanketing the planet. Flying wouldn't be easy when the time came, when their instructors would turn on those defensive stations for their final mission. Jordan scanned the incoming reports. "This is interesting. Scattered iron content in the atmosphere."

"Does that mean anything to you?" Red asked as he reversed their trajectory and headed back over their sector for another sweep.

"Not a thing, but the analysis program is picking it up as a red-flag issue. Do you know who's going over these results when we get back?" Jordan dropped the next probe toward the planet surface.

"Not us. We're just the initial recon team. After us, another team will do site surveys based on what we find."

Jordan crossed her arms and stared at her readouts in frustration. It would take days for the Zapara ship to get them back to the Entari system. She could analyze the iron herself in that time, but the captain of the ship would probably prevent her from doing it. The captain was a grizzled veteran who seemed very put out to have to allow a group of training cadets on her ship at all. She wouldn't grant time on the ship's computer clusters for Jordan to play with the gathered data. Jordan sighed as she watched the data stream by, pondering what her career would be like in the future, when she wasn't at the bottom of the military food chain and could make some command decisions on her own.

STRIDING ACROSS THE covered causeway, Dray made her way through the central administrative dome for the Entari complex. She resented having to spend her day off away from Jordan, but her brother, Kelvin, was visiting and had requested a meeting with her.

Dray's gaze wandered over the intricate artwork displayed from multiple ADF member cultures who were present in the Entari system. Tarquin artwork was easy to spot, with its dependence on fluid contours and contrasting colors, but it was the Aquaran art which drew her off her path. She stood in front of a moving sculpture of deep greens and rusty reds that seemed to ebb and sway to an unseen current.

Someone stepped up beside her. "It's alive, you know."

Dray turned to the voice. An older female Aquaran officer gazed up at the sculpture. "It's from the Cafier Sea. Our moons create rapid tidal changes, so what we call seas are more like perpetual tidal surfs. All life on our planet is amphibian, including the plants."

The woman turned to Dray. "You are Terran, yes?"

"Yes."

"I'm on my way to your world. I've booked a vacation to explore the remnants of your Great Barrier Reef. Have you been there?"

"No," Dray said. "I've never been to Earth. My family's from New Antioch, in the Greco system."

The woman turned back to the sculpture. "Pity. I wanted to ask what a kelp forest was like. We don't have anything like that, and I won't get to see it this visit."

Dray excused herself and continued to her brother's temporary quarters. She buzzed the door to Kelvin's quarters, bouncing on her toes as she waited. Eager as she was to see her brother, she wanted to get back to Jordan as well. When the door slid open, she stepped inside the Spartan apartment. In typical fashion, her brother had the barest essentials for furniture. The main living area had a large table and high-backed chairs, with no kitchen facilities. Kelvin never cooked.

Her brother hopped up from a chair. His red-blond hair framed a face marred by a frown. "You look tired," he said as he pulled a chair out for her.

"We don't all have desk jobs," she said, taking a seat. "So what brings you to Entari?"

He smiled. "That would be classified."

"Fine. How's Cara?"

"She's doing well. You know she wanted to sign up for duty as soon as the war broke out?"

Dray shook her head. "Dad didn't let her, did he? She's too young."

"And that's the only thing keeping her out. She begged him to sign a consent form, but he wouldn't. Not even for his favorite kid."

Dray sensed the bitterness in Kelvin's voice, but she ignored it. Cara was as close to the perfect child as anyone could hope for. She had perfect grades, perfect manners, and, unlike Dray, she obeyed orders to the letter. Dray was proud of her sister, and glad at least one of them had their father's full support and approval.

"So, what's the real point of this visit?" Dray asked.

"I'm sorry, Dray. My classified projects wouldn't allow me to communicate with you until now." Kelvin folded his hands on the table, but she saw the tightness in his jaw. "I wanted to apologize to you."

Dray frowned. "What for?"

Kelvin leaned forward. "For the Tarquin ship. For what happened to you and your friends."

"What's this have to do with you?" she asked.

Kelvin let out a sigh. "Remember when you saw me on Buenos Aires? I took a Tamil transport on a classified mission. The same ship you and your friends escaped on."

Dray stared at him. "So you were responsible for the stolen Baeron drive technology?"

"Indirectly, yes. I didn't steal it, but when the information was presented to me, I authorized the building of that drive and installation into the Tamil-class. I should never have left that ship on Buenos Aires. I wasn't even aware of the problem until I got word of your rescue beacon."

Dray frowned. "The encrypted one? That was sent to Jordan's mother."

Kelvin leaned back. "All beacons from that ship were modified to come directly to my department."

"And the Tarquin ship?"

Kelvin looked away. "My fault, yes." He looked back at her, his blue eyes glistening in the overhead lights. "They knew about the Tamil-class. As soon as you initiated the drive engine, they were after you. We tried to follow, but we've got nothing else in the fleet as fast. Even the Tarquins took days to reach you."

Dray's fists clenched. "So my interrogation was because of you? Because they knew a Draybeck had stolen the information?"

"I didn't know you were interrogated when they found you. That's probably my fault as well. I head the department that created the ship. The work was classified, but it wouldn't take a genius to figure out where the approval came from. I'm sorry, Dray."

Silence filled the room. Dray's mouth opened, but no words came. Her mind swam with the memory of her shock treatment.

"Damn it." She dropped her head in her hands. Everything that happened was because of her brother. She was ashamed of herself for assuming the Tarquins thought her guilty because of her mother. It was Kelvin who'd tarnished their family name. She slammed her hands on the table, frustrated that, like everyone else, she'd blamed her mother unfairly for what happened.

"I'm sorry, Dray." Kelvin wrapped an arm around her, but she pushed him off.

She couldn't bear to look at his face. His actions would counter everything she'd been working toward to clear her family name. She had to get out. "Is that all?" she asked.

"Yes," he said, watching her with his deep-set blue eyes.

Dray pushed back from the table and stood.

"What we had on that ship was the best and the fastest, period. We can build more ships, of course. Now the Tarquins have evidence of what Terran Military has stolen from them, and well, it puts a strain on Tarquin support for the ADF."

Without another word, she saluted him, turned, and marched out of the quarters. When the door closed behind her, she broke into a run. She ran down the hallway and past a startled group of visitors in the main entrance. The administration complex was a vast mesh of interconnected residences and training facilities. Dray ran as far as her legs would take her.

Hours later, Jordan found Dray in the back corner of the biosphere they'd used for Red's ritual. Dray had been watching the accelerated growth, decay, and regrowth of some exotic plant. Jordan sat down and wrapped her arms around Dray.

After a long while, Dray spoke. "It's my fault, you know."

"What is?"

"Everything that's happened since Buenos Aires." Dray looked at Jordan.

"It's no one's fault," Jordan said. "It just happened."

"No." Dray shrugged off Jordan's arms. "That's not true. My brother was responsible. Right down to the building of the stolen Baeron drive technology."

"Oh." Jordan lifted Dray's hands and held them tight. "I don't know how or why he's involved, but it's not you, Dray. It's not your fault."

It was logical, and Dray knew Jordan was right, but Kelvin's involvement was yet another slight against the Draybeck name.

Chapter Eleven

WHEN ALPHA SQUAD arrived in orbit around NL-021, Bello assigned each squad member a section of the planet to investigate before their final training mission. They were responsible for searching out landing sites based on the data Zeta squad had gathered. Dray's survey would take her over the southernmost landmass which was partly covered by the polar ice cap. She was paired with Dai, whose hair now shimmered a chestnut brown that matched her eyes and nails. Dray wondered if there was any color the Chameleon could not blend into, but kept her thoughts to herself. Dai would fly a tight pattern around their section, recording data. Bello assigned Dray the task of controlling twenty decoy drones to protect their ship from the automated defense system. Controlling that many drones haunted Dray, like the ghost of her mother's last, fatal, misson. With only two weeks left under Bello's authority, she wondered if he gave her the task to rattle her nerves.

"Not the fanciest of ships, is it?" Dai said when they found their assigned vessel.

"It's better than sitting on the cruiser and supervising," Dray said. That was an assignment Bello kept for himself.

The shuttle was a modified HV low-orbit reconnaissance flyer. As Dai flew into the planet's atmosphere toward their target coordinates, Dray pulled on the virtual reality helmet and equipment which would allow her to control all twenty drones at once. She started up the program and was bombarded by information from all the drones. It took her a while just to sync communication between the drones and the ship's database.

"Problems?" Dai asked.

"There's too many of them." Dray struggled through the pre-flight check for each of the drones.

"Should I check with Bello and see if you can send out fewer drones?"

"No, thanks." If she'd had command implants, she wouldn't

need a reduced load. She'd have instant multitasking and CPU offloading abilities. Besides, Bello wouldn't cut her any slack, anyway. With effort, she managed to get all twenty drones to hover in the launch pad. "I'm ready."

"Entering target area," Dai said.

Dray opened the lower hatch and launched the drones in pairs. Her control over them slipped as they hit atmospheric conditions and she lost two drones in a mid-air collision before she regained control over the remaining eighteen. "Fly slow," she said, as much to Dai as to herself. She had no time to comprehend the landscape they flew over. She had a fraction of a second to manage each drone and keep each in formation while Dai directed the shuttle in a slow sweep of their target area.

"Novan defense system has been activated," Dai said.

Sweat trickled down Dray's back. She registered three missiles targeting their shuttle. In theory, she knew, they were not strong enough to cripple their ship, but she wanted no more marks against her on this mission. She redirected a cluster of drones to distract the missiles. "All missiles locked onto the decoys," she said. A moment later, she was controlling only fifteen drones.

"We're reaching the end of our sector," Dai said. "I'm turning in ten." Dai counted down the seconds. Dray's mind was locked into the drones as Dai banked in a wide arc. A VR headache pounded through Dray's brain as she hopped from drone to drone to keep them in line with Dai's flight pattern. With fifteen drones, there was no way she could get to each one fast enough.

"I'm losing them," she shouted. She felt, rather than saw, the destruction of three more drones when they collided during the turn.

"We're in line again," Dai said. "One more sweep and we're done."

Dray held onto the remaining twelve drones. Straight-line flight was easy, especially with eight drones fewer than she'd started with. Two more Novan missiles locked onto them, but the decoy drones blocked both. Dray was down to ten drones.

"That's it," Dai said. "Bring them home."

This was the hardest procedure. Dray isolated the first drone. She had to split her focus between flying the drone onto the landing dock and keeping the other drones in formation. It would be a breeze if she had implants to split the load. Instead, she controlled a very shaky drone toward the flight deck.

"Ease up, " Dai warned. "You're coming in too fast."

Dray accepted her advice and slowed the first drone. It clattered onto the landing deck, where the ship took over. "One down," Dray said. She locked onto the next drone and repeated the exercise. Each landing made the remaining drones easier to control. When she had three drones left, she decided to fly them all in together.

"You're showing off now," Dai said.

Dray landed the three in unison and pulled herself out of the VR environment. "Losing five drones to mid-air collisions isn't showing off."

Dai shrugged and set their flyer on a return course to the mother ship. "They're disposable anyway."

Dray didn't think Bello would have the same attitude about her losses, and she wasn't disappointed. When they docked, Bello was addressing the assembled squad. Dai and Dray took their place in the group.

"We'll be returning to the Entari system today," Bello said. "We've done well, with the exception of the drones Draybeck crashed."

Her team glanced back at her, but Dray was used to his taunts by now. *Two weeks left*, she told herself. Then it was reassignment and active duty as far away from this idiot as possible. The squad dispersed after Bello's speech. Dray assumed he was satisfied with his taunts until he brushed past her and Dai.

"The Draybecks are failures when it comes to simultaneous flight controls, aren't they?" he said. "Or maybe you're just practicing to turn spy for the Novans like your mother. Good thing it was only drones you killed this time."

Dray froze, shocked by his insult to her and her mother. She lurched forward to go after him, but a restraining hand on her arm kept her back. She looked back into Dai's brown eyes.

"He's not worth it," Dai said.

"Did you hear him?"

"Yes. But he's our squad leader. And I'm sure he's not the only jerk we'll ever have to report to in our careers." Dai didn't let go until Dray relaxed. "Don't worry about the drones. The rest of the squad only had seven."

"Seven?" Dray asked. "I had twenty." At least her mission report would reflect her skills at navigating double the number of drones compared to the rest of the squad. Bello couldn't take that away from her.

Dai shook her head. "Bello really does have a grudge against you."

"Why are you being so nice? I thought you were dating him."

"Bello? I don't think so." Dai's eyes changed to a deep purple as they roamed up and down Dray. "I've set my eye on a more interesting catch."

Dray turned away, trying to hide the blush creeping up her face.

DRAY'S HAND STROKED Jordan's inner thigh. Jordan arched toward the attention, desperate for Dray's touch, but mentally fought against the urge. She stifled a moan and pushed Dray's hand back. "You have to stop. I mean it," she said. "You know what they did to Jenny and Malory when they found them half-undressed two weeks ago." Jordan remembered the video broadcast of Jenny and Malory making out.

Dray winced, scanning the room. "You think they have cameras in here?"

"I hope not. I don't want to see clips of us on the vid monitors for our last few days here, either." Jordan had installed electronic scramblers in the room to make sure they couldn't be spied on, but she didn't mention that to Dray.

Dray leaned back. "Okay, you win."

Jordan kissed the top of Dray's head and took a deep breath. "There's something I need to tell you," she said. Her voice held, but her body trembled as she waited for Dray's full attention. Dray sat up and Jordan's gaze locked on hers.

Dray held her hand, stroking the top with her thumb. "You're looking very serious," she said. "Did I do something wrong?"

"No, not at all." Jordan tightened her hold on Dray's hand.

"Okay, the death grip is scaring me. Whatever's bothering you, please tell me."

Jordan focused her thoughts. She'd practiced this conversation in her mind for over four weeks, and she didn't want to put it off any longer. "It's about my father," Jordan said. "Well, about me, too." Her heart was beating fast and her hands were turning cold, even in Dray's warm touch. "I've always had a hard time, letting people get close to me, you know, romantically."

Dray chuckled. "Tell me about it. Flying Bello's twenty drones was easier than navigating the way to your heart." Jordan lowered her head, feeling ashamed of how she'd kept Dray at a distance for so long. Dray lifted her chin and smiled. "Hey, you're worth it, believe me. Nothing's going to change between us, okay?"

Please, Jordan prayed. *Let her be okay with this.* It was time for Jordan to tell the truth. "I had to keep people away, because of who I am. I couldn't know if they really cared about me or were just reacting to my body chemistry."

"I understand," Dray said. "You're gorgeous."

Jordan shook her head. "I don't think so, but it's not that. It's me, who I am."

The frown on Dray's face meant Jordan wasn't explaining things properly. She swallowed her fears, trusting in Dray and what they had together. Dray knew what it was like to bear the stigma of an untrusted parent. She would understand. "My father was Novan."

Dray's hands twitched, but she didn't pull away from Jordan. That was a good sign, Jordan thought.

"I don't get it," Dray said. "Your mother's an ambassador. She's powerful enough to be the next Terran Chief Minister."

Jordan nodded. "And she married a Novan on Gilgar."

Dray tried to mask her discomfort by kissing Jordan's hand, but her ploy was obvious. "So what?" Dray said. "Your mother made a mistake. That doesn't mean anything to me, okay?"

Jordan ignored the subtle insult to her mother and father. She was too relieved Dray was taking it all so well. She wouldn't upset her by being defensive.

"I can't believe you were adopted. You look so much like your mother."

Jordan looked up into Dray's blue eyes, realizing Dray still didn't understand. She swallowed hard. "I'm not adopted."

Dray pulled back. "I don't get it. Terra/Nova couples never have offspring."

Jordan folded her empty hands in her lap. "Sometimes they do."

DRAY'S MIND WENT blank for a moment. Jordan's brown eyes pleaded, but they didn't penetrate Dray's confusion. *Jordan is Novan?* Dray wanted to ask for clarification, but the mask of guilt on Jordan's face told her more than she wanted to know. She was in love with a Novan. Dray pushed herself away and stood up.

"Dray."

Dray ignored Jordan as a feeling of betrayal burned through her. Grinding her teeth to keep from crying, Dray slid open the door and stormed down the hallway. She half wanted to hear Jordan's voice calling her back, but she heard nothing. Jordan said nothing, did nothing to stop her. That silence hurt as much as Dray's self-doubts and guilt.

She pushed past a gaggle of her peers, making her way through the common area. Was any of it real? Did she love Jordan, or was she just another slave to the Novan genetic enhancements that made them so attractive to Terrans?

Dray betrayed her mother's memory by being with a Novan. And Bello considered Dray the potential Novan sympathizer. Did he know about Jordan already? Maybe Dray was the last to know. That couldn't be true. Novans weren't allowed in the Terran Military or the ADF. If anyone knew, Jordan would have been tossed from the program.

Dray's pace slowed as she found an isolated section to walk

down. They were at war with the Novans now. Why hadn't Jordan resigned her position? Dray was sure Ambassador Bowers could have gotten Jordan out of the program. Had she stayed for Dray? Would it matter if Jordan truly loved her? Because Dray couldn't know if her feelings for Jordan were real or just Novan pheromones, could she?

Dray wandered aimlessly for hours. Long enough to cast doubt on everything she'd ever felt for Jordan.

WHEN DINNER TIME came, Jordan searched for Dray in the mess hall. She'd just gotten off a vid-link to her mother, confessing what had happened. Instead of sympathy, her mother gave her a lecture about secrecy and unrealistic expectations — and demanded she come back to Gilgar. Jordan had never felt so alone as when she stared at the entry to the hall. Squads were not required to take meals together, but she knew what Alpha squad leader was like, so she started her search around him. When she saw no sign of Dray there, she walked a methodical pattern down every row in the hall. Dray wasn't there. She found Jenny and Malory together, but refused their invitation to join them. Instead, she grabbed a roll of bread and sat on her own, facing the door and hoping Dray would come in soon for food.

The look of disgust on Dray's face when Jordan confessed her background was burned into Jordan's mind. Tears welled up again, but she brushed them away with her uniform sleeve. Self-pity would not help, but she couldn't stop the downward spiral of her emotions. Dray might never take her back. She would be worse than alone. Jordan slumped in her seat, not really noticing the hall was emptying out. Did Dray hate her enough to reveal her secret? Maybe Jordan should take her mother's advice and leave the military before she was arrested.

DRAY HAD ONLY seen Jordan once in the past week, in a corner of the mess hall. Dray sat with her squad, and Jordan left shortly after. Dray didn't trust her feelings when it came to Jordan. She may have fallen in love with a Novan, but she wouldn't betray her mother's memory by acting on those feelings anymore.

They had a combined training exercise in one of the biospheres, in preparation for their final mission to the deserted Novan planet they'd completed the site survey on. They would be searching for any surviving data cores in the city ruins. Alpha and Zeta squads competed against each other. They were all dressed in thin thermo-suits and helmets to deal with the frigid atmosphere simulated in the biosphere. The gravity was less than 1-G, which meant their heavy equipment was less of a burden, but they'd have to be more careful.

"Draybeck," Bello said as they entered the biosphere after Zeta team.

Dray turned to her squad leader, awaiting his instructions.

"You and Dai are Survey Team One. Try not to screw it up." His yellow eyes reflected the dim light in the biosphere like an animal in the dark.

"Yes, Sir." She'd been matched up with Dai twice over the past few days, and the woman's obvious interest was bordering on predatory. Dai preceded her into the biosphere. Dray's eyes darted around, searching for any sign of Jordan. She was ashamed of her weakness, but still wanted to see Jordan, even if she couldn't bring herself to speak to her.

Dai led the way through a forest of trees and stopped outside the remains of an exploded building. "I'll check inside for the data core." She pulled out a portable hydraulic digger and set it on the floor inside the building.

Dray took her proximity monitor out of her backpack and turned it on. A map of their area showed on the small screen, with a marker for her and for Dai, who was moving inside the building.

A large section of the area was blocked from the proximity detector, appearing as a blank gray blob on her readout. She turned on sub-vocal communications. "Dai."

A moment later, Dai responded. "Miss me already?"

Dray ignored her taunt. "I need to reposition to the other side of the building. Something inside there is blocking my detectors."

"Okay," Dai said. "Keep an open link with me."

Dray stuffed her detector back in her pack and climbed over the jagged pieces of wall lying scattered around the main building. Halfway over the pile, she moved too fast, tumbling over a sharp section of metal. Cursing when her side scraped over the topmost edge, she landed in a crouch on the other side.

"What happened?" Dai asked.

"Nothing, just a bruise." Dray ignored the pain and found a good position on the opposite side of the building. She scanned her surroundings. The burnt remains of conifers formed a wide black half-circle around their site, and beyond that, a still forest surrounded them. Dray turned on her proximity detector and saw the same gray blob as before, but this time blocking out where Dai was.

Dray watched and waited. The time passed in slow increments. Nothing moved on her screen. If there were any Novan attackers in this exercise, they made no approach. It was not until Dai announced she had the data core that Dray saw anything interesting on her screen. Three foreign dots appeared on the edge of her readout, moving toward them.

"We've got company," she said.

"How many?" Dai asked.

"Three. Can't tell who they are yet."

Dray put away her detector and made her way back around the building. Dai waited for her on the other side, holding a small gray cylinder Dray assumed was the data core.

"I bet they're supposed to be Novans. " Dai pulled out her gun and checked her fake ammo cartridge.

Their detectors were blind to the approaching targets from this side of the building, but Dray guessed the fake Novans would not be able to see her and Dai, either. She signaled Dai to stay put, and scrambled to separate cover with a better view. It didn't make sense to have Novans in this exercise since none lived on their final mission planet, but she wouldn't put it past Bello to toss in something extra like this to catch her off-guard.

Movement caught Dray's attention. She crouched down and pulled out her gun. Three people walked around the building. One of them was Jordan. Dray stared, unable to move or react. Jordan's weapon was strapped to her side as she looked at the instrument in her hand. The other two members of Zeta team followed Jordan.

Out of the corner of her eye, Dray saw Dai move. She turned and saw Dai point her gun at Jordan. Dray's reaction was instant and unconscious. Before she realized what she was doing, she stood and fired at Dai. Dai's injury marker registered red, a deadly hit. Dai looked down at her marker and then at Dray, her face a mask of confusion. An instant later, Dray's own injury marker flared to life, also red. She looked from the marker to the Zeta team members. Jordan was the only one who didn't have a weapon in her hand.

Dray walked back to her squad with a stiff stride. Bello shouted a stream of insults at her as she approached. The only sympathetic face Dray saw was Jenny's.

"You shot your own teammate," Bello repeated. Dray stared past his angry face, focusing on keeping her expression neutral. She knew the implications of her actions, and she knew why she'd done it. How many times had she and Jordan gone head to head in the simulators and reveled in the destruction they rained down on each other? This time was different. This time, someone had been about to shoot Jordan as a Novan. The exercise was too close to reality, and Dray's instinct was to protect Jordan, no matter the cost.

Bello dismissed the rest of the squad. "Except you, Draybeck."

Jenny lingered just at the edges of Dray's vision, but Dray did not acknowledge her. Bello would not let Jenny stay and hear whatever punishment he was planning for Dray. When the squad drifted off, Bello stared at Dray in silence. She resisted the urge to flinch. Whatever twisted punishment he had in mind, she would take it without complaint. She deserved it. She had jeopardized Dai's position as well as her own. And once again, she'd let down the squad.

"I want you out," Bello said.

"Excuse me?" Dray wondered if Bello would force her to transfer to a different squad.

"I said I want you out of here. Off my squad, out of this training program." He stepped to within centimeters of Dray's face. His breath smelled of decayed plant life, and Dray flinched away as he continued. "You have a choice. You can quit, or I can force you out."

"Why are you doing this?" she asked. "You've been after me from the day we met."

His damp breath blew across her face. "Turin," he said, barely above a whisper. "Did you know Aquarans used to fight as a family unit before we got real independence? A full wing was made up of parents and siblings, and sometimes children. Your bitch of a mother killed my entire family that day. I grew up in an orphanage, hating the name Draybeck."

Dray felt as if she had just stepped out of an airlock without protection. No other sound penetrated her shock but the sound of Bello's breathing.

"You aren't fit for command. Do the honorable thing, Draybeck. Just resign." Bello narrowed his eyes to slits as he glared at Dray one last time, then walked away, leaving her alone.

Dray couldn't move. His words bore into her soul. So many other people had died at Turin. She'd always viewed it as her mother's death and an accident tainting her mother's military record. Now she was faced with someone else whose life was changed forever by that battle, changed because of her mother's actions. And now, he was destroying Dray's hopes and her future. Where would she go, where could she go, but the military? Her father was a general, her mother had been one of the best close-range fighter pilots in the force. Her older brother was military intelligence. What would she be, if not like them?

Activity behind Dray broke the ice surrounding her thoughts. Pride kept her from staying there, facing a blank wall while others came into the room. Mechanically, she dropped her equipment on a bench and walked out. She passed Dai in the corridor, and the Chameleon brushed a hand along Dray's arm.

"I understand why you did it," Dai said. "Very honorable of you to defend your ex-girlfriend. I admire that."

Dray pulled away from her and continued her blind walk. Ex-girlfriend? Is that what people were thinking of her and Jordan? The words sunk deep into Dray's heart as she moved without thought or direction through the corridors.

It wasn't until she recognized Jenny as the lone figure working out on an archaic rower that Dray realized she had wandered into the gym. Physical activity was her life-blood, but even the call of grueling exercise would not block her fear of the future. With a jolt, she realized it would be a future without Jordan. If she quit, she'd never see Jordan again.

"Wow, I've never seen you so down," Jenny said between huffs. A sheen of sweat covered her arms as she pulled on the rower in a smooth, repetitive motion.

"I've failed," Dray said, taking a seat on a workout bench. To her relief, no one else was in the gym. She could not bear anyone seeing her like this, but she needed someone to talk to. And Jenny had proved to be a good friend.

Jenny continued to row. "Come on. You haven't been that bad. It's probably hard for you not to be the top of the squad anymore, but you are still making the marks, overall."

Dray shook her head. "I was just given the choice to quit or be forced out."

"What?" Jenny stopped rowing. The machine hummed to silence as she wiped sweat off her forehead. "That didn't come from Major Duli."

"No. Bello."

Jenny cursed. "Well, he hasn't got the authority. Your pilot scores aren't as high as they used to be, but your weapons and navigation are top of the squad. You won't fail."

Dray dropped her head into her hands. Jenny was right, but Bello was only part of the problem. She'd destroyed her relationship with Jordan. She couldn't keep ignoring the empty ache inside her. Lifting her head, she saw Jenny staring at her, waiting. "Have you ever met a Novan?" Dray asked.

"A few of them, yes. Earth is still the home world to both species."

"Do you hate them?"

Jenny wiped her face with a towel as she repositioned herself to a workout bench. "Not really. They're different, but no more so than any other species we've met in our training. I know there's a lot of bad politics between us and them, but that's more about the government than the Novan people themselves. So, I have no reason to hate them."

Dray stared at the floor. "I've always hated them. They killed my mother." The hatred didn't seem as strong as it had been.

Jordan was Novan. *Part Novan*, Dray corrected herself. She thought about Bello's hostility toward her, because of her mother and Turin. How different was that from her own excuse for detesting all things Novan? For all her bravado, she couldn't control the tears coming down her cheeks. How could she have let her blind prejudice ruin what she had with Jordan? And now, Jordan must hate her for being so stupid.

A hand rested on her shoulder and she looked up to see Jenny's worried expression. "It's not just Bello, is it?" Jenny asked.

"I've messed everything up. Jordan hates me."

Jenny smiled. "Now, that I don't believe, not for an instant."

"You don't understand. I got really mad. I mean, *really* mad. I avoided her like she was a disease."

"It's been pretty obvious the two of you are having problems. What happened?"

Dray thought back to Jordan's revelation, but she couldn't tell Jenny that Jordan was Novan. Or part Novan. "I can't really talk about it, but I overreacted to something and ruined the best thing in my life. I'm sure Jordan hates me by now."

Jenny laughed. The sound stung Dray's ears, but Jenny patted her shoulder. "She still loves you. Red's been all but shaking Jordan to get her to talk about what's wrong, but Jordan is as tight-lipped as you are about whatever happened between you two. She just goes around like a walking zombie. I know she's been talking to her mother almost every day. Do you think she's planning on resigning her post and going back to Gilgar?"

Panic shot through Dray. If Jordan resigned, Dray would never get a chance to see her again. Would Jordan even talk to her after the way she'd been acting? And how could Dray know if her feelings for Jordan were real or just a reaction to Novan pheromones?

"There's no way you are quitting. If Bello wants to try and force you out, he's going to have one major battle ahead of him." Jenny struck a pose of determination that made Dray smile, despite her desolate mood. "Good. That's more like it. Now, I'm off to the showers and food, how about you?"

Dray looked at the exercise equipment surrounding her. "I think I need to think a few things out. I'm going to stay here awhile." She had to decide how to approach Jordan. What could she say to make up for days of avoidance and acting like a narrow-minded bigot?

"Okay, but not too long," Jenny said. "You need to talk to Jordan, for sure."

ZETA SQUAD'S CELEBRATION party for beating Alpha squad was too much for Jordan, and she left. When she'd stood in shocked silence as Dray pulled a weapon on her own teammate, she hadn't realized Sahar was already aiming at Dray's exposed body. If Jordan had seen Sahar about to fire, would she have acted as protectively as Dray had?

Someone tapped Jordan on the shoulder. She turned to see Malory beside her, wearing a creased flight suit. "Just off active duty?" Jordan asked.

"An hour ago, actually. I've been with Jenny." Malory led Jordan off to a side corridor and relayed what Jenny had told her. Jordan leaned against the wall, trying to understand it all.

"Dray's a wreck," Malory said.

Jordan's mind glossed over Malory's final words, stuck instead on the thought Dray might leave or be forced out. She couldn't let that happen. Jordan left Malory in the hallway and rushed out of the dormitory and down the two adjacent corridors to an elevator. She punched in the lowest level where the gym facilities were. The elevator crawled from one level to the next. An eternity later, it came to a slow stop. Jordan was out before the doors fully opened and ran into the open doors of the gym.

Dray sat beside a rowing machine, staring into space. Jordan stood still in the doorway, feeling the gym's cooler air surrounding her. Dray turned in her direction, and Jordan's gaze locked on Dray's pale face. Uncertainty plagued Jordan. Did Dray even want to see her? The thought of losing Dray overcame Jordan's fear of rejection. She walked to Dray, gazing into eyes she hadn't seen in days.

"Please tell me you aren't leaving," Jordan said.

"Do you want me to stay?" Dray asked. Her voice came out raspy, as if she had been crying. Was she the cause of Dray's tears, or was it Bello's threat to force her out?

"I couldn't bear it if you left." Jordan reached out a tentative hand and was surprised when Dray met her halfway. She held Dray's hand tighter than she should have, but couldn't loosen her grasp.

"Tell me you're not resigning, either," Dray said.

"No. I couldn't leave you." Jordan lowered her gaze. "I'm so sorry for all that's happened."

Dray shook her head. "I was being pig-headed."

Jordan brushed a trembling hand along Dray's cheek. "I'm sorry I lied to you."

"You had to," Dray said. "I understand now."

Jordan stared into deep blue eyes. "Where does it leave us now?"

"I don't know."

Jordan loosened her hold on Dray, but Dray didn't let go of her hand. Silence surrounded them in the empty gym for a time.

"You're not an F-K baby, are you?" Dray asked.

"No. I'm natural-born. It's rare, but it can happen."

Dray nodded. "That's why your chip-ID works. It would reject any genetic trace of the Fletcher-Koopman procedure."

"And my DNA is Terran enough to pass, at least for a simple implant like the chip-IDs," Jordan added.

Dray let go of Jordan's hand and sighed. "I'm sorry. I just don't know what's real anymore."

Jordan's jaw tightened. "I'm real. What I feel for you is real."

"This is all so new to me." Dray looked down. "I just need time."

Jordan took a deep breath and let it out slowly. "I understand." It wasn't a perfect reunion, but it was progress. And it was all she had to hold on to for now.

Chapter Twelve

JORDAN WAS RELUCTANT to let Dray out of her sight, but there was only one week of training left. Dray was determined to maintain her first place standing for navigation and was busy training for her last exam. Rather than be alone with her thoughts, Jordan tracked down Jenny for a walk through the tunnels.

"How did your last few days go?" Jordan asked as they turned into a side tunnel that branched off into some of the unused biospheres.

"Nothing like yours, I bet," Jenny said. "I'm happy for you two."

Jordan didn't reveal just how tenuous her situation with Dray was. She waited until they passed the last busy intersection of tunnels before continuing. "So how about you and Malory?"

Jenny stuffed her hands into her uniform pockets. "Not much to tell."

"She came here on her off-time. Did you get a chance, you know, for some alone time?"

"Yes and no. We had the time, but mostly we talked."

"Just talked?"

Jenny laughed. "It's not that bad. Talking was good. We realized something important."

"Which is?" Jordan asked as they neared the end of the tunnel. They turned around and walked back.

"Loving someone isn't the same as being in love with them."

"Oh." Jordan put her arm around her friend as they walked. "I'm sorry."

"Yeah, me, too. I can't force Malory to be in love with me. I'm not sure she ever was, really."

"Why do you say that?" Jordan's mind whirled with guilt. Was she trying to force Dray to be in love with her? It was one of the myths Terrans believed of Novans, but was there a glimmer of truth to it?

Jenny stopped walking as she spoke. "We were alike when we

joined the officer training program. Two outcasts who managed to sneak our way in with all you high-profile folks."

"That's not true. You both deserve to be here, just as much as the rest of us."

"We know that now, but at the time, it was Malory and me against the world. It brought us together, though in a sense, it also isolated us from everyone else. I fell in love with her, and I think she went along with it. She was always my protector, you know?"

Like Dray had been Jordan's protector. "I guess. You seem to be taking it okay."

Jenny continued walking. "I think I've just realized I'd rather keep Malory as a close friend than lose her because I'm clinging to false hope. She loves me and I love her. I'll get over the physical attraction some day."

Jordan gave Jenny a quick hug before they left the tunnel system and entered into the main common room. "Sometimes, I think you're the smartest of all of us." And, Jordan realized, far stronger than she was at the moment. If Dray drifted away, would she be as accepting as Jenny was?

DRAY WAITED WITH anticipation for their final assignments. It was a real mission and it determined what military officer posts they'd be eligible for. Those who didn't pass would transfer to standard military with the grunts. She knew Bello would force her to become a grunt if he could, but Dray wasn't going to let him get the chance. If she passed this final mission, he couldn't touch her. If she failed, his report could lead to her dismissal from officer training.

"What's going on?" Jordan asked.

"Not sure. The assignment board split all the squads up into pairs. Alpha and Zeta are together, that's all I know," Dray said. "Bello doesn't talk to me anymore." She left out that she hadn't forgotten Bello's threat, and likely neither had he.

"Sorry."

Dray shrugged. "It's better this way. At least I'm not getting the drudge assignments. He's leaving it up to Dai to fill me in."

Jordan entwined her fingers with Dray's. Dray smiled, clinging to the warmth of Jordan's hand. She'd missed this contact, though she hadn't yet managed to silence the little voice in her head that wondered still if her reactions to Jordan were love, or a biochemical response to Novan physiology. Red joined them, and the room grew still. Dray looked up to the stage where Major Duli walked to the podium. Duli started talking, and Dray turned her attention to their C.O.

"This will be your last mission with your current squads. This isn't a drill or an exercise. This is a real mission. Your squads have been paired up for combined teams. Alpha squad did recon on NL-021, and Zeta provided the initial site survey. Your squad leaders have separated you into task groups. From here on, you are under the command of Cadet Corporal Bello." Dray's enthusiasm for the mission dimmed with that news. She'd been hoping Sahar would command the combined squads. Duli continued with a brief lecture on how far they'd all come since their first week and wished them luck. He would not be joining them on the mission.

Jordan gave Dray a feather-light kiss on the cheek as they waited for Sahar to take his place on the podium and go over their mission details. Dray tried not to let the rush of arousal show at Jordan's touch. At least they were together on this mission. Red joined them as she listened to Sahar's speech next.

"We will rendezvous with another ship for a search and retrieval operation on NL-021 in the Ko'akiat system. The mission details have been downloaded to your personal databases. The commander of the other ship will act in an advisory role only."

Sahar's face physically altered as he spoke.

"Why does his face keep shifting?" Dray asked.

"He is part Chameleon. When he is over-tired, his face shows the strain." Red smiled. "He is a fascinating person, but troubled by his limitations. Did you know, Chameleons can change everything about themselves, including their sex? It is truly a fascinating culture, from what Sahar has told me of it."

Dray wondered what it was like to live in a culture where sexual characteristics were so fluid. After his speech, Sahar marched the two squads down the tunnel and into the Cygna-major transport they would be taking to join the *Exelon*, a recon vessel that would explore the Ko'akiat system with them.

As they cleared the entrance, Alpha squad split off and lined up on the far wall with Bello in front. Dray caught Jordan's eye for an instant, but had to wait until Bello finished before they could speak. Sahar presented Zeta team to him, and Bello marched over.

"Most of you know me," he said. "For those who don't, I am Cadet Corporal Bello, and I will be your C.O. for this mission. You've been briefed and have your mission summary by now, so I won't keep you here." He paced in front of the team as he spoke. "We are one team now. Sahar is my second in command, but I expect us to work as one. You know the importance of this mission." He backed up a pace to address both teams. "You will bunk four to a room. Sahar will coordinate room assignments. Dismissed."

Jordan joined Dray in the queue for bunk assignments. When

their turn came, Sahar gave them a tired smile and assigned them bunks in the same room.

"Bunkmates again," Jordan said.

"Looks like it," Dray said with a smile. Red and Sahar were their other roommates.

Bello did not let them sit idle for the two days it took to reach the *Exelon*. The Cygna-major was armed with long-range missiles, forward and aft gun turrets, and a series of armed scout ships like the one Dray had flown in her exercise with the defensive drones. Bello hadn't handed out final mission assignments, so the combined unit took turns operating and running drills on every aspect of the Cygna and its scout ships.

It was a busy two days, but Dray was glad for the distraction the daytime exercises gave her. With the added presence of Red and Sahar in their room at night, Dray and Jordan had no privacy. Dray was frustrated on more than one level. How could she explore her feelings for Jordan if they never had time together?

By the time they joined the *Exelon*, both squads were working as a coordinated unit. Dray spotted the *Exelon* out of the starboard view port as she watched Red pilot a shuttle to the larger ship. He would return soon with the recon commander they would be working with. She studied the larger ship as they waited. The *Exelon* was longer than their ship, with multiple short-range probes offsetting its streamlined shape. Dray wondered how many of those probes the recon team would use.

When Red returned from the *Exelon*, he emerged from the docking hatch, followed by a squat, balding man with pale skin who wore a gray commander's uniform.

Bello ordered the squad to attention. "I am honored to introduce the head of the recon expedition, Commander Resil." He saluted as Resil stepped to the front.

"Thank you, Cadet Corporal." Resil addressed the assembled unit. "I will be working with your C.O. to coordinate smaller teams to visit the *Exelon*. You will be using our equipment for recon and retrieval on this mission." His expression betrayed extreme boredom. "Your teams will be split, with some of you landing at the survey sites you investigated earlier, and some of you flying high-orbit defensive maneuvers with the Cygna's ships to take out any defensive missiles targeting the site teams."

JORDAN AND DRAY stepped off the Cygna-major's shuttle, along with four other unit members, for their scheduled visit to the *Exelon*. A staff sergeant waited for them all to emerge and led them out of the docking area. Jordan studied the interior of the *Exelon* as they walked down the corridor and through a lab cluttered with equipment in various stages of repair. As they left the lab, Jordan recognized Dai's annoying voice behind them. She turned to see Dai chatting up the other three cadets in the rear. Dai looked at her and winked. Jordan frowned in return. As Dai spoke, her hair changed to a deep brown, bordering on black. It still shocked Jordan to see how quickly Dai could modify her appearance. She didn't trust her fellow cadet, especially when she gave Dray a seductive smile.

Dai approached and shook Jordan's hand. "I don't believe we've been introduced. I'm Dai," she said. "I've had the pleasure of being with Dray multiple times."

Jordan ignored her innuendo. "We should continue with the tour," she said, trying to extricate herself from Dai's strong grasp.

Dai let go. "You're looking forward to this mission?"

"There's still data cores left on this planet. We might learn more about the Novan genetics program," Jordan said.

"Brains and beauty." Dai turned to Dray. "How exciting."

Jordan kept rigid control over her frustration as they were led through the ship's two main launch pads to view the landers the retrieval teams would use. When Dai's arms brushed against Dray's for the third time, Jordan stepped between them and started up a conversation with the Chameleon about how Bello would divide up the unit for the mission. Dai accepted the change with a sardonic smile.

An hour later, Jordan relaxed when she stepped back onto the shuttle, leaving Dai and Bello on the *Exelon* to coordinate with the *Exelon*'s commander. "That was exhausting."

Dray strapped into the seat between Jordan and Sahar. "Your mother would be proud, Jordan. Who knew diplomatic skills were an inherited trait," she teased.

"Would you rather I'd left Dai free to taunt you some more?"

"No, thanks. She's a little too touchy-feely. I didn't think she'd ever let go of your hand in the end."

"That's one of the reasons I can't stand Dai," Sahar said. "She's imprinting everyone on the ship."

"What's that do?" Dray asked.

"It's how Chameleons learn new ways to adapt their appearance and such. If I was any good at it, I could hold your hand and shift my eyes to match yours, for instance."

"Nice," Jordan said. At least Dray wasn't the one being copied. Dai's hair had shifted from its original blue to black and her skin was taking on more of a tanned look. That didn't come from Dray's short blond hair and freckles, anyway.

JORDAN COULD HAVE screamed. She nearly did when she read the final assignment sheet Bello had prepared, obviously under Dai's influence. All of Zeta squad would remain on the Cygna-major with half of Alpha squad. Bello was taking Dray with him and his cronies to the *Exelon*. "Limiting the landing teams," she said. "What kind of excuse is that?"

"It's not that bad," Dray said. "I didn't expect him to let me fly drone patrol anyway."

"That's not what this is, you know. She's making him take you away from me."

Dray lifted Jordan's hand to her lips, kissing her palm. "It's just two days, then I'll be back."

Jordan's frustrations did not abate while she sat and watched Dray pack. Dai was manipulating Dray, forcing herself between them. And the worst part was that Dray didn't seem to care. Jordan felt her fragile relationship with Dray slipping away, and she had no idea how to prevent it.

"We'll talk on the vid-link every night," Dray said, hoisting her pack over one shoulder.

Jordan threw her arms around Dray and held her close. "Give me one good reason why I should let you go," she whispered.

Dray kissed her cheek, then pressed her lips to Jordan's. Heat flooded Jordan's body as she clung to Dray, sinking into the first real kiss they'd shared in weeks.

"Because I'll be thinking of you the whole time," Dray said, her pale face flushing.

Jordan let Dray go and walked with her to the shuttle Dray would take to the *Exelon*. At least Dai wasn't present to ruin their goodbye. Jordan watched the shuttle leave the Cygna-major, but did not linger to see it dock on the *Exelon*. She had to hope Dray was learning to trust their relationship. And that she wouldn't let Dai come between them.

DRAY FELT A hand on her shoulder and her pulse quickened, thinking of Jordan. She smiled and turned around, but her smile faded when she saw it was Dai. Of course. Jordan was on the Cygna-major.

Dai's long hair was brown-black now, as were her eyes. "We're in geosynchronous orbit around Ko'akiat Seven. You're with me," Dai said quietly. Her hand trailed down Dray's arm. Dray backed away, annoyed she was reacting to Dai's touch. Dai wandered back to her temporary quarters, smiling in a way Dray found disturbing. Dray had enough to worry about with Bello controlling her last mission. She didn't need Dai's unwelcome attention throwing her even further off-balance.

Dray waited until after the lunch before searching out Dai to coordinate their mission. When she didn't find her with Bello, she was forced to seek out Dai's private quarters. Dray stood outside the door, clamping down on her frustration. She wouldn't let Dai get under her skin.

The door slid open before Dray had asked for entry. Dai's appraising gaze wandered up and down as Dray stood in the hallway, forcing herself not to react. Dai's uniform jacket was unbuttoned, as was the top of her blouse, revealing well-defined cleavage.

"Come in," Dai said.

Dray clenched her jaw and stepped into Dai's quarters.

Dai tucked her hand under Dray's elbow. "Not much to show here, but please, come sit." She led Dray to a deep, wide floor cushion. Dray studied it for a moment, unsure how to sit in or on it. She gave up and lowered herself, feeling the cushion surround her. Dai relaxed beside her and the cushion reformed as a cocoon around the two of them. Dray found her leg pressed against Dai's thigh. She tried to pull away but her movements only tightened the cushion's grip on them both.

"It's a Dregar love cushion," Dai said, resting a hand on Dray's knee. "It's best if you just stay still or we'll end up in a most uncompromising position."

Dray felt the heat from Dai's hand. If she closed her eyes, she could almost feel as if Jordan were next to her. This was bad. Why was she reacting to Dai now, when she hadn't ever before? "Where did you get this furniture?" Dray asked.

"A gift from Bello. He's so easily manipulated."

"Excuse me?"

Dai stretched. The cushion moved and reformed around them. "He still thinks he can win me over, but I have other plans."

Dray kept her mouth shut, waiting for Dai to get tired of her little game and get on with the mission. She wasn't disappointed.

"You do carry the strong, silent act well," Dai said. "Anyway, you and I are responsible for site two. We head down in one of the *Exelon*'s survey shuttles tomorrow morning."

"What information do you have on our assigned site?"

Dai pulled herself out of the cushion and walked to her desk. She took out a vid-display and handed it to Dray. It showed a moving image of multiple collapsed structures, surrounded by tall weeds, what Dray assumed was the natural plant life reclaiming the abandoned site.

"Anything we find could be as important as records of Novan genetic programs or as dull as a stack of old recipes. The planet was home to both private and government genetic facilities before they were bombed in the last war."

Dray shifted out of the cushion and stood up. "If there's nothing else, I'd like to familiarize myself with the shuttle I'll be piloting."

Dai took the vid-display from Dray, letting her fingertips brush against the back of Dray's hand. She stepped closer, her chest pressing against Dray's arm. Dray took a step back, struggling to regain control of her feelings. She stared into Dai's brown eyes, trying to force her body into behaving. Dai leaned closer, her breath tickling the side of Dray's neck. Too close, Dray thought, back stepping once more. Her boot caught on the edge of the cushion, and her arms flew out.

Dai's arm was around her in an instant, steadying her. The press of Dai's body sent an unwelcome heat through Dray, and she extricated herself. "Sorry. I have to go," Dray said and rushed out of the room, ignoring Dai's half-closed eyes and languid smile.

JORDAN KEYED IN a private video link to Dray for the third time that night. She was caught off-guard when the link went through. "Where have you been?" she asked.

"Checking out the shuttle I'll be taking to the planet tomorrow. Sorry."

"You look tired. Has Bello been bothering you?"

"Him? No."

"It's Dai, isn't it?"

Dray's blue eyes widened. "No, it's nothing. What about you? What's your task for tomorrow?"

"Defensive flights in short shifts. We make sure no missiles come within range while you all are on the planet. It's an interesting combination of real work and simulated battle conditions. The old Novan missile defense was designed so that missiles self-destruct in the lower atmosphere. Terran records estimate there are over a thousand data cores buried in the rubble on this planet. Who knows what we could learn about pre-war Novan operations?"

Dray's hand touched the monitor screen. "I wish I was there."

"What's wrong?" Jordan shifted to the edge of her chair, studying Dray's image.

"Nothing, I'm okay." Dray looked down at something out of view. "I should be going, though."

Jordan signed off after they agreed to chat again at the same time the next night. She leaned across the table, wondering what was bothering Dray. It wasn't Bello. Even at his worst, he never had that effect on Dray. Jordan knew the real cause for Dray's odd behavior. Dai was getting to her.

BELLO WAS PACKING his shuttle when Dray walked into the launch area, followed by Dai. They both wore the thin thermal suits for protection against the cold atmosphere on the planet. With something to focus on, Dray was less threatened by her mission partner, managing to engage in small-talk while she stowed her gear and double-checked the shuttle's provisions. The shuttle came with the standard emergency stock, so Dray was surprised when Bello walked over and gave her extra food rations and a portable survival dome.

"Commander Resil's insisting we all take these," he said, dumping the package at Dray's feet. Dray glanced at Dai, but the woman shrugged and went back to storing the survey gear in the back of the small shuttle.

Bello's lips curled into a cold smile. "Good luck, Draybeck."

Dray watched him return to his shuttle. *What's he planning?* They were scheduled for only a four-hour shift on the planet. Even the unnerving prospect of spending that much time in close quarters with Dai was worth it, just to be away from Bello for a while. She finished packing and strapped herself into the pilot seat. She turned on the shuttle command panel and started her pre-flight check. Dai locked the shuttle door and took the copilot seat next to her.

Something in the pre-flight caught Dray's eye. She pulled on a headset and linked to Bello. "You logged into my shuttle this morning," she said.

"I logged into all the shuttles," Bello replied. "Most of your pre-flight's already done. Same for the rest of us."

"That wasn't necessary."

Bello's voice reflected his usual disdain. "I control every aspect of this mission, Cadet. Remember that." He terminated the conversation.

Dray swore at him over the dead link. What else was he controlling, and how would he use it against her?

The *Exelon* controlled each shuttle launch. Dray had little to do until her ship launched after Bello's, following his shuttle into high orbit. Shuttle control was returned to her, and she veered off toward their landing site. When the surface came into view in front of them, Dai pressed forward against her safety straps.

"We can take a short loop around the landing area if you want," Dray offered.

Dai looked at her with unmasked excitement. Dray took that as a yes and started a slow arc. No sign of missiles showed up on her scanners, so the defensive teams were doing their job. The heavy cloud cover blocked out more light than Dray had anticipated. She flew the shuttle lower, turning on search beams. The remains of an abandoned city came to life beneath them. Unlike her last trip, Dray got to see the landscape. Nothing substantial remained of what must have been a sizable city. The Terrans were thorough when it came to destroying genetic labs. The natural plant life had taken over most of the hilly terrain, with outcroppings of stone dotting the landscape.

"Any idea what this was?" Dray asked.

"According to planetary records, this used to be a prisoner-of-war camp, and there was a genetic research center in the city."

Dray circled closer to their landing coordinates. There was a wide, flat area next to one of a set of remains. She brought the shuttle down to a smooth stop and turned the engines off. Dai worked her way out of her safety harness and strapped an air filter to her back.

Dray kept her helmet on. It had a built-in air filter and communicator. "I'll do an initial sweep of the site and leave markers for you where there is evidence of underground facilities."

Dray left Dai in the shuttle where she was preparing the portable hydraulic digger. Dray scanned their immediate area. They were near a flat expanse of stone less than 50 meters wide, surrounded by tall, fern-like plants leading up to a small hill. The remnants of two buildings dominated the site's far side. The structures must have been massive if the remains were any indication. She wondered what kind of prisoners were kept here, and how long ago it had been abandoned. Dray turned on her site meter and stepped onto the stone slab. She walked a methodical pattern across the site. Dai joined her slow progress, but Dray hadn't found anything worth digging yet.

Her meter registered a hit inside what was left of the first building. "Looks like a basement is still intact under here." She looked around, but the building's rubble had covered over any easy access to the basement. Dray waited while Dai set up a digger to bore though the stone floor. Dray wandered around what was left of the walls, listening to the noise of the digger chipping through the stone. The surface of the walls was smooth except for a regular series of holes. She poked a gloved finger into the top of one hole. A layer of metallic dust came off on her glove. She pulled out a light and examined it closer. The holes bored through the stone were lined with the metal dust, probably from support rods. She brushed off her gloves on a nearby big-leaf plant. The sound of crashing stone brought Dray's focus back to their mission.

"We're through," Dai said. She lowered a floodlight into the circular hole and the two of them peered over the edge.

Dray was uncomfortably aware of Dai leaning next to her. She took a step back. "I'll get the ladder." She took off her pack and pulled out a cable ladder, set the power grapple hooks, and fired them into the stone. "The ladder's anchored."

Dai pushed the ladder into the hole and climbed down. Dray followed her. They were in a large room, covered in debris. "Not much down here," Dai said, shining the floodlight in a wide arc as she walked around the perimeter of the room.

Dray examined the two cabinets lining the nearest wall. One was collapsed on its side, with the doors ajar. "Nothing in here," she said.

Dai struggled with the handles of the second cabinet, but couldn't get it open.

"Let me," Dray said. She pulled a laser drill out of her pack and cut through the door handle in minutes.

Dai leaned over her shoulder, her black hair cascading over Dray. For an instant, Dray was tempted to touch the hair with her gloved hand. It reminded her of Jordan. She was glad for the protection of her helmet as it prevented Dai from seeing the heat rushing to her cheeks. She stepped back. "It's all yours," she said, struggling for self-control.

She watched Dai examining the contents of the cabinet. She didn't want Dai. Watching her from a distance, she felt nothing. And even when she was close to Dai, she thought of Jordan. So why did she feel so off-balance when she was close to Dai? As Dai pulled out and discarded the contents of the cabinet, Dray recognized that her physical attraction to Dai lacked the emotional bond she shared with Jordan. It made Dray realize how much she missed her girlfriend. Jordan was sharp, intuitive, and sensitive in ways Dai could never be.

"We've got it!" Dai said, standing up. "If we're lucky, these data cores will have something other than grandma's quilting designs."

"Good. Let's pack up." Dray wanted to get off this planet and away from Dai. She didn't care what the data cores held, so long as it was a good mark for her team and got them back to the Cygna-major sooner.

Dai packed up the digger and followed Dray back to the shuttle. Dray strapped into the pilot seat while Dai stowed her equipment. Turning on the command console, Dray started her pre-flight check. A red, flashing indicator glared at her when she tested the launch engines. She stared at the readout, then restarted the flight check. When it came to testing the launch engines, the red indicator lit up again. She cursed under her breath, considering her options.

Hands rested on her shoulders. Dai's long hair brushed against her, and she blushed.

"Is there a problem?" Dai asked, leaning over Dray.

Dray unstrapped from her chair and stood up to get away from Dai. "The launch engines are showing critical failures." Instead of looking surprised, Dai only smiled at her. "I'm going out to take a look," Dray said.

She stepped out of the shuttle and searched the rear underside until she found the launch engine access panel. She snapped off the latch, opened the panel, and looked around in frustration. She didn't know what she expected to see. A dangling cord? A burnt-out component? It wouldn't have mattered. She wasn't trained in ship repair anyway. The need to get away from Dai kept her outside the shuttle for a while as she weighed their options. She couldn't repair the shuttle on her own, and she couldn't get it in the air without the launch engines. They were stranded. Someone would have to send a rescue ship for them and a mechanic from the *Exelon* for the shuttle. She'd fail her final mission.

Bello. Dray studied the inside of the maintenance panel again. He had controlled her pre-flight check before they left the *Exelon*. If their launch engines were inoperable, why hadn't he detected it? She slammed the panel shut and stormed back into the shuttle.

Dray pulled off her helmet. "So, did you set me up, or did Bello?"

Dai stepped close to Dray. "Maybe I should be asking you that." She traced one finger along Dray's jaw. "If you wanted to be alone with me, you only had to ask."

Dray shut her eyes. It was all going wrong. The mission. Her reactions to Dai. She stuffed her head back into her helmet and left the shuttle. She stomped across the landing site, passed the crumbling buildings, and made her way up to the top of the small hill. She could look down on her useless shuttle from that vantage, but that was the last thing she wanted to see. She turned her back to it and leaned against a fern tree.

What would she do if she were ejected from officer training? Could she accept a position in standard military, or would she resign in disgrace. She glanced back toward her crippled ship where Dai waited. Why did she react to Dai? She loved Jordan. Even when Dai aroused her, she thought of Jordan. It didn't make sense, and yet she couldn't stop it.

She looked down at her gloved hand, realizing she still held the metal latch to the maintenance panel. She threw it on the ground. She'd failed her mission, and the longer she delayed, the longer it would be before a ship came to retrieve them. She switched on her helmet com-link, about to call the *Exelon*. Instead, she switched to a different channel and tried to reach the Cygna-major. The defensive teams were on thirty minute rotations. Jordan's rotation should be over by now.

"Dray?" Jordan's voice washed over her, calming Dray's fragile mind.

"I've got problems down here," Dray said, poking at the dirt with her boot. "The shuttle won't fly."

"Did it get damaged on landing?"

"No. It was an easy flight." A cloud of dust hovered over the ground and Dray stopped playing with the dirt. "I want to say Bello did something, but I have no proof."

"What do you mean?"

"He overrode my pre-flight check before we left. And the *Exelon* launched us, so I had no idea the shuttle's launch engines were bad until just now."

"Who are you there with?" Jordan's voice had an edge to it Dray had never heard before.

"Dai."

Silence. Dray waited, but when Jordan didn't speak again, she said, "I have to call the *Exelon* and tell Bello."

"Okay." Jordan terminated the call. Dray slid down and sat on the ground, not caring what the dirt did to her suit. Everything was falling apart. Dray was finally realizing what made her feelings for Jordan real and not just chemical, and now she'd be a grunt, Jordan would be an officer, and their chances of finding an assignment together would be practically zero.

"THAT BITCH." JORDAN turned her chair around to face Red, who sat next to her at the Cygna-major's communications deck.

"An Earth-based female dog?" he asked. "I do not follow you."

"It's an old-world curse Jenny taught me. And it fits Dai perfectly."

Sahar walked in on their discussion. "What's going on?"

"Either Dai or Bello sabotaged Dray's shuttle," Jordan said. "She's stranded at site two."

Sahar glanced between Red and Jordan. "That's a serious accusation. I don't recommend you repeat it unless you have proof."

Jordan turned back to her console. "I'll find the proof."

"Should we send someone to get them?" Red asked.

"Dray's under Bello's command. He'll send a shuttle and tech to retrieve them," Sahar said.

Jordan linked the Cygna-major to Dray's shuttle logs. She retrieved the data for the past two days and disconnected the link. If anyone deliberately tampered with Dray's ship, the information would be there somewhere.

DRAY COULDN'T POSTPONE contacting Bello any longer. She stared down at her stranded shuttle and switched her com-link to the *Exelon*.

"Draybeck. What do you want?" Bello asked.

Dray closed her eyes and took a deep breath. "The launch engines malfunctioned, Sir. I can't get the shuttle off the ground." Her face burned when she heard laughter in the background. Bello didn't reply right away. She was about to repeat her status when he answered.

"The rest of the shuttles are on their way back. You'll have to wait until we can refuel one of them."

He didn't berate her for screwing up the mission, which convinced her even more he was responsible for her state, either on his own or with Dai's consent. Either way, Bello had enough to ruin her career if she failed this mission. She needed to go back to the shuttle. Maybe she could figure out something to get them off the planet. Dray scanned the ground, looking for the latch she'd tossed away in anger. When she couldn't find it right away, she squatted down to look closer, brushing her gloved hand over the exposed dirt. She didn't find the latch. All she found was a small clump of metal dust. She stood back up, giving up the search. Looking back at the shuttle, her view was partially blocked by a low-lying cloud mass surrounding the landing site. She headed back to the shuttle to find her way off the planet, or more likely, to wait for Bello's rescue ship.

"TAKE A LOOK at this," Jordan said. She leaned back from the console where she'd been studying Dray's shuttle logs.

Red walked up to her and leaned over to read the console output. "Did you find proof Bello sabotaged the ship?"

"Not yet, but what do you make of these status warnings? They were in the transmissions I got from Dray's shuttle fifteen minutes ago."

Red traced the screen with his finger. "Are these all the logs?"

"No, just level three and above." Jordan's fingers flew over the controls. "There. Now we're showing all the logs, right down to minor diagnostics." She scrolled through the messages along with Red. He made her stop at a series of diagnostic readings.

"Bring up the planetary survey we started yesterday," he said, taking the chair next to her. Jordan searched the ship database until she found the report Red requested. She put it onscreen, next to the shuttle logs. She reconnected to the shuttle and pulled up the raw data currently being collected as well. Red flipped through the three sets of information. Jordan tried to correlate the data, but she didn't know what Red was looking for.

He shifted to the edge of his chair and turned to her. "Contact the shuttle," he ordered.

Jordan switched on the command com and searched for the shuttle's com-link. "It's not here."

"What do you mean?"

"I mean I can't find the shuttle's frequency. Their communications are down." She looked back at the data screen. "The raw data's stopped." She brought up the survey program and verified it was still running. "We've lost contact with the shuttle." A rising panic overwhelmed her for a moment, and she didn't hear what Red said.

"Jordan. I need you in control." His hands were holding her shoulder. "I asked if you had spoken to Dray via the shuttle or her helmet com?"

"Her helmet, I think."

DRAY STARTED DOWN the slope toward the landing site. The fern trees blocked her view of the shuttle, but she followed her own boot tracks back down the trail. She didn't look forward to being alone with Dai. Just thinking about her made Dray feel guilty.

She slipped on dead leaves and had to grab hold of a tree to keep from falling. She straightened up and continued down the slope until the ground leveled. The trees gave way to low brush, and Dray got her first close view of the shuttle. She paused, trying to see through the gray cloud that blocked her view. She heard a low-pitched buzzing noise, but couldn't determine its source.

Her helmet com-link rang for attention. Bello, she thought. She contemplated not answering. She couldn't get in much more trouble, could she? If he had his way, she'd be ejected from officer training and turned into a military grunt.

Her helmet rang again. She gave in and answered. "Draybeck."

"Dray! Are you in the shuttle?" Jordan's voice sounded on the edge of panic.

Dray responded, suddenly alert. "Not yet. I'm about fifty meters from it."

"We lost all contact with the shuttle about two minutes ago.

What can you see?"

Dray peered into the cloud. "I can barely make out the outline of the shuttle. It's surrounded by a low cloud. What's going on?"

Red's voice replaced Jordan's. "We are trying to figure that out now. It is not an ordinary cloud, and from the last readouts, it looks like it is attacking the shuttle's iron content."

Dai was still in there. "I have to go into the cloud. Dai's in the shuttle," Dray said.

"Don't do it," Jordan said.

Dray shut her eyes. "I can't leave her behind. She might not even know what's happening."

Red let out a stream of words in his native language that Dray didn't recognize. She considered her options. "I'm going to try to raise her on the com-link. It might work for me."

Dray switched her helmet com-link to the shuttle's frequency. No luck. If she was reaching the shuttle at all, Dai wasn't answering. She had no other choice. She switched back to the Cygna-major. "Jordan?"

"Did you reach her?" Jordan asked.

"No."

"Dray, please. Don't do this."

Dray clenched her fists. "You know I have to. We have spare breathers and a survival tent in the shuttle."

Red broke in again. "Jordan is right. We do not even know if Dai is still alive. Sahar is getting approval to send a Cygna-major shuttle for you."

Dray studied the buzzing cloud around her ship. "Our shuttle may not survive until then." She inventoried her gear and pulled off anything with iron content. Except her helmet. She needed that to filter the air. Her thermal suit had metal filaments, but they were embedded inside a layer of cloth, and she didn't know if they had iron in them. She considered the distance to the shuttle. At a fast run, she'd still need her helmet to breathe. She couldn't leave it behind. "I'm ready."

"Dray." Jordan's voice pulled at her, but she didn't give in.

"Promise you won't leave me down here," Dray said.

"Oh, God. Please, don't."

"Jordan. I love you. Get me off this planet." Dray switched off her com-link. She couldn't bear hearing Jordan crying. She studied the cloud as she stepped closer. It wasn't just hovering over the shuttle. Her heart raced as she prepared to make a run for it. The cloud formed a moving circle between the bare ground and the shuttle's hull. A tendril reached out from the cloud, drifting toward Dray. Her time was up. She inhaled and ran for the shuttle. Her legs pumped as fast as she could make them move, but the nonstandard gravity upset her equilibrium. She fell, sprawling across the stone not more than ten meters from the shuttle. She could see the damage to the hull, now. Huge tracts of the ship seemed to be melting in front of her. The noise of the cloud turned into a thundering roar. She scrambled back to her feet. Dust sprinkled down across her visor. She wiped it off and touched the top of her helmet. It was being eaten away.

    She inhaled. The air filter still worked. She ran the remaining distance to the shuttle and hit the door open latch. Nothing moved. She brushed away more dust from her visor and took another breath. It tasted metallic. Her air filters were failing. She fumbled to open the side panel covering the manual release. Holding her breath, she yanked on the release lever. The shuttle door groaned as it lifted. She pulled harder, but the door opened less than a meter wide. Dray crawled into the opening and pushed the door shut as her lungs burned for air.

Chapter Thirteen

JORDAN'S TEARS DRIED as she did the only thing she could. She set up a remote link to the nearest ADF base station and searched for information on the bio-cloud attacking her lover. Behind her, Sahar paced the small open space in the Cygna-major's communications room, waiting for word from Bello.

"Why hasn't he approved the launch yet?" Sahar asked.

"Because he's incompetent," Jordan said. She pivoted in her chair to look at him. "And if anything happens to Dray, he's a dead man."

Sahar stared at her, but didn't reply. Jordan returned to her screen, scanning the information coming back from the base station. There were five matches to her search, but the last one caught her attention. The Odahim. She pulled up the report. Her finger traced the screen as she read, going faster as the full details of what they faced sunk in.

She turned to Sahar. "They're called the Odahim and they're a borderline-sentient iron-eating bio-cloud left behind on Novan planets as a defense mechanism. Dray's shuttle hasn't got a chance."

Sahar's fists clenched at his side. "Bello should have known this. Planetary security was his responsibility."

Sahar bypassed Bello's command and spoke directly to Commander Resil. When he ended his conversation with Resil, he turned to Jordan. "Go get a lander ready for flight," he said. "You're going down there."

DRAY TORE OFF her helmet and breathed the stale air inside the shuttle. It wasn't tainted yet, but she could tell the external air filters had failed. "Dai?" She searched in the dusty dimness of the shuttle's interior for Dai. She found her huddled over the command console.

The relief in Dai's eyes turned to anger in a flash. "Where have you been? What's happening?"

"The shuttle is being eaten by some kind of cloud. Put on your thermal suit. We're leaving. I'll pack the survival tent."

"Bello," Dai said. "That bastard's responsible for this."

Dray filed that information away. Right now, she needed to pack as much food and water as she could find. She started stuffing supplies into the two backpacks. Dray shouldered one pack and handed Dai the other.

Dai struggled into the harness. Dray handed her one of the air filters and placed the other one on herself. She'd packed two spares in her bag.

"When we landed," Dray said, "we passed another series of structures. I estimate they are less than a kilometer away. That's where we're headed."

"Why so far from the shuttle?"

"I'm hoping something there will provide additional shelter." She turned on her air filter. "Most of what we're carrying has no iron content, but not all of it. We need as much space between us and the cloud as we can get." She didn't bother adding that they had no way of telling their would-be rescuers where they were. Ship communications didn't work and Dai's helmet would only attract the cloud to them. Dray pulled on the shuttle's exterior door. It didn't budge. "Give me a hand," she said.

Dai stepped up next to her and they both pulled on the door. Metal dust sprinkled down on them as the door creaked, then jolted up. It stopped at knee height and a rush of air brought in the gray cloud. "Out," Dray said. Dai scrambled out of the shuttle, and Dray followed. Their air filters held up to the initial onslaught of the cloud. Dray trotted off in the direction she thought the structures were in. Dai matched her pace, her face a grim, pale reflection of the dark beauty she'd been just an hour ago.

JORDAN'S FISTS WRAPPED around the Cygna-major lander's pilot seat. "We need to go," she repeated.

"We can't yet," Red said. "Regulations require our C.O.'s clearance."

"Screw regulations. Dray's down there."

Sahar's voice crackled over the com-link. "The planet's automated defense missiles have been deactivated. You've got clearance to go."

Jordan strapped in her seat and fired up the engines.

Red turned on his com-link. "Who gave clearance?"

"Resil. Bello's been sidelined for now on the *Exelon*. Resil's calling the shots."

A sense of renewed hope filled Jordan as the Cygna-major's launch doors slid open in front of her. A patch of darkness waited as she gave power to the take-off engines and maneuvered the lander out beyond the Cygna-major. Red keyed in the coordinates for Dray's landing site. The darkness in front of them became dominated by the half-illuminated view of the planet. Clouds swirled over the planet, but it was impossible to tell which were the Odahim and which were normal atmospheric clouds. Jordan flew the lander toward the planet, preparing for entry into the atmosphere. They flew at an angle toward landing site two. As they got closer, the front viewer transitioned into a useless view of grayness. Red projected a holo-screen over the front viewer, showing an electronic image of their surroundings. A red beacon pointed to the landing site. Jordan turned the lander toward it.

"We've lost three external sensors," Red said.

The Odahim surrounded the landing site, extending a kilometer into the atmosphere. Jordan's jaw tightened. She was already flying faster than she should have been able to without pilot reflex implants, but risk of exposing her Novan origins was far from her mind. The stranded shuttle beacon seemed to float, tantalizing but distant in front of her.

"Yellow warnings on both wing flaps. This ship has too many metal alloys. The Odahim are tearing it apart."

Her hands tightened on the controls. They were less than two clicks from the landing site. "Lower the landing gear," she said.

Red's hands moved over the controls. Jordan waited for the familiar rumble of the landing gear lowering and locking into place. Nothing happened. She stole a quick glance at Red, but his concentration was focused on his controls. Jordan looked down at ship status. It was sprinkled with yellow warnings and a red flashing indicator on the landing gear.

"The landing gear will not work," Red said.

Less than one click to the beacon. "What the hell is wrong with it?" Jordan asked.

Red's fingers flew over his controls. "I do not know. Jammed or destroyed. Either way, we cannot land this thing."

DRAY GUESSED THE remains they finally found were more than two kilometers from their landing site. They'd reached the site after jogging up a narrow path and forcing their way through a native bramble bush that scraped at their suits but didn't penetrate the reinforced material. A very good thing, Dray thought, since exposed iron fibers would open them to another cloud attack. If the iron was covered, it seemed the cloud ignored it. At least so far.

The ground beneath them hardened. Dray paused to kick at the dirt. A few centimeters underneath was stone. They walked past the crumbled remains that were overtaken by weeds and small fern trees. A massive collapsed structure blocked their path. Dray scanned the perimeter, but it was blocked in by the bramble bush. She didn't want to risk their suits any more than necessary. "We'll have to climb over this." She led the way, pulling Dai up as necessary over the steep sections. They were at the top of the structure when Dray heard a familiar rumble overhead. She scanned the sky, searching for the source.

"What is it?" Dai asked.

A chill ran through Dray's body. In the distance, she saw what looked like a fast-approaching gray cloud. It was heading toward their original landing site. The rumbling grew louder. The gray cloud seemed to grow, but not in proportion to how much closer it was getting. *They won't make it*, Dray thought, knowing it was their rescue ship. As it flew closer, she got a good look at the twisted mess of the underside of the ship that was being attacked by the iron-eating cloud. The ship veered. She didn't watch as it flew up higher and disappeared into the upper atmosphere. When the sound of its engines faded, she turned back to the landscape around them. "There." She pointed to the right. "That building looks almost intact." Her voice sounded hoarse, but one look at Dai told her that her fellow cadet knew what had happened to their rescue. They were stranded.

TEARS OF FRUSTRATION streamed down Jordan's cheeks. Red took over and piloted the lander back to the Cygna-major. Without landing gear, they'd have to effectively crash on the Cygna-major's emergency deck. She should have worried about how they would escape their own crippled lander, but the failed rescue attempt overwhelmed her. For all she knew, Dray was dying or already dead, and Jordan was helpless to do anything. *Get me off this planet*. Dray's last words echoed in her mind. Jordan wouldn't even be able to retrieve her body. Not with the Odahim attacking so successfully.

"Prepare for emergency landing," Red said.

Jordan pulled on the pilot seat head brace and tightened her harness. Her tears stopped as the amber lights of the emergency deck glowed in front of them. The crash foam covering the deck reflected yellow from the lights. Jordan's breath came in short gasps. Statistics rattled through her brain. Three out of five emergency landings result in fatalities. Three out of five. Red cut the flight engines. The ship slowed, but still, the amber lighting approached at a frightening pace.

"Forward engines are offline," he said. "I cannot slow us down any more."

Three out of five. The foam-covered deck dominated their view. The sounds of screaming metal filled Jordan's ears as she was slammed forward into her harness. Pain laced across her head and chest. She closed her eyes as a wall of foam surrounded the front view screen.

DAI CRAWLED INTO the dome-shaped survival tent as soon as Dray had it opened. They hadn't found any sections of the ruins that were still whole or stable enough to provide real protection, so Dray chose a wide floor with three existing walls to house their tent. She passed Dai her pack and crawled into the tent. She sealed it shut and maneuvered around Dai to set up the air filter. It would normally be outside the tent, but with its metal content, Dray kept it inside. She didn't mention the risk that the cloud would find it even inside the tent. One look at Dai's tense form told Dray she was one step away from hysterical already.

Dray sensed it was night, but slow planetary rotation meant it would remain light for several Terran-standard days. She couldn't sleep anyway. Her stomach growled, but they had only a few emergency ration bars, so she wouldn't eat yet. They wouldn't starve to death. They'd die of dehydration first. With less than three liters of water remaining, they didn't stand a chance, even assuming they weren't attacked by the cloud first.

"I'm going outside to try and make a signal for the rescue team," Dray said. Dai didn't answer. She just stared at the tent wall, slowly rocking herself. "You can take your portable air filter off. The tent filter will keep the air clean for us." She waited, but Dai still didn't react, so she leaned across, unclipped the filter, and pulled it off Dai's head. There was nothing she could do to help Dai, so she crawled out of the tent and sealed it shut.

Dray stood up and surveyed the area. They were in a cluster of crumbled buildings in the middle of the ruins. Dray thought the cloud avoided stone, which is why she'd chosen the innermost position to set up the tent. She could be wrong, but after remembering what had happened to the shuttle latch in the dirt, she surmised the cloud might lie dormant in the ground itself. If she had any kind of functional electronics left, she might have been able to prove her theory. She'd stripped down the survival packs to the barest essentials, leaving behind anything with significant metal content.

She scanned the area again, trying to figure out a way to make a marker. The Cygna-major needed to know where they were. She didn't want to depend on being found based on their life signs. Not with the kind of interference the cloud probably made. There wasn't much around them. They were well away from the vegetation that surrounded the ruins. She started exploring the nearest building sites, looking for anything she might use to show their location.

STALE AIR FILLED Jordan's lungs as she struggled to release her harness. She worked the latch with frantic fingers and scrambled free. Gasping for air, she felt a sharp pain in her chest and collapsed on the floor, dark spots filling her vision. She bit down hard on her lip to regain control and crawled to Red, who was unconscious, still strapped into his seat.

"Wake up." She shook his arm, then unlatched the head-brace. Red's head dropped forward. Deep orange blood streamed down his forehead. "Damn it. Wake up. I can't haul you out of this wreck." She looked out of the front view port, or what remained of it. It was a spiderweb of cracks looking out into a thick blanket of foam. She pulled herself up using Red's chair. Pain throbbed where the head restraint had been, but it wasn't as bad as the pain in her chest, which became worse if she breathed too deeply.

Sweat streamed down her chest. Banging to her right made her gasp. A sharp pain stabbed her side and she doubled over. The black dots appeared again, this time covering her vision. Before she blacked out, she heard voices shouting.

Consciousness returned to Jordan in pain-filled dreams. When her eyes flickered open, she saw a familiar orange face leaning over her. "That's not fair," she croaked.

Red smiled. "Being a fast healer has advantages."

Jordan looked around her. She was on a bed surrounded by a guard rail. A thin, white curtain blocked her from seeing the rest of the facility, but she recognized it anyway. She was in the Cygna-major's med clinic. "How long have I been out?"

"Just a couple of hours. You have a bad concussion and two broken ribs, but otherwise, you are doing well."

Jordan saw the broad discoloration covering the top half of Red's face. He didn't heal that fast. She struggled to sit up, but stabbing pain made her collapse into the bed. "Dray?"

Red's smile faded. "We do not know yet. We are working on an idea Bello had."

"Bello? I don't trust that slimy bastard."

"Your vocabulary has expanded in interesting directions," he said.

Jordan sat up, slower this time. When she was up, her head pounded harder, but she ignored it. "What's his idea?"

"Use one of the *Exelon* shuttles we have on board the Cygna-major. The *Exelon* is a more modern ship, made predominantly of composite materials. They lasted longer than the Cygna-major lander against the Odahim."

"You think it will work?"

Red looked away. "It is our only option, if Commander Resil gets authorization. We have already lost the lander we crashed."

"They won't leave Dray there. She's a general's daughter."

"That is the only reason Resil has pursued the matter with his superiors. There is no other ADF ship in the area that could help us, and Resil is reluctant to risk any of the *Exelon*'s assets in another rescue attempt."

He'll be overruled, Jordan thought. Resil was Terran Military, and that meant Dray's father was the final decision-maker. Jordan grabbed the guard rail and pulled herself up to a sitting position.

"You should stay in bed," he said.

"I can't. I'm piloting the *Exelon* shuttle." She stared at him, daring him to deny her the rescue attempt.

He smiled. "Sahar has already agreed, assuming you can walk far enough on your own to report to him. Hopefully, we will hear from Resil soon."

"I can walk."

DRAY HAULED THE last of the plastic crates she'd found under a collapsed wall. She'd scratched her thigh in the process, but as she stood back and surveyed the end result, she was satisfied. In a flat space not far from the tent, she'd built a wide circle around a central triangle, logo of the ADF. If any ship flew as close as the last rescue attempt had, they'd see it.

She brushed the dust off her gloves and suit and grinned at her handiwork. An icy sensation on her leg drew her attention. She looked down. Where there had been a deep scratch in the material of her suit, there was now a hole. The skin of her thigh showed through. A wave of panic rushed over her as she examined the hole. The edges of the material were covered in gray dots. She scrubbed at them, brushing them off, but an instant later, they returned, settling on the fabric edges. She froze as she watched more gray dots float over and land on her.

They were communicating! They were calling other cloud elements in. She scanned the area. She didn't see anything like the large gray cloud that had surrounded the shuttle, but looking down, she saw more gray dots around her thigh. She unzipped her thermal suit and pulled it off. She had to bend over and pull off her boots to get the suit off completely. The frigid air stung at her exposed flesh as she stuffed her feet back into the boots and threw the suit away.

She ran as fast as her legs would take her back to the survival tent, wearing only her boxers, tank top, gloves, and boots. She prayed the cloud wasn't smart enough to follow her back to the tent. Without a thermal suit, she wouldn't survive outside in the freezing temperatures for more than an hour.

She scrambled at the tent seal with shaking hands. She couldn't unseal it. From inside, Dai unsealed the tent, and Dray tumbled inside. Dai resealed the tent as Dray curled up, shivering. Their body heat would warm the tent eventually. *How long will it take?* she wondered as her teeth chattered.

"Where's your suit?" Dai asked.

"Had to strip," Dray said in a shaky voice. "Cloud."

Dai let out a small gasp. "It found us?"

Dray shook her head. "I tore the suit. It found the iron fibers inside." Dai looked down at her own suit as if it had turned against her. "You're safe," Dray said. "Your suit is intact." Her body shook.

Dai shuffled closer to her and wrapped an arm around her. Dray tensed. Even with the extreme cold, she sensed Dai's presence in a sexual way and hated herself for it. She pushed Dai away.

"Don't be an idiot," Dai said. "You're going to freeze to death."

"I'll survive." Dray shook so hard she could hardly talk.

Dai's eyes narrowed. "You hate me so much you won't let me help you, even this small bit?"

"I don't hate you."

"Then what?"

Dray closed her eyes, holding her legs up to her chest as she shivered. "You make me feel something I only want to feel for my girlfriend, for Jordan."

When Dai didn't respond, Dray opened her eyes.

A wry smile curled Dai's lips. "So I was having an effect after all."

Dray just stared at her. What was she talking about?

"And I thought you were impossible to break," Dai said. "Just give me a moment." She shut her eyes. As Dray watched, her features shimmered and changed. Her hair and skin lightened. When she opened her eyes, they were a hazy gray instead of brown. "Better?" When Dray didn't answer, Dai shifted closer and wrapped her arms around Dray.

Dray felt none of the arousal Dai's presence usually signaled. "What did you do?"

"Pheromones, I believe you call them. Chameleons have a different word, but the meaning's the same."

"I don't understand."

Dai sighed. "I imprinted your lover. I effectively became her. Looks, smell, body language, and pheromones. Right down to the chemical signals she gives off. She has a delicious scent. I'll have to use it again some day."

Dray waited, tense. Dai didn't elaborate on Jordan's scent, so she must not have recognized it as Novan. What Dai said made sense, but it didn't make her feel any better about herself. She should have realized what was happening. She'd noticed Dai's subtle changes over time, but never connected it with Jordan. She'd been too busy fighting her attraction to Dai to realize the underlying cause. "Why'd you do it?" she asked.

Dai frowned. "It was Bello's idea. We are, were, lovers. I can't believe I let him manipulate me into this mess."

Dray wanted to push Dai away again, but her body warmth was slowing down Dray's shivering. And without the pheromones or whatever, she felt no attraction to Dai at all. So she stayed there, using Dai's body heat, and hoping Dai never equated Jordan's unique scent with her Novan genetics.

Chapter Fourteen

JORDAN STARTED HER pre-flight check. She would fly solo. Commander Resil had given reluctant approval, but ordered them to abort the mission if this attempt failed. Jordan pulled the pilot harness over her head and groaned when the straps pressed against her broken ribs.

"Everything okay in there?" Red asked over the open com-link.

"Fine," Jordan said. She wouldn't take painkillers. Not before this flight. The medical technician had managed to reduce the pain in her head to a persistent, dull ache, but bones were bones. Even her partial Novan genetics wouldn't speed up their healing fast enough to matter on this mission. She switched on the launch engines and looked out the front view port. She had clearance to fly and piloted the shuttle out of the Cygna-major.

"When you approach the upper atmosphere, stay high until you reach Dray's landing site," Red said.

The surface appeared in front of Jordan. She shifted the shuttle to top speed, hoping she could outrun the bio-cloud. With Red acting as her link to the Cygna, there was no risk anyone would notice how smoothly she handled the extreme speed. She saw an expanse of untouched forest give way to jagged stone shapes. "Landing site one beneath me," she said. It wasn't Dray's site. She kept her shuttle high for another five minutes, waiting until the last moment before she dipped into a steep dive as she approached site two.

Jordan scanned her equipment. "It's working," she said, ignoring the G forces on her descent. Novan physiology had been modified for extremes like this, and for once she was glad she'd inherited that much from her father. "No sign of the Odahim yet."

Red's voice came out scratchy over the com-link. Jordan couldn't make out what he was saying. "I'm two minutes away from Dray's site," she said, hoping her signal was still reaching the Cygna-major.

She leveled her flight trajectory so she was flying just over the tree tops. As site two appeared on her horizon, she cut the rear engines and used reverse engines to slow down. The shuttle groaned in protest, but it would hold under the pressure. She saw a wide, flat stone slab below her that represented site two. A thin, gray cloud lingered over the crumbled remains of Dray's shuttle. She saw nothing else. Dray wasn't there.

DRAY WANTED TO sleep. Even with Dai lying on top of her, she was so cold. She'd thought their body heat would be enough to warm up the survival tent, but she was wrong. Her body ached, and she didn't want to fight to stay awake anymore. Her eyes drifted shut.

"No you don't," Dai said, shaking her. "You fall asleep, and you'll never wake up."

Dray groaned. *Why can't she just leave me alone?* "We're dying," she said, her voice hoarse. "Just let me go." Her thoughts drifted. "Do you believe in an afterlife?"

"Stop it," Dai said. "We're not going to die."

Dray thought about Jordan, apologizing mentally for not loving her as she deserved. "I'm sorry, Jordan," she whispered. "Sorry I didn't make it."

"What?" Dai shook her again. "You're getting delirious. Jordan's not here. Open your eyes."

Dray slipped into a dreamland. She wasn't as cold anymore. She heard a distant rumbling that sounded like thunder.

"DAMN IT, WHERE are you?" Jordan banked her lander in a wide sweep around the ruins. She didn't dare go as fast as she wanted to, for fear of missing signs of Dray. She saw nothing but stone and large-leaf trees. So far, the Odahim had left her alone, but for how long? And where was Dray?

She slowed her engines further, doing a visual sweep. The ship's sensors were useless. Everything that wasn't stone turned up as a dim life sign. The sensors should have been able to block out vegetation, but something was scrambling the readouts. She assumed Dray and Dai would show up as stronger life signs but so far, the ship found nothing else. Jordan forced back the tears. Dray had to be alive. She had to. Something caught Jordan's attention to her right, and she veered the shuttle to investigate. She wanted to laugh and cry at the same time when she saw the makeshift logo of the ADF. *Dray.*

Jordan pulled the shuttle out in a narrow circle around the small site. She saw the survival tent tucked in between two stone slabs. Dray was here. She'd made it this far. Jordan lowered the landing gear and cut the main engines. She used the thrusters to maneuver the shuttle next to Dray's symbol, the only place clear enough to land.

When the ship settled on the ground, Jordan unstrapped and jumped out of the seat. Pain shot across her chest from moving too fast. She held onto her seat until she could steady herself again, then pushed a helmet on and exited the ship. She had to pause for a moment to remember from which direction she'd seen the tent. She trotted as fast as she could, ignoring the pain in her ribs. *Dray is here.*

DRAY'S DREAMLAND BECAME more real. Dai's insistent shaking had stopped, and so had the noisy rumbling she'd heard. She heard Dai's voice, but the words weren't making any sense. She heard Jordan's voice. It was such a sweet, painful sound. She wanted to cry. Dai shook her. *No*, she thought. *Don't wake me up. Jordan's here in my dreams.*

"Dray. Dray." Dai's voice held a new urgency to it that pulled Dray out of her dream. She opened her eyes. The same drab tent hovered over her, and Dai's body still wrapped around her, for what little warmth it provided.

"Someone's out there," Dai said.

Dray heard her name being called. "Jordan," she croaked. "It's Jordan."

Dai turned her head and shouted Jordan's name. Dray tried to help, but all she could do was cling to Dai and wait. She wasn't going to die. Jordan was here.

JORDAN FOLLOWED THE sound of Dai's voice to the tent. Why wasn't Dray calling to her? She knelt at the base of the tent, her gloved fingers working the seal. She peeled open the tent flap and pushed her body halfway inside. Dray was lying on the floor of the tent, barely clothed and in Dai's arms.

"It's about time you got here," Dai said, trying to sit up. Dray sat up with her, still clinging to Dai, like lovers.

Lovers. Jordan squirmed back out of the tent. "Get out."

"A little help would be nice," Dai said. "Your girlfriend is hardly mobile."

"She's hurt?" Jordan stuck her head back into the tent, forcing herself to view the painful sight again. Dray was shivering so hard Jordan could hear her teeth chattering. Jordan crawled into the tent. "Where's your suit?" she asked.

"Compromised. Cloud." Dray could barely talk.

Feeling foolish and embarrassed, Jordan turned to Dai. "We'll need to carry her. My shuttle's not far away."

Dai nodded and crawled out of the tent. Dray managed to crawl to the edge. "It's too cold," Dray said.

"It's not far. Please, Dray, you have to get outside. We'll carry you from there."

Dray tumbled out of the tent. Jordan followed, crawling over Dray's curled-up, shivering body. She and Dai put their arms under Dray and lifted. It felt like two knives were being driven into Jordan's chest, and she stumbled back to one knee.

"What's wrong?" Dai asked.

"Nothing." Jordan bit her lip and hoisted Dray up. Every step sent excruciating pain through her, but Jordan kept moving. Dray's head dropped forward as they walked, and she stopped shivering. Jordan didn't think it was a good sign and tried to quicken her step. She saw the clearing ahead of them. When they got there, she stopped, staring at her ship.

Or what she could see of her ship. A gray cloud was forming around it. "Hurry," she said, forcing herself to trot the short distance to the ship. She had to lower Dray to the ground so she could open the shuttle's hatch. As soon as it opened, she pushed Dray in. Dai followed, tugging Dray up the short ramp while Jordan shut the hatch. Jordan stepped over Dray and scrambled into the pilot seat.

"I can't get her into a seat," Dai said.

Jordan turned around. Dray was curled up in a ball on the floor of the shuttle. "There's a thermal blanket in the compartment to your left. Cover her up and strap yourself in."

Jordan couldn't take the time to force Dray into a safety harness. She fired up the launch engines and scanned the ship's readouts. She'd sustained only minor damage so far. Dai sat in the chair next to her and pulled on her harness. Jordan yanked her own down, then fed more power to the take-off engines. The ship lifted off. She could just make out the surroundings through the gray haze of the bio-cloud attacking them. "Sorry, Dray," she whispered as she turned on the flight engines fully and launched the shuttle.

She heard Dray roll on the floor and bang into a wall, but she couldn't take the time to turn around. Dray would be fine, she told herself, so long as Jordan could get them out of the planetary pull without too much turbulence. The front view port was blocked by a gray haze. She flew by electronic navigation, but kept the speed and ascent to within normal Terran flight standards.

Accelerating into the upper atmosphere, they emerged from the bio-cloud into a dark sky. Jordan checked the shuttle for damage. Landing gear and reverse engines were intact. She would not have to survive another crash landing. After getting them beyond the planet's orbit, Jordan turned toward the Cygna-major ship.

Dray was huddled in the corner under the thermal blanket. "Let's get her into a seat," Jordan said. She turned on auto flight controls and unstrapped herself.

Dai unbuckled and helped Jordan maneuver Dray into a passenger seat with the blanket tucked around her. Jordan strapped her in. She pulled off her gloves and touched Dray's cheek, lifting her head to look at her. Dray's skin was paler than normal against Jordan's darker hand. And cold. Her lips looked purple. Dray never opened her eyes.

Jordan returned to her pilot seat, preparing to dock on the Cygna-major.

Dai sat next to her. "Nothing happened, you know."

"Excuse me?"

"Between me and your lover. Not for lack of trying on my part."

Jordan glared at Dai. "Just shut up." In other circumstances, she'd have given in to her desire to slap Dai across the face. She didn't want to know how far Dai had gone to seduce Dray. She had an inkling of Dai's tricks and hated her for it.

Jordan signaled ahead for a medical team, and they were waiting when she landed the ship. She watched as they strapped Dray to a gurney and carried her away. She wanted to follow, but had to report to Sahar. She walked at a slow pace through the ship in search of him.

STINGING PAIN RADIATED along Dray's arms and legs like a thousand little pins pricking her flesh. She groaned and opened her eyes, blinking into the harsh overhead lights. When her eyes adjusted, she recognized the med clinic.

A gray-haired med-tech leaned over her. "I know things feel unpleasant, but consider it a positive sign. You have no permanent frostbite damage."

It was more than unpleasant, but at least she was alive. She remembered only bits and pieces of her rescue, including who came for her. "Jordan?" she asked. Her voice came out as a whisper.

"Cadet Bowers?" The technician frowned. "She left the facility before her treatment was completed. If you ask me, she should never have been released to fly. Not with that concussion."

Concussion? What had happened to her? Dray struggled to sit up.

"No you don't." The med-tech pushed her back down on the

bed. "You are here for the rest of the day, at least. I have authority to use restraints if necessary."

Dray sank back onto her soft pillow. The effort to move proved too much. If she couldn't get up to see Jordan, she hoped Jordan would come to see her soon.

JORDAN LEANED AGAINST the wall on the command deck, watching black space through the view port. Their mission was over and they were heading back to the Entari system.

"You should be down in the med clinic, you know," Sahar said.

Her eyes flicked to his dark, worried face and back to the view port. She wasn't ready to face Dray. The memory of finding her almost naked in another woman's arms still haunted her. She understood the need for it. She'd stayed with the med-tech long enough to realize how close Dray had come to severe hypothermia, but that was a mental understanding. Jordan's heart betrayed her insecurities. How much had gone on between the two women while they were stranded? Sahar explained what Dai had tried to do with her Chameleon abilities. What had Dray felt? Her relationship with Dray was already strained before all this. Jordan didn't think she could handle it if Dray decided Jordan had manipulated her just like Dai had.

"I could order you to the med clinic," Sahar said.

"Don't make me regret that Commander Resil put you in charge over Bello," she said.

"Bello won't be leading anything for a good, long time."

"Why?"

Sahar pulled up something on his command screen and waved Jordan over. "I think this was the evidence you were looking for."

Jordan read through the report Sahar had sent to Resil. It included command traces that highlighted Bello's manipulations on Dray's craft. So, she was right. He had sabotaged Dray's ship so she'd be stranded on the planet. She felt a cold satisfaction in that. "What happens to him now?"

"He came back from the *Exelon* with the rest of his team, but he is stripped of all responsibilities. He'll go before a military review board when we get back. Probably not severe enough to warrant a court-martial, but he faces some serious disciplinary action." Sahar closed his report and turned back to Jordan. "What he did was wrong, but I don't think even he knew how bad it would get down there. He wanted Dray out of his unit, not dead."

The thought that Dray could have died on this mission sent a shiver through Jordan. She shouldn't be here talking to Sahar. "I'm going to the med clinic," she announced. She saw a faint smile on Sahar's dark face before she turned and walked away.

JORDAN FOUND EACH step painful as she made steady progress through the ship to the med clinic on the lower level. No one talked to her as she passed them in the hall. The unit seemed subdued by the events of the last few hours. She felt it herself, an uncertainty and bone-weariness no simulated exercise could match. She turned the final corner and saw the white double doors emblazoned with a red cross marking the ship's medical facilities. The doors opened as she approached, and she was greeted by a med-tech whose name she'd forgotten.

"Not surprised to see you back here, Cadet Bowers," he said. "I was just telling your teammate you should never have been dismissed from here."

"Can I see her?" she asked.

He frowned, studying her for a moment. "You should be admitted yourself. How are those ribs?"

Jordan touched her side and winced.

The med-tech was up from his chair in an instant. "I thought as much. I'm admitting you for further treatment."

"I need to see Dray."

"No arguments. Your injuries first, then I'll put you both in the same room, and you can chat until the stars burn out." He took her by the arm and led her to a stretcher along the wall.

DRAY WOKE TO the sound of someone humming. At first, she thought she was dreaming as the soothing melody wrapped itself around her drowsy thoughts. She not only recognized the tune, but the voice, and opened her eyes. Her first thought was that she was in a different room. There were no overhead lights, just a glowing lamp to her left. She turned and saw Jordan sitting up in a bed next to hers.

Jordan turned to her. "You're awake."

"Yes." Dray's voice sounded weak in her own ears. She cleared her throat and tried again. "Why are you here?" The words hadn't come out right. "I mean, in a bed."

Jordan touched the medical patch on her forehead. "This is for the concussion." She lifted her hospital-gray T-shirt to reveal a tight bandage around her chest. "And this is for the stress I put on my cracked ribs."

"Cracked? How?"

"In the first rescue shuttle Red and I flew to help you."

Dray sat up and swung her bare feet over the edge of her bed. A wave of lightheadedness passed over her.

"You shouldn't be moving," Jordan said.

Dray waited for the nausea to pass, then looked up to Jordan. "You got all that trying to rescue me, didn't you?"

"The first trip, yes."

"I saw you, your shuttle. I didn't think it would make it."

Jordan pulled her sheet up to her sides. "We almost didn't. We lost our landing gear and forward engines."

Dray felt a renewed sense of guilt. "So not only did I fail my own mission, I nearly got you and Red killed."

Jordan smiled at her. "Some day you'll stop blaming yourself for all the problems in the universe."

"This time, it's true."

"No, actually, it's not." Jordan repositioned herself on the bed to face Dray. "First, Bello's been stripped of command for sabotaging your mission. So, that's not your fault. And second, the aborted rescue attempt was more my fault than yours, for not waiting until we'd done a complete analysis of what was happening to your shuttle. When we lost communications, I panicked."

Dray watched the mask of worry cover Jordan's face. "When you aborted the rescue, I thought we were done for. The cloud attacked my suit. I was sure I wouldn't make it." She shivered, remembering feeling so cold it burned.

"I should probably be grateful Dai was there." The edge to Jordan's voice told Dray there was more hurt there.

"I'm sorry for that as well. And this time it was my fault," Dray said.

Jordan's eyes locked with hers. "Not entirely. From what both Sahar and Dai told me, she's been manipulating you from the start. And using me to do it."

Dray looked down at the floor. "Even so, I shouldn't have reacted the way I did."

"Did anything happen?"

Dray looked up into Jordan's worried brown eyes. "I didn't want her, but whenever she was close, it felt like you next to me. I was so confused, but nothing happened."

Jordan let out a long, slow breath. "Good. Why did Bello sabotage your ship? I mean, he wasn't doing it just to get you and Dai alone."

Dray stared at the ceiling. "Turin. Some of his family were part of the squads my mother led into battle. His family were part of those disposable Aquaran troops Franklin talked about. They all died."

"And Bello blames you for that?"

Dray shrugged. "He said it was my mother's fault. He can't stand the thought that I'll have officer rank after this mission."

"And what do you think?"

Dray heard the worry in Jordan's voice. She had to think before she answered. A few weeks ago, she would have said Bello was wrong, that the whole historical record of Turin was wrong. Being faced with a person at least as deeply affected by that ill-fated mission as she was, Dray was no longer as confident of her mother's innocence.

"I'm not sure," Dray said. "I mean, he's deranged, but a lot of people died. And my mother directed that attack." She didn't want to say what she was thinking: that it really had been her mother's fault. Her vision of her mother wavered as she accepted that maybe she wasn't perfect. Dray looked over to Jordan. "I don't think children should bear the sins of their parents."

JORDAN FROWNED. "WHAT do you mean?"

Dray stared at her hands. "Dai taught me something down there. She taught me that physical attraction isn't enough." She looked up at Jordan, her blue eyes glistening. "I realized what I felt for you was so much more than just your body chemistry."

Jordan's heart pounded. Was Dray accepting her at last? "So, what's this have to do with sins of the parents?"

"I was blaming you for your parents. That's what Bello did to me, and I realize just how unfair it is."

Jordan felt a stab of frustration. "My parents committed no sins."

Dray winced. "I'm not saying this right, am I? I love you, Jordan. I don't care what your genetics are." Jordan frowned, but Dray held up her hand. "Please, let me finish. I've spent most of my life blaming Novans for my mother's death. I learned to hate them when I was just a kid. I don't really know what happened at Turin, but I know now my mother caused a lot of deaths besides her own. I can't blame Novans for that."

"What a relief," Jordan said, turning away from Dray.

"Jordan, please. I'm trying to get over years of prejudice. Can't you give me some time?"

Jordan looked into Dray's pleading eyes and reined in her frustration. "I'm sorry, you're right. I've been dealing with my mixed heritage for years. I can't expect you to accept it immediately."

"I do accept it," Dray said. "But it will take me a while to accept Novans as something other than my enemy."

Jordan smiled. "Not an easy task if we're at war with them again."

"No," Dray said. "No, it's not."

Chapter Fifteen

DRAY STOOD ALONE in the Alpha squad dorm and straightened out the sleeves on her new blue dress uniform. They were graduating at last.

Major Duli arranged the graduation banquet for the cadets two days after their squads had returned. Dray scrutinized her appearance in the full-length mirror as she prepared for the banquet. She'd pressed her new uniform and even visited the site's barber to get her hair trimmed. She placed her new name tag on the right side of her uniform, adjusting it to make sure it was perfectly straight. "Draybeck, Lt.," it said. Lieutenant. Dray smiled at her image in the mirror and walked out of their dorm. She looked as good as she was going to.

Jordan had left to help Jenny dress for the banquet and Dray hadn't seen her since lunch. When Dray opened the doors to the banquet hall, she was overcome by the delicious scent from the buffet tables lining the near wall. Her stomach urged her to seek out food, but her priority was to find Jordan. She scanned the crowd, some lining the walls, some eating, and a good many dancing on the large open floor space in front of a live band. Major Duli got bonus points for that touch, in Dray's mind. She walked around the periphery of the dance floor until she found Red standing by the side wall and joined him.

"Good evening, Lieutenant," he said, smiling.

"Yeah, yeah. I feel like a poser."

"You earned your status. Just like the rest of us."

Not as well as the rest of you, Dray thought. "Have you chosen your reassignment, yet?"

"My assessment gave me clearance for Ship Warfare Officer. I will be taking a post with the Third Fleet, on the *Rubicon*. What about you?"

"I haven't decided yet." She didn't mention that her assessment gave her a marginal fighter-pilot rating. "Have you seen Jordan?" she asked, changing the subject.

"No, but if she looks as beautiful as you this evening, I must beg for the honor of a dance with each of you."

"No guarantees," Dray said, grinning.

When Red's skin rippled a deeper orange, she laughed, elbowing him in the ribs. "Who's got you getting all colored this time?"

Red stared across the room, and Dray followed his gaze. She saw Venkata enter the hall in civilian clothes. The Gilgaran scanned the crowd until she saw Red.

"You will excuse me?" Red said as he moved off.

"Have a good time." Dray watched him make his way past the stage where the band was beating out a fast tune.

Dray saw Jenny near the buffet tables. Jenny's hair was pulled up into a loose bun, with tendrils of black hair curling around her ears. *Definitely Jordan's touch*, Dray thought. She watched for a moment as Malory Grace approached Jenny. Dray could sense Malory's uncertainty from across the dance floor. Jenny reached out and pulled Malory closer, whispering something in her ear that made Malory's face redden as she smiled.

Dray scanned the banquet hall. Jordan should be somewhere in the crowd by now. As the band started a slow instrumental, Dray found Jordan standing on the edge of the dance floor opposite her. Jordan's hair was similarly styled to Jenny's, her long black hair pulled up off a graceful neck. Jordan's eyes met hers, and Dray's heart skipped. She moved through the dancers as Jordan walked toward her. They met halfway across the floor.

"You're beautiful," Dray said.

Jordan blushed. "So are you."

Dray smiled, tracing her finger along the rigid bar on Jordan's uniform that signified her promotion as well. "Would you like to dance?" she asked.

Jordan slipped her arms over Dray's shoulders. "Yes, please."

Dray wrapped her arms around Jordan's waist and pulled her closer as they moved to the slow music. She sighed when Jordan's body pressed against hers, and Jordan laid her head on Dray's shoulder.

"I love you," Dray whispered.

Jordan lifted her head and gazed into Dray's eyes, smiling. She leaned in and placed a slow, lingering kiss on Dray's lips. When Jordan pulled back, tears glistened in her eyes. "I love you, too."

"IT'S JUST A family visit," Jordan said. "I'm excited to see my mother, but not as jumpy as you are about seeing your father and brother. Besides, we'll have a one-week leave after this before reassignment. That's something to be happy about."

Dray sat in the shuttle, her legs bouncing as she waited to dock on the Denali Orbital Station. Yesterday's banquet had been fantastic, but today's events were another matter. Red sat across from her, looking just as nervous. Only Jordan seemed at ease.

"How can you be so calm?" Dray asked. "You're not the least bit nervous about meeting my family? And, do I really have to meet your mother? I mean, the Ambassador to Gilgar?"

Jordan reached over and took her hand. "She'll love you. I've already told her all about you."

Dray's eyes widened. "You did what? What did you say?" Her voice squeaked, and she coughed to mask her fear. It didn't help when Jordan laughed. Even Red was hiding a smirk behind his big orange hand.

"What are you laughing about, Big Red? How many brothers and sisters do you have waiting for you, eh?"

Red's smile faded. "Three middle sisters and one brother, though he has not matured yet."

"Why are you nervous?" Jordan asked.

"I know I should not be. My family compares me to my eldest sister in ways I wish they would not."

"This is the sister who's the Tarquin delegate to the ADF?" Dray asked.

"Yes. And I am sure she is not the only one who is displeased with my decision to stay in an ADF military division. They believe I should transfer to Tarquin military."

"Why don't you?" Jordan asked.

"You have experienced in part what Tarquin military is like. They are warriors at heart. When I accepted the Eternal Flame, I chose a different, less aggressive path. And I wish to remain with friends."

"Right," Dray said. "You just like having a variety of women from difference species to flirt with."

Red grinned as he nodded. "It is a unique benefit the ADF military units offer."

Dray relaxed some as she poked fun at Red's problems. Anything was better than wondering how she'd face Jordan's mother in less than an hour. Was she supposed to introduce her father and brother to Jordan's mother as well? Her legs twitched double-time as the shuttle's engines slowed.

The shuttle landed twenty minutes later, the quiet hum of its engines replaced with the hiss of fresh air being taken in from the station. Dray, Jordan, and Red, along with another twenty graduates, filed down the connector ramp, through a long tunnel, and into the greeting area. The lighting seemed excessively bright to Dray as she scanned the waiting crowd. Her father would be the easiest to see, she thought, since people tended to give four-star generals a wide berth. She saw her brother Kelvin first, his red hair looking nearly orange in the overly bright lighting. He was wearing his crisp black Military Intelligence uniform. She smiled and waved, then saw her father standing next to Kelvin, smaller in stature, but, as she expected, isolated by a wide space from the rest of the visitors.

"There they are, over there," she said, pointing. "Have you found your mother yet?"

Jordan turned to follow Dray's direction. "No, not yet." Jordan's voice drifted as she turned away. Dray itched to join her family, but she waited for Jordan to find hers before leaving.

"Mom!" Jordan shouted as she waved. Dray looked where Jordan was staring but could not make out who among the crowd was Jordan's mother. Jordan pulled away from her. "I'll bring her over to you, okay?"

Jordan ran off. Dray looked around to find Red. The tall Tarquin was easy to spot. He stood in a cluster of orange faces, a wide grin plastered on his face. Dray turned back and worked her way through the throng to her brother and father.

"Hey," Kelvin said. Dray saw the tension in his face from their last meeting. So much had happened since then.

Not wanting anything to stand between them anymore, Dray threw her arms around her brother and felt a low rumbling chuckle inside his chest. She pulled away and turned to her father. "Good to see you, Sir."

"And you, Lieutenant," he said, his arms relaxed at his side.

Dray didn't expect any other greeting. Her father was always distant, but now that she was in the military, he would keep a strict officer/subordinate distance between them. *Even during visitor times, generals maintain a certain decorum,* she thought.

"How was your training?" her father asked.

Dray refrained from going into details. She would not burden her family with the minor squabbles of her training. And she wasn't sure how long Kelvin and her father could remain civil to one another. The male Draybecks held a longstanding animosity with each other that neither would discuss with Dray or her sister, Cara.

CHANDRIKA'S SMALL ARMS surrounded Jordan. Jordan knew there would be at least two of her mother's security guards nearby, but they kept away from mother and daughter and for that, Jordan was grateful. She preferred some semblance of a normal family. Her mother was her adviser, her confidante, and sometimes, her best friend.

"You are a lieutenant now, I see." Her mother's voice held the familiar accent she'd acquired after years of speaking Gilgaran. "Are you still determined to play this military game?"

"It's not a game, Mother."

"No it is not. It's a war."

Jordan held her mother's gaze, recognizing the cool expression of the master politician. "I swore allegiance to the Terran Military. War with the Novans doesn't change that."

"If you are discovered, I cannot help you. Whatever influence I have within the Terran government would be destroyed."

"I understand." Jordan was on her own. For the first time, she would not have the safety net her mother represented. This was her future, and it would be with Dray, not hiding in her mother's shadow. "Dray's here," she said to break the tension.

"Do I get to meet her?" And just as fast, the career politician was gone, replaced by the caring mother. Chandrika's relaxed gaze washed over Jordan like a warm bath, erasing Jordan's remaining doubts. She'd always have her mother as confidante and companion, even if they disagreed about Jordan's career.

"Yes, come on." Jordan pulled her mother, weaving them through the crowd of families. She spotted the two guards shadowing them, but knew they'd keep up without a problem. It took her longer than she expected to find Dray, but she spotted Dray's blond head being patted by a lanky male version of Dray.

Jordan slowed down, and her mother bumped into her. "Can't you find her?" Chandrika asked.

"Yes, she's over there, with the tall, red-headed guy." Jordan pushed back her hair, wishing she'd worn it in a pony tail or something.

Her mother tried to hide her smile. "Nervous?"

"Kind of," Jordan said. "She talks a lot about her sister and brother, but hasn't told me much about her father."

"General Draybeck would be the aloof man to her left."

Jordan turned to her mother. "You know him?"

"Of course," her mother said, leading Jordan toward the family. "We've debated the role of neutral planets in Terran economic and political strategy. I'm afraid we don't see eye to eye on very many issues."

Jordan blanched. She hadn't considered that her mother and Dray's father would be political combatants. Her mother gave Jordan no time to react to the news as she wove her way to Dray's family. Her mother stood a few centimeters shorter than Jordan, but the crowd seemed to make a path for the older woman.

Everything about her demeanor radiated power. Jordan followed in her mother's wake, wishing she'd spent more time preparing herself for meeting Dray's family. A dozen other conversations drifted around them as they progressed across the greeting area, but that all faded away when Jordan stood in front of Dray's father.

"General Draybeck. It is good to see you again." Her mother held the gaze of the general.

Dray's father extended his hand. "And you, Ambassador. I see our children have already met."

Jordan wrapped her hand around Dray's as Dray introduced her to her brother and father. She needn't have worried about what to say, since her mother dominated most of the conversation. At the urging of her guards, Chandrika offered to host both families in her private suite. Jordan slipped her arm around Dray's back and let the warmth of her lover calm her as they followed their parents into the elite quarters. At least she would have a week to spend alone with Dray. They just had to get through the next two days they would be required to spend with both families.

DRAY MANAGED TO convince her father to let her spend the first night with Jordan at the Ambassador's suite if they agreed to spend the second night with him. After entertaining Dray with stories of Jordan's childhood, Chandrika retired to her own room, leaving Dray and Jordan alone. Dray wiped her sweaty palms on the knees of her pants, unsure of herself now that they were alone.

Jordan stood up from the wide sofa. "We should probably go to our room, too." Dray let herself be pulled up from the seat as her heart pounded. She had not been alone with Jordan since the transport ship brought them to the Entari system. After all that had passed between them, she didn't know how to act. What did Jordan expect of her?

The room Jordan led her into was more like a suite within a suite. A love seat, chair, and end tables formed a compact living room, and the opposite wall had the largest bed Dray had ever seen. She turned away from the bed and its implications, eyeing a tiny kitchen. "Is it stocked with food?" she asked.

Jordan sat on the love seat, pulling off her boots. "Probably, knowing my mother. Are you hungry?"

"Not really, just curious." Dray walked to the kitchen and opened up cabinets, peering inside. She let out a low whistle. "Your mom knows how to stock a pantry." She pulled out an oddly shaped box with indecipherable lettering. "What's this stuff?"

"No idea. My mother will eat just about anything from any culture so long as it's safe for Terrans." Jordan stretched out on the love seat, her long legs dangling over the edge. "Are you eating?"

Dray put the food back and closed the cabinet door. She stood on the threshold between the kitchen and living area, rocking from foot to foot. Jordan had pulled off her uniform jacket and rolled up the sleeves of the white blouse she wore underneath. Her exposed forearms showed muscle tone under her light brown skin that hadn't been there before their final training had started. Dray's pulse quickened.

"Why are you standing there?" Jordan asked, looking at her through sleepy eyes.

"I'm nervous," Dray confessed.

Jordan sat up, her eyes widening. "Why? Have I done something wrong?"

Dray took a few steps closer. "No, it's just... A lot's happened between us. And not all of it was good."

"Will you sit with me?" Jordan asked. She folded her hands on her lap as Dray sat down. "Do we need to talk?"

Dray inhaled the scent of Jordan, a sweet mix of her natural scent and perfume from a planetary system Dray forgot the name of. It brought back memories of when they shared a room on Buenos Aires. It seemed so long ago, yet it hadn't been. She took a deep, steadying breath. "Do you know what you want to do next? We have until tomorrow night to choose our first assignments."

Jordan hands clasped and unclasped as she thought. "I want a military career. My family background doesn't change that."

"There is one option. I talked to Kelvin. His department openly employs Novans."

"As spies," Jordan said. "I don't know. I mean, I know it's the safer route, but it's not what I've pictured for my future. You can tell him about me, but I don't know if I want to join his department." Jordan took Dray's hand. "Do we have anything else we need to talk about?"

Dray's cheeks turned red. "Maybe not talk, but just, take things slow."

Jordan shifted closer. Dray felt the heat of Jordan's body where it touched hers, a warmth which was both calming and exciting, heightening the effect of Jordan's unique scent. Jordan's free hand brushed through Dray's short hair. Dray shut her eyes, living only through the sensations of Jordan's touch for a moment. Jordan edged nearer, but Dray didn't open her eyes just yet. Warm lips brushed against hers, and her body arched toward that contact. The kiss lingered, then Jordan pulled back. Dray cupped the back of Jordan's head, pulling her closer. Their lips met again. Dray sucked on Jordan's lower lip, and a tremor ran through her lover's body. Dray's hand slipped from Jordan's neck to stroke her back. Jordan moaned, leaning down on Dray and pushing her further into the love seat's cushions.

Dray felt a slow, languorous heat building in response to her lover's tender caress. Jordan's fingers traced down Dray's arm, but Dray could barely feel it. She pulled back for a moment and took off her uniform jacket, tossing it on the floor. Jordan unsnapped Dray's cuffs and pushed the sleeves up with her stroking hand, leaving a trail of fire on Dray's skin. Dray wanted more, but she didn't want to rush. She wanted this time to extend into forever.

JORDAN SHIFTED AS Dray's head dipped lower, and the warm trail of Dray's tongue on her flesh set her on fire. "You don't make it easy to go slowly."

"Maybe slow just isn't right for us," Dray said with a mischievous smile.

Jordan closed her eyes as Dray kissed her neck and moved lower. With an awkward tug, the first snap on Jordan's blouse came undone. Jordan looked down to see Dray grinning as she held Jordan's blouse between her teeth. Her lover gave another tug, and the second snap popped open, revealing Jordan's lace bra. Jordan burned wherever Dray's lips touched her. Those lips brushed the exposed curve of her breast, leaving Jordan breathless. "Can we move to the bed?" she asked, fighting to catch her breath. She wanted Dray, but she worried about pushing her too fast. It had to be perfect this time, to show how much she loved Dray.

Dray pulled Jordan up with her. She led Jordan to the bed and pulled down the off-white cover, revealing a set of deep green, satiny sheets. Jordan watched Dray's eyes widen as she gazed at the luxurious bed.

"Please don't weird out because my mother ordered these sheets for us," Jordan said, hiding her embarrassment.

Dray turned to her, eyes widening further. "Your mother ordered these?"

"No. Well. Yes. I mean, she knew I wanted you to stay here with me, and she knows I love you."

Dray's hand covered Jordan's mouth. "We'll talk about how freakishly close you and your mother are some other time. For now, no more talking." Dray lifted her hand and replaced it with her lips, silencing Jordan's reply. They sat on the edge of the bed while Dray pulled off her boots. With perfect comic timing, Dray scrambled up to the top of the bed and stretched out, patting the pillow next to her. Jordan stifled a laugh as she joined Dray.

Jordan traced the outline of Dray's collar, clasped the first snap of Dray's shirt, and popped it open. She looked into Dray's eyes, watching them dilate as she worked her way to the next snap, and the next, popping each open between her fingers. When she finished, she caressed Dray's tight stomach and moved up, lingering on the warm underside of Dray's breasts. "No bra," Jordan said. "Is that regulation?"

Dray took Jordan's hand and slipped it higher until it cupped her breast. A fire shot through Jordan from where her hand covered Dray's breast. The heat centered between her legs. She pinched the nipple between her fingers, and Dray arched into her. Jordan pushed the open shirt out of her way and wrapped the hardened nipple between her lips, sucking to the rhythm of Dray's breathing.

Jordan traced her kisses along Dray's stomach as she tugged at Dray's belt. Working it and the zipper open, she slipped her hand inside her boxers and cupped Dray's warm, moist mound. Dray pushed into Jordan's hand, grinding against the pressure, but that wasn't what Jordan wanted. She sat up and pulled off Dray's pants and boxers. Dray watched her through half-closed eyes as Jordan pushed her legs apart and positioned herself between Dray's thighs. She could smell Dray's heady scent as she kissed and nibbled her way from Dray's knees to her damp curls. Dray's hips pushed up to her as Jordan traced her tongue in circles around Dray's swollen folds. Jordan tasted her lover, teasing her, loving her until Dray's thighs shook. With her free hand, Jordan slipped two fingers into Dray and felt Dray tighten around her. Jordan matched her rhythm to Dray's thrusting hips, feeling her own wetness growing as Dray's body arched in one final thrust against her. She could feel the climax around her fingers and collapsed onto Dray's thighs when it ebbed. She wanted to stay there, just feeling Dray's heat, but Dray had other ideas. Ideas Jordan was more than eager to join in as she maneuvered out of her pants and dampened panties. Whatever drowsiness she'd felt earlier in the evening disappeared when she gazed into Dray's mischievous face. This night would be as special as she had hoped.

DRAY BOUNCED DOWN the escalator from Ambassador Bowers' suite with a wide grin on her face. Jordan's mother had kept her in stitches all morning with tales of political fiascoes. Dray's best laugh came from the old vids the Ambassador showed her, much to Jordan's embarrassment. "I loved your princess costume," she teased. The memory of seeing five-year-old Jordan dancing around as the Crystal Princess from Y'taria would keep Dray laughing for days.

Jordan gave her a playful punch in the arm. "Are you telling me there are no compromising vids of you as a child? Maybe I'll ask your brother."

"You better not."

Kelvin was waiting for them in a conference room on the next level, but he wasn't alone. Dray and Jordan walked into the room and the door clicked shut behind them. The room had a small circular table where Kelvin sat in one of the four mesh chairs. Dray looked at the man standing behind Kelvin. He wasn't hard to recognize, even though he was clean-shaven and dressed in a black Military Intel uniform.

"Franklin?" Jordan asked.

He smiled. "It's Jeffrey Franklin, actually. I'm glad you remembered me."

Kelvin looked up at Jeffrey. "Jeff was a covert agent planted with the Novans."

Dray took a seat and Jordan pulled up the chair next to her. "You shot N'Gollo," Jordan said.

Jeffrey shook his head. "Your lieutenant wasn't too observant. I shot the man who was dead at my feet. He'd already fired a round at your chief instructor."

Kelvin interrupted them. "We didn't have enough intelligence on the Novans to know what they were planning on Buenos Aires."

Jordan glared at Jeffrey. "So you came with them and did nothing to stop the attack?"

"No. Each group came to the station at different times. I'd been on Buenos Aires since the time Dray saw Kelvin in the recon landing dock."

"That was you in the shadows," Dray said.

Jeffrey rested his hand on Kelvin's shoulder. His stance was too close, suggesting his relationship with her brother was more than just professional. Dray wondered if he was Kelvin's lover.

"He had to maintain his cover," Kelvin said. "What little we knew of the Novans' plans came from him."

"It wasn't enough," Jordan said.

"No, it wasn't." Kelvin folded his hands on the table. "Jeff's cell wasn't given orders until the attack on Buenos Aires had already begun. He broke cover and fought for the ADF."

Dray looked at Kelvin and waited for him to broach the subject she'd spoken to him about over the com-link this morning.

He leaned forward. "And that brings us to the two of you. You're ranking officers now, but you need to choose your assignments. Dray's explained your unique situation, Jordan." He paused, but Jordan didn't say anything. "I can get you on my team, with clearance. With your Novan background, you'd be an asset to the team. I can pull the right strings to make sure you stay in the same unit, if that's what you want."

Kelvin explained his organization in detail, including the kinds of assignments and projects they took on. Most involved covert operations on Novan planets. Dray masked her disappointment that her fighter-pilot training would be useless in Kelvin's division. But, she wasn't the top pilot she'd imagined she was.

"One other thing before you go. Even in my department, Novans can't get implants. We've experimented a few times, but the end results are too unpredictable. Other military departments will expect you to sign up for implants now that you are officers."

"I've taken steps to avoid that," Jordan said. "I was raised as a Catholic Universalist. I'll be exempt from implants on religious grounds."

"Thank you for considering us," Jordan finally said. "We haven't made our decision yet, but thanks."

"Good. I'll await your decision," Kelvin said.

They left Kelvin and Jeffrey in the conference room. The sounds of distant conversations drifted around them as they made their way back through the busy station to the Ambassador's suite. Dray waited until Jordan closed the door before she asked what Jordan thought of Kelvin's proposal.

Jordan collapsed onto the sofa. "I don't know. When I signed up, I was focused entirely on a long-term military career. The Entari training broadened our options, but the war brings its own set of worries."

"So what options do you see for us?" Dray knew she was avoiding her own assignment decision.

Jordan sighed. "There are two areas that interest me. Fighter pilot or the Security Force."

"Not Kelvin's Military Intel?"

"No. I appreciate what you did for me, but I won't be a spy. I can defend Terran resources because that is where my loyalty lies. But I won't use the genetics my father gave me to spy on his own people."

Jordan wrapped her arms around her legs, staring at the floor. Dray sat next to her on the sofa and lifted Jordan's face to look into her deep brown eyes. "I'll go wherever you want," Dray said.

"What about being a top pilot, like your mother?"

Dray caressed Jordan's cheek, marveling at its softness. She dropped her hands so she could concentrate. "You saw my assessment."

"That score doesn't reflect your real skills. Bello was manipulating your training missions from the start."

"Maybe. I could still take a fighter-pilot position, but my top marks were in weapons and navigation. Some day, I'd like to know what really happened at Turin. I've built my mother up as a hero, but I realize now her mistakes cost a lot of lives besides her own." Glancing up, she was caught by Jordan's penetrating stare.

"I understand. How does that affect our decision?"

"It's not as important as being with you." Dray smiled and leaned across her, wrapping her arms around Jordan. Someday, she'd get more information on Turin. Today, her thoughts were for Jordan and their future. She kissed Jordan's neck, enjoying Jordan's quick intake of breath.

"That's not helping us concentrate," Jordan said, smiling.

"Where do you want to go?" Dray asked.

Jordan looked at Dray. "Should we stay with what we joined for?"

Dray smiled. "Fighter pilots? I checked the assignment options. There's openings on the *Rubicon* for fighter pilots and weapons officers."

"So, which will you sign up for?"

Dray took a deep breath. "I can't chase my mother's ghost forever. I think I'm a good pilot, but I know I've got the skills to be a top weapons officer. And if I get the right implants, I can fly the drones."

Jordan stood up and unsnapped the top of her uniform. "We're agreed on what ship to join, then?"

"Yes. Red will be there, too. He's already signed on for the *Rubicon*."

Dray's eyes followed Jordan's movement as Jordan pulled off her dark blue jacket. Jordan smiled at her as she loosened the collar of her shirt. "Did you want to officially sign up right now, or..." She traced a finger along the open collar of her blouse.

Dray hopped off the sofa and whipped off her own jacket. "Later," she said. Jordan's sultry stare sent a shiver through Dray. Later was good, she thought.

DRAY'S EYES CLOSED as she listened to the soft sounds of Jordan sleeping, cradled in her arms. *How did I get so lucky?* she wondered. Jordan meant everything to her. She had so much in her life now, a future she could build with Jordan. She was still very much the daughter of Lieutenant Commander Katherine Draybeck, but now, for the first time, she wanted to be more than that.

Jordan sighed and draped a leg across Dray. *Time enough for the future*, Dray thought, but never enough time to be alone with Jordan.

Another Sandra Barret title:

Lavender Secrets

Emma LeVanteur has written off any chance of true love and is focused on her graduate thesis, when Nicole Davis, a beautiful British instructor, turns Emma's world upside down. Emma thinks she can finally break out of a comatose love-life, but when Nicole convinces Emma to help with her upcoming wedding, Emma's brief hope for romance seems lost. But is it?

Nicole Davis is marrying into a socialite family. But Emma's friendship pulls her in another direction, sending her tumbling into a world of undeniable longing. When Nicole can no longer silence her feelings for Emma, will she give up her picture-perfect future to gamble on a love she can barely comprehend, or will she stick with the life she's always known?

Set in New England, "Lavender Secrets" explores the boundaries that define love, lust, and friendship for Emma, Nicole, and the world they live in.

ISBN 978-1-932300-73-4
1-932300-73-2

Available at booksellers everywhere.

FORTHCOMING TITLES

published by
Quest Books

Deadly Vision:
Book One of the Cassandra Chronicles
by Rick R. Reed

Deadly Vision is inspired by the mythical seer Cassandra, who was given the gift of prophecy only to be cursed by having no one believe her. Reed's story is about a small-town single mom, Cass D'Angelo, whose life changes when a thunderstorm sweeps into her small Ohio River town. Cass must venture out in it to hunt for her son, seven-year-old Max. Lightning strikes a tree near her and a branch crashes onto her head, knocking her unconscious; when Cass awakens a couple of days later, she sees into the deepest secrets of those around her. Worse, some teenage girls have gone missing, and Cass can see their grisly fates. She tries to interest law enforcement and the mother of one of the girls in her visions and is rebuffed. The only one who will believe her is the father of the first missing girl. Reluctantly, Cass agrees to help him find his daughter and she does, in a shallow grave by the river.

The discovery opens the door to a whole new life. The police are suspicious. The press wants to make her a celebrity. And the killers are desperate to know how she found their carefully concealed grave. Cass's visions continue, frustrating and terrifying her. She finds an ally in Dani Westwood, a local reporter. The two women begin to probe into the disappearances/murders and start to forge a romance. When Cass's little boy, Max, disappears, Dani and Cass must race against the clock to find him...before it's too late.

Will Cass find her son in time? Will the parents of the other missing girl get closure? Will the killers escape? These are all questions answered by the time the reader comes to the breathtaking conclusion of Deadly Vision: Book One of the Cassandra Chronicles.

Available January 2008

Land of Entrapment
by Andi Marquette

K.C. Fontero left Albuquerque for Texas in the wake of a bitter break-up, headed for a teaching and research post-doc at the University of Texas, Austin. With a doctorate in sociology and expertise in American while supremacist groups, she's well on her way to an established academic life. But the past has a way of catching up with you and as K.C. spends a summer helping her grandfather on his central Texas farm, her past shows up in the form of her ex, Melissa Crown, an Albuquerque lawyer who left K.C. for another woman three years earlier. Melissa's younger sister, Megan, has gone missing—she's hooked up with a man Melissa suspects is part of an underground white supremacist group and Melissa needs K.C.'s help to find her and hopefully bring her out of the movement.

K.C. knows she has the knowledge and contacts to track the group. She knows that, in the interests of public service, she'd be helping law enforcement as well. What she doesn't know is how far into her past she'll have to go in order to find not only Megan, but herself as well. Working to locate the group without alerting members' suspicions, K.C. finds herself drawn to Megan's friend and neighbor, Sage Crandall, a photographer who challenges K.C.'s attempts to keep her heart esconced in the safety of research and analysis. Confronted with her growing feelings for Sage while unraveling her complicated past with Melissa, K.C. delves into the racist and apocalyptic beliefs of the mysterious group, but the deeper she goes, the greater the danger she faces.

Available September 2008

OTHER QUEST PUBLICATIONS

Brenda Adcock	Pipeline	978-1-932300-64-2
Brenda Adcock	Redress of Grievances	978-1-932300-86-4
Sandra Barret	Face of the Enemy	978-1-932300-91-8
Blayne Cooper	Cobb Island	978-1-932300-67-3
Blayne Cooper	Echoes From The Mist	978-1-932300-68-0
Gabrielle Goldsby	Never Wake	978-1-932300-61-1
Nancy Griffis	Mind Games	1-932300-53-8
Lori L. Lake	Gun Shy	978-1-932300-56-7
Lori L. Lake	Have Gun We'll Travel	1-932300-33-3
Lori L. Lake	Under the Gun	978-1-932300-57-4
Helen M. Macpherson	Colder Than Ice	1-932300-29-5
Meghan O'Brien	The Three	978-1-932300-51-2
C. Paradee	Deep Cover	1-932300-23-6
John F. Parker	Come Clean	978-1-932300-43-7
Radclyffe	In Pursuit of Justice	978-1-932300-69-7
Rick R. Reed	IM	978-1-932300-79-6
Rick R. Reed	In the Blood	978-1-932300-90-1

About the Author:

Sandra Barret grew up in New England, where she spent more years than she cares to mention as a software programmer. She lives on a small farm with her partner, two children, and more pets than are probably legal to own. She's an avid reader of lesbian SF, fantasy, horror, and romance and is now writing her own stories in these genres.

VISIT US ONLINE AT
www.regalcrest.biz

At the Regal Crest Website You'll Find

- The latest news about forthcoming titles and new releases

- Our complete backlist of romance, mystery, thriller and adventure titles

- Information about your favorite authors

- Current bestsellers

- Media tearsheets to print and take with you when you shop

Regal Crest titles are available from all progressive booksellers and online at StarCrossed Productions, (www.scp-inc.biz), or at www.amazon.com, www.bamm.com, www.barnesandnoble.com, and many others.